THE ARENA OF ANTS

BOOKS BY JAMES SCHEVILL

Tensions *(Poems)*	Bern Porter Books	1947
The American Fantasies *(Poems)*	Bern Porter Books	1951
Sherwood Anderson: His Life and Work	University of Denver Press	1951
High Sinners, Low Angels *(Play with Music)*	Bern Porter Books	1953
The Right To Greet *(Poems)*	Bern Porter Books	1956
The Roaring Market and The Silent Tomb *(Biography)*	Abbey Press	1956
The Bloody Tenet *(Verse Play)*	Meridan Books	1957
Selected Poems: 1945-1959	Bern Porter Books	1959
The Cid *(Translation of Corneille's Le Cid)*	Anchor Books	1961
Private Dooms and Public Destinations: Poems 1945-1962	Alan Swallow	1962
Voices of Mass and Capital A *(A Play for Voices)*	Friendship Press	1962
The Stalingrad Elegies *(Dramatic Poem)*	Alan Swallow	1964
The Black President and Other Plays	Alan Swallow	1965
Violence and Glory: Poems 1962-1968	Swallow Press Inc.	1969
Lovecraft's Follies *(A Play)*	Swallow Press Inc.	1971
Breakout: In Search of New Theatrical Environments	Swallow Press Inc.	1973
The Buddist Car and Other Characters *(Poems)*	Swallow Press Inc.	1973
Pursuing Elegy: A Poem About Haiti	Copper Beech Press	1974
Cathedral of Ice *(Play)*	Pourboire Press	1975
The Arena of Ants *(Novel)*	Copper Beech Press	1977
Collected Short Plays	Swallow Press Inc.	1977

JAMES SCHEVILL

Drawings by Walter Feldman

THE ARENA OF ANTS
a novel

This book was supported by a grant from the Rhode Island State Council on the Arts.

LC: 77-29531

ISBN: 0-914278-11-8

Copper Beech Press
Box 1852
Brown University
Providence, R. I. 02912

To Carl D. Brandt and Ferol Egan

ENEMY VOICES: GERMAN AND AMERICAN

"A hundred and fifty years ago, people became sentimental about lakes and forests. Today we have the lyricism of the prison cell."

Albert Camus, *The Fall*

"One of the first things the student of atomic structure must come to understand is the rather deep and subtle principle which has turned out to be a clue to unraveling the whole domain of physical experience. This is the principle of complementarity, which recognizes that various ways of talking about physical experience may each have validity and may each be necessary for adequate description of the physical world, and may yet stand in a mutually contradictory relationship to each other. . ."

J. Robert Oppenheimer

THE AMERICAN   TRINIDAD, COLORADO

Trinidad, Colorado. Why expect this godforsaken town to be unusual? Stepping off the train hot, dry air hit my face. Except for the porter the station seemed deserted. The German prisoner of war camp to which I was assigned was miles away in the desert. After the long trip from Mobile, Alabama, I was tired, disgusted. Another screw-up. Someone from the Internment Camp (why the hell did they call a prisoner of war camp an Internment Camp?) was supposed to meet me. That was the least they could do after the recent mess. Especially since they'd called me *Absent Without Leave. . .*

I walked to the edge of the station platform, stared down the main street. Even in front of the bar no truck or staff car was visible. The Victorian Catholic church, the massive stone bulk of a school loomed darkly against the sky. A movie marquee blazed in broken neon lights:

ROY R.GER AND T.IG.ER

Sitting on a wooden bench carved with names and initials I tried to relax. Trinidad I remembered vaguely was a half-Mexican mining town. Didn't the Ludlow Massacre take place around here some time in the 1920s? Troops and guards fired at random into the striking miners and their families. How old was I then? Four or five, easy and safe at home in Berkeley, California. . .

A Mexican in cowboy hat, boots, chewing gum, sauntered up. Grinning he stared at my uniform, trying to make out my branch of service. If only I were still wearing Air Force wings. . . I folded my arms over the crossed pistols of my Military Police insignia. . .

No one arrived to pick me up. It was almost 8 P.M. What the hell to do? Call the camp, announce my arrival. No, better wait a while, let things happen by themselves. Try to avoid any more trouble. . .

At the Air Force base in Mobile, despite my ignorance about Air Force positions and qualifications, I'd been assigned to work as a Classification Officer. After two weeks, just as I was beginning to feel a little more secure in translating the manuals' technical jargon, the Pentagon accused me of being *Absent Without Leave* from a new German Prisoner of War Camp at Trinidad, Colorado.

Actually the Pentagon word was a telegram signed by General George C. Marshall, the Chief of Staff himself. Why should General Marshall send me, a mere Limited Service Second Lieutenant, a personal telegram at the peak of the African campaign when American tanks were rolling towards Cairo? It turned out that Limited Service personnel with some knowledge of German were desperately needed to man the prisoner of war camps throughout the country where thousands of captured Africa Corps troops were arriving daily.

Major Thompson, my superior Classification Officer, was forced to explain on the telephone to General Marshall's aide that I was not *Absent Without Leave*. I was undergoing intensive, important training as an Air Force Classification Officer. The error of this assignment almost blew up the telephone. Major Thompson's face turned purple.

"You're supposed to be a god damn MP officer in a Nazi prison camp," he hissed at me. "How the hell did you get here?"

"I don't know, Sir."

The next day another personal telegram arrived from General Marshall ordering me to proceed immediately to:

7th Serv C Trinidad Internment Cp, Trinidad, Colo, for ltd serv only

I noted the fact that *ltd serv only* was printed in lower case. Supposedly Limited Service was an Army classification designed to use men with physical ailments, but to keep them from combat service. Stamped in heavy letters over my service records, this classification had caused me nothing but trouble. I was even guilty of forging a physical examination to escape from this segregated lower class to which my poor eyes and heavy glasses condemned me. Certainly I didn't look forward to serving in a prison camp guarded entirely by untrained Limited Service personnel. The camp was full of Nazi prisoners who had been crack combat troops in Africa. . .

My stomach nagged. Nothing to eat since lunch. Looking at my watch I saw it was 8:15. What if something had happened at the camp? Better call. I walked over to the battered phone booth. Green paint had faded and cracked into patterns on the door. All I could get was a busy signal. Impossible. . .How could the switchboard of a large prisoner of war camp be tied up at this time of night? Wrong number maybe. Squinting through my glasses in the dim light, I looked up the number again. Another buzzing busy signal. Nothing to do but wait. . .

*Limited Service. . .*After getting burned by General Marshall's aide, Major Thompson, the Air Force Classification officer, had started to bawl me out for concealing the facts of my case:

"Why the hell didn't you tell me you were trained especially for prisoner of war work?"

"I'm sorry, Sir. I wasn't just trained for prisoner of war work, I graduated from one of the Adjutant General's schools. Anyway I didn't think my Limited Service classification was fair." *Shut up. Don't say any more. How could I explain to him all my experiences in Limited Service?*

"You didn't think. . .*Fair*. . .Who the hell are you to think what's fair?" Suddenly Major Thompson began to chuckle. Then he burst into a laugh. Not a sympathetic laugh either.

"How old are you kid?"

"Twenty-two, Sir."

"Twenty-two, hell. You're much older than that. In fact you're over-age."

"I don't understand."

"You're a god damn *over-age* officer."

"Over *what,* Sir?"

"Damn right you're *over-age* in grade. That's why you got sent here. A god damn hyphen was left out of your order in transmission." He started laughing again.

"A *hyphen?*"

"Yeah, you're the victim of a hyphen, kid. It seems the Seventh Service Command in Omaha, Nebraska, received an order from the War Department to transfer so many officers '*over-age in grade.*' The idea was to find excess officers jobs where they could be promoted and sent overseas."

"What's that got to do with me?"

"When that order arrived you were at some god damn Italian prison camp in Nevada, Missouri, under the jurisdiction of the Seventh Service Command. You never told me about that. Right?"

"Yes, Sir. I was only there for temporary training after graduating from Officers' School. I don't see. . ."

"When the order was transmitted, they left out the hyphen so it read, 'Transfer so many officers *overage.*' "

"What's *overage?*"

"Jesus Christ, you're supposed to be an administrative officer. Overage means too damn many officers, get rid of 'em. That was you, kid, hanging around there doing nothing. So the camp authorities seized the opportunity to transfer you and keep the officers they wanted."

Staring at him, I struggled to comprehend the difference between *over-age* and *overage.* Was that really the cause of my transfer from Military Police to Air Force?

"Look out when you get your ass back to the Seventh Service Command," the Major grinned. "Already they're beginning to call you The Hyphen Kid."

The Hyphen Kid. . .All right so it was a screwed-up hyphen that caused all this. What good does it do to create illusions of myself as a Limited Service martyr?. . .

Roaring up to the station a dusty green staff car startled me out of my revery. A corporal climbed ponderously out, hurried toward me, saluted. Short, paunchy, grey haired, he looked at least fifty. As a new, young officer, I still felt peculiar being saluted by older men.

"Sorry to be so late, Sir. I'm afraid we've got some real trouble at the camp."

Trouble. . .No hyphen in that word. . .As we roared out of town, the dry, severe landscape was relieved only by the sharp edges of high mountains towering south in New Mexico. Barren, lonely country. I began to feel younger and younger.

The corporal's fingers drummed on the wheel, poked at gadgets on the instrument panel. "You picked a great time to arrive, Lieutenant."

"What happened?"

"One of the tower guards blew his lid and fired into the officers' compound. You wouldn't believe what happened. He killed two German officers with one bullet."

"Two?"

"Yeah, the shot went through one officer, ricocheted off a stone or something and hit another officer. Bingo! That wouldn't happen in a million years if you spent full-time trying to duplicate it."

For a wild moment I felt like ordering him to turn around and drive me back to the station to begin a million years of solitary research. "How are the German prisoners taking it?"

"Rough. We've got a thousand tough line officers from the Africa Corps out there. They've started a strike in the whole camp. Mostly they're just sitting in their barracks, waiting. You can't tell what those bastards will do next."

"What do they want?"

"They're angry because they claim Colonel Williams, our camp commander, won't court-martial old One-Eyed Nellie."

"One-Eyed Nellie?"

"He's the guy who fired into the compound."

"Why did he fire?"

"Who knows? Probably he panicked and fired blind. How else with one eye could you kill two guys with one shot?"

Another Limited Service specialist. . . "What do you think's going to happen?"

"The trouble is we don't have a German-speaking officer in that compound to negotiate with them. Captain Stevens was our liaison officer, but he doesn't speak any German. Anyway he couldn't take it and got sick. You speak German, Lieutenant?"

"Not much," I said. I began to sweat.

"The Colonel seems to think you do. He wants to see you as soon as we arrive."

Colonel Williams was seated at his desk when I was ushered into his office. His crewcut white hair bristled in the light as he waved away my salute impatiently. He rapped on the desk with his hand and the ring on his finger glistened. "I'm glad you're here, Lieutenant. We sure could have used you earlier. I still don't know what the hell happened. You were supposed to be here days ago."

Wearily, trying to suppress my hunger and my anxiety, I began to explain the complicated administrative maneuvers that had brought me from the Air Force in Alabama to the Military Police in Colorado. He listened, paying sudden attention at the mention of General Marshall, then growing bored and cutting me off sharply. "Never mind the excuses. We've got a job to do." He jumped up from his desk and motioned me to the window. "Look out there. The whole place is so damn quiet you can hear a jackrabbit jump. All those Krauts do every hour is send me another list of demands. We've got to settle this before the place explodes. I want you to go in there and talk to those officers. We need a real good German speaker."

"I'm afraid my German is a little rusty, Sir." *Don't admit it's lousy.*

"I don't care if it's so rusty they only understand every fourth word." The Colonel's trim white mustache trembled as he bit into the words with irritation. "It's a matter of putting up a front. We don't have any officer in that compound now. I can't go in there myself. That'd be running up the white flag, wouldn't it?"

"Yes, Sir."

"So you just go in, open your ears, and listen. That's all I want. I don't expect you to be a genius. I don't expect you to arrange everything right away. All I want you to do is be the valve through which they blow off steam. Then it should be easier to settle things."

"How do we settle things, Sir?"

"They want a full-scale funeral with all military honors. At first, believe it or not, they wanted the whole damn camp to go marching off into the desert." The Colonel gestured out the window with indignation. "Can you imagine what would happen if we let them get away with that? Still we can bend a little about the funeral. The real problem is the guard who fired that shot."

"Are you going to court-martial him, Sir?"

"I hope so. We haven't finished the investigation yet," the Colonel hedged. "But if we court-martial him what's to prevent every guard from looking the other way whenever a Kraut tries to escape? As it is we've got a bunch of damn Limited Service men here who've barely fired a gun."

With a shock I remembered that when I was transfered abruptly to the Air Force, I had been assigned first to a Military Police Aviation Company destined for overseas service. I was marched out immediately to the firing range to make sure that I qualified for the pistol. A Master Sergeant, a grizzled twenty year veteran, had to cope with me. After I missed the target completely on the first three shots, everyone began to duck instinctively. Struck dumb the Master Sergeant gaped at me. "My eyes are not too good," I apologized lamely. "You ain't just a roostapoopin', Lieutenant," he muttered. I didn't have the courage to ask him what *roostapoopin'* meant. . .

"Listen, Lieutenant. You know what the trouble is in this country?"

"No, Sir." I jerked back to attention.

"We're too soft. How can you expect guards like they give me to watch these Krauts who are in the peak of condition? Most of my troops here can't even stand up straight. They don't teach real Physical Education any more in the schools. In my day they started you right out with ten push-ups the first day you hit gym. I've got a son and you know what they started him out with?"

"No, Sir."

"Dancing, believe it or not, dancing." Colonel Williams stared out of the window into the dark.

"Excuse me, Colonel, do you think I can get some food? There wasn't any on the train."

"For Christ' sake, Lieutenant, why didn't you say you're hungry. We don't starve our people around here." He called the corporal who was waiting outside and asked him to find me some food. "Don't worry," Colonel Williams smiled as he clapped me on the back, "We'll take care of you."

"When do I go into the compound, Sir?"

"Tomorrow morning first thing. Get yourself a good sleep first. The corporal here will drive you out to the gate of the officers' compound. You walk in, down the road about half a mile to their headquarters building. Don't let the silence throw you even if it seems like a tomb."

Tomb...

"Ask for their commanding officer, Major Weimann. Tall, stiff, blond man with blue eyes. A real soldier. Probably he won't speak to you."

"What do I do then, Sir?"

The Colonel glared at my stupidity. "Don't let it throw you if they make you sit around and wait. After all you're only a second lieutenant. What's your date of rank?"

"March 3, 1943, Sir."

"Jesus Christ. . .You know something, Lieutenant?" His face wrinkled in a grin.

"No, Sir."

"My date of rank is the same as General Eisenhower's. We were classmates together at West Point."

"Really, Sir?" *What's he doing in this godforskaen camp then?*

"God damn right. Ike and I still keep in touch. If it weren't for a touch of asthma, you can bet your last dollar I'd be with him in Africa, not in this desert hole with a bunch of broken-down Limited Service assholes whom the Krauts laugh at." He pulled a thick book out of his top desk drawer. "You see this book?"

"Yes, Sir." *Even with my magnifying glassed Limited Service eyes. . .*

"We get a lot of visiting inspectors here because they've never seen a Kraut before and they're consumed with curiosity. Whenever some visiting bastard shows up and tries to pull rank on me, I show 'em this book and ask their date of rank. That cools 'em off. They know they're still babies. You ever see any German soliders before, Lieutenant?"

"A few, Sir. In Europe."

He looked at me suspiciously, his shrewed eyes tightening over the white mustache. "Where in Europe? You mean you really know something about the German army?"

"Not really, Sir. Just before the war started I was a student in Switzerland. When I traveled in Germany and Austria I saw some German soldiers in action."

"If you were a student, son, you didn't see any troops like the ones we've got here. In the four compounds out there we've got four thousand top combat men from the Africa Corps. Paratroopers, infantry, tank corps, all mixed together. That's a mess of trouble if they try to escape."

"Yes, Sir."

"If we had just a few guards with half their training and discipline, maybe we could make things work. But all we've got is untrained, unsound Limited Service men up in the guard towers. I know we need our healthy soldiers overseas, but, Jesus Christ, the least they could do would be to train some of these Limited Service spectres."

"Can't you train them here, Sir?"

"With what? They don't give us equipment. They don't give us personnel. We couldn't even train a herd of sheep here."

*Limited Service sheep. . .*Colonel Williams broke into a smile and patted my arm. "Don't worry, Lieutenant," he assured me. "I'm not sending a kid to the slaughter. The worst the Krauts can give you is the ice treatment."

"What's the ice treatment, Sir?"

"The cold shoulder. Any questions?"

"No, Sir."

The Colonel grunted, walked to the door, and called the corporal: "After he gets some food show the lieutenant to his quarters." Turning to me he said: "You'll be called tomorrow morning at six. Any further instructions will be given to you at breakfast. Have a good sleep and don't spend all night brushing up on your German."

"Yes, Sir." I pulled myself together, saluted. The Colonel had already turned away. I saluted his back.

My stupid room in the officers' barrack seemed like the inside of a cardboard box. Colorless walls made out of cheap wallboard. The only furnishings were a cot and a chair. *At least it's some privacy--the privacy of a cell. Still you can escape to go to the can down the hall.* I escaped frequently.

Tossing on the cot, thumbing through two German books to brush up on useful phrases, I remembered guiltily Colonel Williams's instructions: *Don't spend all night brushing up on your German.* Turning out the light I lay there sleepless, rolling over and over, haunted by the Colonel's scorn of Limited Service personnel. . .

What a category, I-B, Limited Service, pigeonholing thousands of men age eighteen to forty-five, men with all kinds of ailments from bad eyes and bad feet to ulcers and God Knows What. All of these miserable draftees were dedicated to the idealistic concept: *Save these men from their fleshly failures and by their military salvation save healthier men for combat* *service. . .*Great theory, but here we are up against the Africa Corps in Colorado yet. From the day that we were drafted we'd been segregated, restricted, prevented from applying for positions and schools that were supposedly open to any free American soldier.

How could I forget my first Army day at the Reception Center in Monterey, California? Still clinging to our civilian clothes, dazed, we waited in line for lunch. Below us on the shore curled wind-shaped cypress trees. The blue waves of the Pacific lashed against the rocks. Farewell civilian life. An incongruous group of fifty socalled men we ranged from pimply adolescents to greyhaired middle-agers with potbellies. We were united only by the huge imprint on our papers, LIMITED SERVICE, that already marked us for special treatment.

In front of me stood a brilliant linguistics research specialist at the University of California. His name was Sandor Walkowsky, a true American foreigner with ancestors deep in three or four Slavic countries. He seemed to live eternally against time. A master of six languages he thrived on abstract questions that made it difficult to penetrate his verbal maze. As a result his academic colleagues had confined him to research and kept him as far as possible away from teaching. When Sandor encountered a student the meeting was dangerous. He would soon become outraged by the inability of young Californians to speak any foreign language and poured his scorn over their heads. When the war came Sandor was classified I-B because he was allergic to any trace of house dust, an infinite variety of pollens, and a large number of foods. Also his eyes were almost as bad as mine. This made us immediate friends as we met struggling in vain without glasses to read the enormous E on the optical chart. All of us I-B's predicted that Sandor would end up in Army Intelligence. How many draftees were there who could speak not only several European languages, but also Russian and Greek? At the Reception Center Sandor surprised all of us by scoring very high on the Mechanical Aptitude Test. As potential aviation mechanics were needed urgently, he was shipped off to a south-western air base to become a mechanic. After the Reception Center I'd never seen Sandor again. We promised to correspond and never did. During my brief Air Force assignment in Alabama, every time I heard of some accident, I couldn't suppress a vision of Sandor's long, white, fumbling fingers servicing the plane. . .

Behind me in the lunch-counter line at the Reception Center stood a grey-haired, forty-five year old owner of a stationery store, Cedric Baxter. Cedric was a perfect family man who wrote every day to his wife and two children. He had the natural politeness and honesty of an ideal storekeeper devoted diligently to record-keeping and the correct display of proper materials for proper offices. After meeting Cedric naked in the physical examination line, I could see that something had gone wrong. Clutched firmly in his hand was a letter from his civilian doctor:

To Whom It May Concern:

> The bearer of this letter, Mr. Cedric Baxter, has been a patient of mine for several years. Mr. Baxter suffers from a potentially dangerous gastric ulcer which he controls by a rigid diet. Consequently, I hope that the Army will permit Mr. Baxter to adhere to the diet that he needs. Otherwise, the result might be dangerous to Mr. Baxter's health to say nothing of the danger to the Army if Mr. Baxter were in a combat situation.
>
> Signed: E. Benjamin Harris, M. D.

Either E. Benjamin Harris was on some Army list of medical quacks, or else the Army had a firm policy of ignoring medical letters brought in by draftees. No doubt the latter as I admit that a lot of the letters displayed by my companions were pretty unbelievable. In any case Baxter's letter counted for zero. The military doctors sympathized with him, told him his ulcer seemed under control, and to watch what food he ate. After lunch, when as far as I could see Cedric merely picked at the food, he slumped to the floor, holding his stomach with both hands, moaning, "Call a doctor."

Some time later a Major appeared leisurely, a baldheaded, tall man with a row of ribbons on his chest indicating the length of his service. His mouth curled into a pleasant grin. Only his eyes weren't smiling. Cedric gasped up at him, "Are you a doctor?"

The Major corrected him: "A doctor, *Sir.* What's the matter with you?" He felt Cedric's pulse.

Without thinking I intervened: "He's got a letter from his doctor, Sir."

"Shut up," snapped the Major. "I'm talking to *him,* soldier."

"It's my ulcer, Sir," moaned Cedric. "I guess it's the Army food. I'm supposed to be on a special diet. In my pocket there's a letter. . . ."

"All you guys have letters," said the Major. "You're just a little nervous, that's all. If you keep this up you know what I'm going to do?"

"Please read my letter, Sir."

"I don't need your letter, you god damn faker. I'm a Major in the Regular Army Medical Corps. What you're asking for is the Mussolini Treatment. You know what that is?"

"No, Sir."

"Castor oil four times a day. That's what we give you fakers. So you'd better get up. Get about your business."

The next morning Cedric could not get up. With Sandor and another friend we carried him to the Station Hospital. Luckily the Major wasn't on duty that morning. What happened to Cedric I never learned. When you meet people in the Army you lose them fast. . .

Unable to sleep I got up, walked to the window, and looked at the dark barbed wire fence. Behind that fence all of the lights were out in the compounds. Which one was the officers' compound that I'd have to enter in the morning? What kind of Limited Service guard would be up in the tower protecting me? Stupid to blame everything on Limited Service. . .Those events at the Reception Center could have happened anywhere. Every institution has certain power-crazy officials like that Major. . .

Still what bothered me was the category of Limited Service as a group of scorned men, men to be used merely as servants, as work animals in menial jobs. After the Reception Center, I'd been sent with other I-B servants to Fort Stevens, a coast guard installation in Oregon on the ocean at the mouth of the Columbia River. As we drove through the gate in our bus a huge sign greeted our eyes: THE ONLY FORT IN THE CONTINENTAL UNITED STATES TO BE AT-

TACKED BY THE JAPANESE. The day after Pearl Harbor a Japanese mini-submarine had surfaced off the coast and lobbed a shell ashore wildly into the empty dunes. The commanding officer put the post under strict blackout regulations. Since no blackout curtains were available to cover windows except in the post theatre, you had two choices. Either you went to bed like a baby at sundown, staring into the dark or listening to the radio until you fell asleep, or you went to so many bad movies that your eyes began to ache with what we called "the shit movie twitch." With other I-Bs I was assigned to work in the Station Hospital where I typed admission forms laboriously with two fingers.

Early one foggy morning it happened. I resolved to leave Fort Stevens at any cost. I was on duty in the reception office, reading a detective story to pass the time. It was 5 AM and the building was full of the silence that comes to a hospital only in the early hours before dawn. Outside the mist was so thick you could hear it dropping from trees. A truck pulled up. Ten newly inducted soldiers entered wearily, dragging their gear behind them. Dragging, because they were physically incapable of carrying anything. Their "leader" was a short, stubby man with a battered nose and cauliflower ears. He didn't need to tell me that he was an ex-boxer. He accosted me belligerently about his former profession: "Which one of my eyes do you think is bad?"

"I don't know. . ." *I couldn't care less,* my tone implied, but he was too obsessed to notice.

"Come on, guess. I'll bet you can't tell. You're runnin' this office. You gotta take care of me."

Only one way to get rid of him--play along. . ."It's your right eye," I said.

"Jesus Christ, how'd you guess?" He drew back in amazement.

"I'm a prophet." *Please go away,* I signalled, turning back to my desk with my two fingers ready to type.

"Man, you're somethin'. You hit it on the button." He reached up, took out his right eye, spun me around, and set it carefully in my hand. I stood there, shaking, terribly afraid of dropping the glass eye that seemed to slither in my palm like a piece of jelly.

Suddenly the alarm bell clanged. I was glad to escape into a real emergency. An army patrol plane had crashed two miles offshore. With a doctor and two medics I rode out to the beach in an ambulance to hunt for survivors. Near the shore the fog lifted a little, although the visibility was still poor. Grey gulls swooped overhead. Huge chunks of twisted driftwood loomed through the mist, strange sentinels guarding the entrance to the ocean world. Ahead of us a jeep veered into the surf. A dark-clothed figure staggered out of the sea waving his arms frantically as if freed from a net. As it turned out, the radio operator and navigator had parachuted out of the disabled plane and were blown out to sea to their deaths. The other two crew members, the pilot and co-pilot, had not been able to parachute in time. After ditching the plane, they started to swim together toward the land. With the shore in sight they were separated. Only the pilot had swum safely ashore.

Draping blankets around the shivering pilot who refused to enter the ambulance, we waited tensely for what seemed an eternity. Somehow I felt released from my petty administrative chores. The sea was a natural adversary, a source of life and death that united men instinctively against its force. After a long wait, fifty yards down the beach, a body pitched head-first out of the waves. It was sucked slowly backward by the undertow. Running into the surf, we dragged the body onto the sand and started artificial respiration. All the long, bouncing way back to the hospital in the ambulance, we took turns with the doctor, fighting desperately, hopelessly, to revive the co-pilot.

That afternoon, since the hospital had no storage facilities for corpses, a mortician was summoned from Portland, ninety miles away. To preserve the body until the mortician's arrival, the head of the hospital assigned me and another I–B slave to pack the body in ice. As we descended into the basement locker room, where the corpse was lying on a table covered with a sheet, I promised myself bitterly to escape from that hospital, from Limited Service any way I could. Two bare feet protruded from one end of the sheet, a blond, young face shone like a pale mask from the other end. Several enormous blocks of ice stood on the floor. A sergeant handed us two icepicks. "Get to work," he said, leaving us alone. We started chipping chunks of ice from the blocks to cover the body, trying to keep our eyes averted from the face.

In the evening the mortician, a middle-aged man in heavy, black spectacles, blue suit with a grey tie and a red carnation in his buttonhole, arrived from Portland. As we escorted him down to the corpse he chattered his regrets about "this unfortunate accident." In the basement, as we watched, condemned to carry out our assignment to the end, the mortician circled the table, cleared away a little of the ice tentatively as if it were mountainous, and turned to us with a slight smile: "You did a good job, fellows, even if you didn't need so much ice. Come on, we'll have to scrape it off." Mechanically we started to clear the ice away. The mortician lifted the sheet and inspected the tag on the co-pilot's leg. Shaking his head, he patted the naked leg affectionately as if expressing his sympathy for lost youth and said: "Too bad. Nice boy."...

Staring into the night through my prison camp window, I remembered abruptly that the bodies of the two murdered German officers were still in that officers' compound, frozen in the refrigerator for safekeeping. Would I be assigned to take care of them too? Had I forged my way out of that Coast Guard Hospital in Oregon merely to encounter another kind of frozen death in Colorado?

Forgery wasn't quite accurate. In order to get into officers' school, I had persuaded a doctor to certify on my physical examination papers that my myopic eyes were actually good enough to see the large E on the optical chart. Since the doctor, a recent graduate from medical school, was also Limited Service and desired to escape from its restrictions, it was easy to persuade him of my just cause. With my two-fingered typing ability and my assistant mortician's service, I ended up in an Officers' Candidate School supervised by The Adjutant General in a former teachers' college in Fargo, North Dakota. Hardly the place where I dreamt equal opportunity would prevail. When I arrived in December the temperature was ten degrees below zero. The aura of Limited Service still haunted me at that socalled officers' training school. Many candidates in my class were at least twenty years older than I was. The curriculum seemed designed to weed out psychological frailties from physical ailments. The first was taken care of by a battery of daily true and false and multiple choice examinations. These forced your brain increasingly into wild assumptions and cunning maneuvers to survive your impossible lack of knowledge. Everyone's face was dazed with the blank continuity of examination time from which there was no escape.

The matter of physical ailments was taken care of by daily outdoor calisthenics in the ice at 6 AM, and by the afternoon "recreation" of long hikes. On the hikes an ambulance followed slowly behind the columns to receive elderly figures when they began to sag behind in the below zero weather and fall like stiff, frozen statues. There seemed to be no escape. Even this officers' school became a battlefield of youthful Limited Service versus aged Limited Service. The practise of the school was to eliminate older administrators with serious physical ailments that could not survive the army's strenuous administrative routine. When our golden bars were pinned on our shoulders at graduation and we saluted our first proud salute as officers, I looked around to perceive that youth had eliminated age in the fierce struggle for administrative authority. . .

Beyond the barbed wire fence that rose jaggedly outside of the window of my room, I could see the dark shadow of a guard tower. Was that the tower from which One-Eyed Nellie fired his shot that killed two German officers? At least I wouldn't have to pull much guard duty in this camp. After graduating from officers' school, all I did in the Italian prisoner of war camp was guard duty, then sit around in the officers' club. Guard duty scared hell out of me. It was easy enough. Strap a pistol around my waist, march the guards to the towers, climb up into the towers once in a while for sudden inspections to keep the guards on their toes. The trouble was I'd only fired a pistol once in basic training. To climb into the towers unannounced was to court disaster. Machine guns up there rotated in any direction, although they were supposed to be trained into the compounds. One night during a storm I climbed into a tower to discover a frightened guard riveting his machine gun on me. After calming him down I discovered that he had as little experience with a machine gun as I did with a pistol.

The sitting around in the officers' club trying to make friends proved fruitful momentarily in that the camp commanding officer saw me there and put me in charge of the club's books as an additional duty. The books of most officers' clubs, I learned, were balanced by money from slot machines. This involved collecting money from the ten slot machines that stood in a corridor at the back of the club and depositing the money in the bank in town. The money was entered in the club's books under ENTERTAINMENT, DANCES, PARTIES, etc. Although it wasn't difficult to learn the club's operating procedures, I failed to appreciate the danger confronted by administrative officers in charge of the slot machines.

An older, dark-skinned woman hovered constantly in front of the slots. At first she was very pleasant to me. She talked passionately about the fact that good slot machines weren't really machines. All of those symbolic, brightly colored fruits that spun around and clicked into place were really like the astrological images of a horoscope, designs for destiny. Her right arm seemed twice as strong as the left because of the zeal with which she pulled down the lever, as if her whole body were riding into the machine. "This is *it,* baby!" she cried out, never losing her confidence.

When she lost she always wrote out a check to "Cash," and gave it to me with a grin. "The trick is to keep looking for *it,*" she'd laugh. Then she'd pour her money again into the slots and the drinks that were brought to her by a Filipino waiter.

She turned out to be the commanding officer's wife. I turned out to be a fool. The checks always bounced. Finally I made the mistake of going to her husband and complaining.

As soon as I walked into his office, I knew it was another mistake. He stared at me, disturbed, and began to lecture me about the illness of gambling. "You've never seen real gamblers have you, son. They're sick. You have to treat them like sick people, not crooks. How come you think my wife's a crook, huh? Have you made any attempt to understand her sickness?"

"Of course I have, Sir," I mumbled, knowing I was in trouble. "It's just I don't know what to do about the bad checks." Two days later I received orders transfering me to the Air Force Base in Mobile, Alabama. . .

Anyway I've seen a lot of the country in Limited Service. What a destiny. . .I'd better learn to live with it. The German Army in America. . .That's a Limited Service paradox. The healthy service men go overseas to fight, but it's here in the U.S.A. that the Limited Service guys really encounter the Nazis. Come on, cut the crap. . .I come to bury them, to negotiate with them about a funeral. Do these Nazis still think they're going to win the war? What the hell's going on out there in the compound? Colonel Williams didn't seem to think there's much danger if the Nazis organize the camp. I turned away from the window, the threatening barbed wire outside, and returned to my cot. Lying there, still unable to sleep, I picked up a German book again and turned the pages frantically looking for colloquial phrases that would help my morning doom-step into the compound. Christ, it was an anthology of classical German poetry given to me by Frau Hedda Simmelstein, who had taught me German in 1938 when I was a music student in Switzerland. What good would Goethe and Schiller be to me when I walked into that compound and needed some sharp colloquial language? I turned the pages idly. Her inscription flashed out: *"To my dear American student, Peter Enders, in the hope that he will learn the real German culture."* In the morning I wouldn't need the real German culture if it still existed. Women seemed so far away from this prisoner of war camp. All you could do was dream of them, plenty of wet dreams.

Frau Hedda, as she asked me to call her, was the Jewish second wife of a well-known, Austrian Catholic novelist. Her husband died in 1935, three years before the Nazi Anschluss of Austria. Until 1938 she managed to live on the small royalties and the house her husband left to her. His first wife had absorbed the major portion of his income. After the Anschluss the Nazis confiscated everything that belonged to Frau Hedda because of her Jewish background. Without her husband's distinguished name she couldn't have escaped. In Zürich, in a tiny boarding house room, she eked out a living teaching German and writing occasional book and concert reviews for Swiss newspapers.

A small, fluttering woman, tense with the energy needed for survival, she resembled a humming bird. She hovered, pounced, fussed over me with darting physical touches that fired my youthful lethargy about German studies. In her early forties she was more attractive than beautiful, I thought, in the instinctively cruel way that eighteen-year-old boy-men catalogue women. Short, carefully cut black hair framed a freckled face in which her quick, glittering eyes changed incessantly from scorn to affectionate humor depending on my ability to learn. Despite her lack of money, she wore stylish clothes with an elegant, sexual flare as if to emphasize that clothes could make the woman who had to brave newspaper offices for a freelance living.

Frau Hedda lived with a fat, grey cat called Oskar, whom she fed more than herself. The cat was named after her brother, a famous Viennese comedian until the Nazis occupied the city. When she tired in her fervent attempts to teach me German, she would talk to me suddenly as if she were the cat speaking and I would have to answer. Since it was Frau Hedda's voice and uncanny cat-spirit that issued from Oskar's mouth, we came to delight in the game of Oskar discoursing on whatever entered his mind. I learned more German from Oskar than from the books we used.

Oskar on American Young Men-- Open your ears! Do all Americans have tin ears? How can you learn *anything,* let alone the intricate sounds of a language, if your ear is deaf to subtleties? The United States must be a land of excessive noise because it seems to produce only deaf people. Well, anyway, deaf people are better than ignorant Nazi swine. But how can you hear the singing world of nature unless you open your ears?

Oskar on German Literature-- Except for an occasional perception in Goethe and Schiller--even those giants tended to sentimentalize women--German literature contains no real women, only shadows of male fantasies. The Germans have always resented women. That is why they consign *das ewig weibliche* to bed, kitchen, and church. With Hitler they have another woman-hater in power. When men have no real relationship with women society becomes sadistic.

Oskar on Frau Hedda-- Look at Frau Hedda, Oskar. Look closely. What do you see? A lost, frightened woman who's suddenly discovered that she's a Jew. So many Jews tried to be Catholic in Austria to fit in. Even Mahler was a Catholic! Now poor Frau Hedda wonders what to do when war breaks out as it must because no one is willing to stop the Nazi insanity. Perhaps Frau Hedda should marry a wealthy man who would take care of her. Take her away even to America if she could learn to stand the noise there. Have you any money, American? But you're too young. . .Where can Frau Hedda find a wealthy, handsome man?. . .

If I only had money I would take care of you, I burst out interrupting Oskar. After that our lessons began to flow past the appointed time. Through the mask of Oskar she revealed an increasing affection for me. While we read together often her slender, nervous hand would rest intimately on my arm . .

Deep in my sexual memory of Frau Hedda I woke with a start to a banging on the door of my room. The corporal's voice sounded loudly through the door, jolting me out of bed: "Come on, Lieutenant, it's time. The Colonel's waiting to brief you."

Brief me? Jesus Christ, that sounds like a combat mission. At breakfast, even though I insisted I wasn't hungry, Colonel Williams sat across the table from me and made me eat an enormous meal. "You need something that'll stick to your ribs, kid. The first tough spot I got into in the Army, that's what I learned. I was starving and I got scared as hell. So I learned to eat when anything tough was coming up. Remember what I said last night. . ."

"Would you please repeat it, Sir?" I said forcing myself to drink the bitter, black coffee.

"When you get into the compound, walk down the road about half a mile. You'll see their headquarters building on the right. They've got a fancy sign on the door so you can't miss it. Walk in, say you have a message from the American commanding officer. Then, as I mentioned last night, you've got to play it cool. . ."

"You said to ask for Major Weimann, Sir."

"Right, but you'll probably have to talk to someone else. Weimann will treat you like a messenger boy."

I'm a messenger boy. . .

"When they finally come up with someone to talk to, all you discuss is the funeral arrangements. Anything they want to do about the funeral arrangements is all right with me, but I want their plans in writing. That way they can't doublecross me. I want to know the exact number of their men who are going outside of the barbed wire to the graveyard site, so we can count 'em back in. According to the Geneva Convention they're entitled to military funerals with all honors. So tell them they can make whatever speeches they want."

"Nazi speeches, Sir?"

"What choice have we got? Tell them we want a religious ceremony, not a political ceremony. If they want to talk about One-Eyed Nellie, no soap. Tell them he's gone, out of our hands. Tell them he's been charged appropriately and will be tried by a military court at the highest level of the Seventh Service Command. If we're lucky they won't know what the hell the Seventh Service Command is."

How do I say all that in German? Struggling desperately to keep all of the Colonel's instructions in mind and all of that food in my stomach, I couldn't think of the right German words. . .

The corporal drove me out to the officers' compound in a jeep. He chattered along as I sat stiff, silent, in the side seat, my mind focused on the German language. The gate to the compound seemed impossibly tall. After it clanged shut behind me, I felt as if I were entering some strange arena surrounded by barbed wire with the indifferent vastness of the early morning desert sky as a roof. What sound would I find in that tense silence?

Suddenly a line from a game that I had played with my dead, older brother when I was a child in California flashed through my mind. *"Enter a silence and find a sound. . ."* To keep me occupied when my independent mother asked him to take care of me, my brother used to make up games. He'd hide from me deep in the green bushes and trees in the canyon where we lived and call out, *"Enter a silence and find a sound."* Going down into that silent canyon of wonder and fear was like entering a threatening paradise. Dodging through the woods, my brother would make all kinds of sounds, bird and animal sounds that he'd learned to imitate in our freedom from our parents. I'd have to pursue his sounds through the canyon silence. . .

The trouble was I might not find any sounds in this compound. Everything was so still. What if they ignored me completely? What would I do then? In the distance, around the edge of a building near a coal pile, I saw a small cluster of prisoners kneeling over something on the ground. What did they see in that barren soil? A lizard, a snake? They were talking excitedly, gesturing, but I couldn't hear anything that far away. Maybe they were playing some game as they seemed to be betting. Nonsense. What game could you play there on the desert? *Keep your mind on finding their headquarters building. . .*

My shoes scuffed up dust as I walked along the dusty, rocky road. *Try not to hurry too much. Walk casually in correct military posture. Don't slouch along the way you usually do. That'll really give them a target to laugh at.* Dear god, please let me speak a few words of German without messing up their stupid syntax. If they don't let me speak, how do I protest in German with the right authority? I'll tell them I'm Limited Service. It's not my fault I'm here. You damn coward, Limited Service has nothing to do with it. These are Africa Corps troops. So hot all of a sudden. At night in the desert you freeze. Then the sun's barely up and you burn. On top of everything else I have to show these Nazis a wet shirt.

Look there's the sign. *Hauptquartier* painted in extraordinary, black Gothic lettering on a white background. Spectacular. A triumph of tradition in this vacant place. Should I knock or just walk in? There's a certain protocol you have to observe with these bastards. Why the hell didn't the Colonel tell me? Otherwise they won't respect me. I'll be in trouble from the start. I should have studied the Geneva Convention harder, but what could you learn in officers' school with all those true and false tests? Damned if I'll knock. That's too timid. After all I'm an American officer. Compromise. Knock to announce my presence, then walk in without waiting.

I knocked loudly and strode into the office. A German enlisted man was cleaning up the outer waiting room. No officers were visible. In an inner room I heard as if in some dream world someone playing a Beethoven sonata. *The "Les Adieux" Sonata at 8:30 in the morning.* Anyone who could play Beethoven like that couldn't be so bad. Maybe things would work out after all.

Over the mop with which he'd been cleaning the floor the German soldier stared at me with surprise. "The American Camp Commander has sent me to see Major Weimann," I announced in German.

Back came the answer *in English,* "The Major is playing the piano."

Frustrated by my inability to even try my German, I said as sharply as I could in English that I had an important message for Major Weimann.

"Yes, Sir. Please wait." The German soldier disappeared. He seemed strangely agitated, his thin fingers poking through his hair nervously. The Beethoven sonata continued in the inner room. Not professional, perhaps, but damn good. I knew good playing when I heard it. The scales, the fast passages, were a little muddy, but the phrasing, the romantic warmth, were there. What was it in these Germans that combined this natural feeling for music and this Nazi military terror? Probably Weimann wasn't really a strong Nazi if he was a professional officer. The conservative General Staff of the Army had been opposed to the Nazis even if only because, as aristocrats, they'd disdained the Nazi bourgeoisie.

I started to fidget. The soldier had been gone a long time. Major Weimann was almost finishing the second movement of the sonata. Was he scared of interrupting Weimann to tell him I was here? Or was Weimann just continuing playing to give me the silent treatment? I sat down beside a table on which copies of *Esquire, Time,* and *The Denver Post,* were neatly arranged. Not so bad--almost like an American waiting room. There didn't seem to be any censorship here. Suddenly the German enlisted man, a lowly private judging from the lack of rank on his uniform, emerged and shut the door quietly behind him. He held a finger up to his lips. *What's going on?* He darted across the room, slipped a folded piece of paper into my hand, and whispered: "Please, very important. Put it in your pocket and read it later."

Dazed I started to unfold the paper and read it on the spot. "No", he clutched me, his voice begging. "Captain Dampfstoff is coming to talk to you. You must read it later for my safety. I will get the Captain."

He disappeared again through the door. *For my safety...* For a moment I was tempted to read the message anyway. Was it some kind of trick they were playing on me? Don't trust these Germans. The rapid, exultant final movement of the "Les Adieux" Sonata began. Slowly I tucked the piece of paper away in my pocket. I looked at my watch. Should I sit down, start reading a magazine? If I do that how do I get back up? I'll stick to the furniture and won't be able to get up. That happens every time when I sweat. . .

Clicking his heels together the German private appeared again, announced: *"Hauptmann Dampfstoff!"* A stocky, powerfully built officer in a pair of shorts and shirt with his captain's insignia gleaming on his shoulders, marched through the door and saluted me formally. Automatically I returned the salute. I gave my name and rank in pure, frightened American. Goodbye German. . . Dampfstoff motioned impatiently with his hand and the German soldier withdrew. Should I mention the note to keep everything in the open? Somehow I didn't like the arrogant way in which he dismissed the soldier.

Dampfstoff started to address me in heavily accented English. Stumbling but adequate enough to be understood, designed to put me in my place. Look he's wearing a medal too, pinned to his shirt, swastika dangling. His nostrils are twitching. Probably allergic to all this dust. With those twitching nostrils he looks like a hunting dog--except for his hands. I wouldn't like those big, meaty hands to get hold of me.

The captain informed me that he was the *Adjutant* of Major Weimann. What the hell does a Nazi Adjutant do? We settled down to negotiate the funeral arrangements. He talked and I listened to his garbled English. It sounded as if it had been strained through a grinder. He wanted the compound gate opened tomorrow morning at 8 AM. Arranged in companies with standard bearers leading the march, the entire compound of officers, together with a matching number of enlisted men from other compounds, would escort the bodies to the funeral site on a hillside near the camp. Naturally there would be no question of escape. *On the word of honor of a German officer. Word of honor?* Remembering Colonel Williams's instructions, I insisted on a head count of all the German prisoners who would attend the funeral. I smothered my naive vision of all the prisoners marching off in columns over the mountains south to Mexico. That was all I needed to negotiate. I told the twitching Captain that I would relay the demands to Colonel Williams. In the adjacent room I heard occasional noises as if other officers were listening.

When the subject of One-Eyed Nellie came up, Dampfstoff stared at me out of two ice eyes and twitched coldly: "Ve demand yustiss!" Suddenly I couldn't stand his accusing English. In amazement I heard myself speaking in German. With absolute conviction I told Dampfstoff that One-Eyed Nellie had been transfered to Omaha, Nebraska, where he was imprisoned awaiting trial at Seventh Service Command Headquarters.

Now it was stubborn English versus stubborn German. Dampfstoff clung scornfully to his guttural version of what I came to think of as Germlish: "You vill tell your Colonel zat ve *inseest* zat yustiss be done for unser murdered offiziere. Ve must hear ze reports effery day from ze trial of ziss murderer. Oderweiss zere vill be great troobles!"

I kept on trying to re-assure him in German that the guard would be adequately punished even if he was Limited Service. *Did I say that?* "Vot iss Leemitive Ser-vess?" Dampfstoff asked. I tried to stammer an explanation. Dampfstoff only grew more puzzled. We ended in a battle of confused languages and absurdly misunderstood terms, sticking to our defiant confusion. On my way out of the compound, as if by some invisible order, masses of officers in all stages of dress and undress emerged from their barracks. They watched my lonely exit in silence. I kept my shoulders back, scuffed up the dust occasionally in a few defiant clouds.

When the gate slammed shut behind me I collapsed into the waiting jeep. The corporal grinned at me. "Good going, Lieutenant." My sopping shirt fastened to the seat like adhesive tape. As we jolted along I remembered abruptly the piece of paper in my pocket. Pulling it out I unfolded it and read: "*Please, I must escape from these Nazis. They are holding this camp in their power. They threaten my life. I am anti-Nazi. Please help me.*" The note in a large, hasty scrawl was signed Hans Armind. . .

THE GERMAN DEATH AND THE NAZI CAMP ORGANIZATION

"They (prisoners of war) must at all times be humanely treated and protected particularly against acts of violence, insults, and public curiosity."

Geneva Convention, 1929

From the doorway of Major Weimann's office in evening half-light, I watch hundreds of German officers surge out of their barracks toward a body lying on the ground. . .*Are there two bodies?*. . .Impossible. . .I heard only one shot. . .Officers converge around the body, obscure my vision. . .Suddenly like an umbrella snapped up, the circle of officers opens as Weimann's voice cracks through the air, *"Zurück!"*. . . Through the angle of retreating officers, I see Weimann kneeling over a body. . .Clothed only in shorts, his heavy body burned dark by the sun, Captain Dampfstoff runs up to join Weimann. . .Weimann shakes his head at Dampfstoff and gestures behind him. . .Dampfstoff moves away, kneels down . . .*There is another body*. . .Have two men been shot by one bullet?. . .

Several officers point furiously at the dark American guard tower looming over the barbed wire fence that surrounds the compound. . ."Murder! The Guard!". . .Cursing officers throw rocks at the tower. . .More join the attack. . .As they surge forward I think they're going to rush the tower. . .*Insane*. . .A machine gun watches there. . .Weimann calls furious orders. . Like trained automatons the officers halt their attack. . . Under Weimann's command they lift up the two bodies. . . They bear them toward the headquarters office where I'm standing. . .No place to hide. . .Wait. . .

A funeral cortege moves across the desert. . .Marching slowly step, pause. . .Step, pause. . .Exact rhythm. . .The bodies are thrust high on the shoulders of the marching officers. . .

As I huddle in a corner the bodies are lowered gently to the floor. . .Outside all officers in the compound--at Weimann's and Dampfstoff's order--are drawn up facing the guard tower in rigid ranks of defiance. . .A medical officer kneels to examine the bodies. . .

"How is it possible?" asks Weimann. "There was only one shot."

"Incredible, Major. I can't believe it. Almost an impossibility. The bullet must have ricocheted. It looks as though it penetrated through one officer, hit some object, and was deflected into the other officer."

From the corner I glimpse the dead officers' faces, eyes

still open, mouths gaping, almost grinning, as if caught playing some childhood game. . .Weimann confers with Dampfstoff . . .They argue. . .The doctor throws a blanket across the officers' bodies. . .Everyone waits in silent expectation for Dampfstoff's orders. . .I wait afraid. . .

Two months before the shooting I arrived in this prison camp under the Sangre de Cristos mountains. . .*The Blood of Christ*. . .Two American guards accompanied my solitary presence. . .Immediately Weimann and Dampfstoff suspected my arrival. . .How could I lie convincingly about my status in the Africa Corps?. . .I'd served in a battalion of political prisoners in the 999th Division that surrendered en masse to the Americans. . .Sick for many months, physically and mentally, I recovered slowly in an American military hospital . . .Suddenly I was sent despite my protests to this camp in western America. . .

After our arrival by train, an army truck transported us to the prison camp. . .Flat arid desert broken only by enormous cactus and sagebrush. . .The sun was setting when we reached the barbed wire. . .A strange, clear light glistened in the western sky, a light which my fellow prisoners came to call *the glow*. . .I don't know why. . .Perhaps because so much of our time in confinement was spent watching the sky change color. . .When your life is fixed in a rigid pattern, you turn your eyes away from earth. . .With its infinite distances the sky becomes the only mirror of possible change. . .

Through the barbed wire in the gathering dusk all of the buildings looked identical--long, squat tarpaper shacks. . . The windows sagged as if inserted by carpenters who hated symmetry. . .From the rooftops protruded black stovepipes bulging out at the top like tin scarecrows with hats. . .Huge wooden coalbins loomed between the barracks. . .Dirt roads, carved with rectangular precision, divided the four compounds of the camp. . .Always the dust blew. . .According to the strength of the wind that hissed constantly across the desert, the dust surged gently or threw an insistent brown haze across your face and body. . .

I dreamt often of *Dust-Demons*, enormous brown clouds that whirled against me in the form of grotesque faces. . . The Dust-Demons were conquerors of the middle air, that territory in which the prison camp hung suspended between earth and sky. . .With a power of transparency that concealed invisible, sharp-pointed weapons, the Dust-Demons flashed through my mind. . .One moment they flared by darkly--beyond man's small possibilities of humility and compassion. . . Next they assumed more graceful forms, dead, cremated bodies seeking wistfully a joyous dance of life. . *My wife, my wife*. . .Her cool presence. . .

With a word of farewell, as if even a formal goodbye symbolized dangerous communication, my guards abandoned me in front of the processing building. . .A long line of prisoners, defiant newly arrived soldiers from the Africa Corps, waited there. . .Eyes glared at me suspiciously. . .*"Line up single file for inspection."*. . .I was jostled around, pushed back to the end of the line. . .How many units, paratroopers, artillery, anti-aircraft, infantry, mixed together. . .Combat-tough faces unwilling to surrender. . .Someone began to sing. . .Slowly other voices joined in. . .At first only a few sang eagerly, willingly. . .Then the familiar undercurrent of discipline tightened. . .For a moment I remained silent against the surge of voices. . .Then I began to sing with a fierce irony, *"Die Fahne hoch, die Reihen fest geschlossen"*. . .The American guards didn't seem to care. . *.Don't you know what they're singing?. . .In honor of a pimp-martyr*. . .The *Horst Wessel* song. . .

After a long wait, I entered the building to see various American officers and enlisted men standing behind the inspection tables. . .They seemed young, unsure of themselves. . . They made no attempt to conceal their curiosity about us prisoners. . .Suddenly I realized it was the first time that they had ever seen Germans, let alone German soldiers. . .

In front of me two American sergeants, one with a limp and the other with a hearing aid, conversed loudly as they waited for us to approach. . .They seemed oblivious to the fact that many of us prisoners had been educated to understand at least some English. . .

"Christ, look at those dirty bastards". . .

"We ought to wear gas masks to look 'em over". . .

"I'm sure going to take a shower when this is finished". . .

"You can say that again". . .

In front of me the second prisoner was short, about five feet four inches, with long, black greasy hair. . .He stood before the sergeants with a blank face like a marionette waiting for the strings to be pulled. . .

"Superman," muttered the sergeant to his companion without making any attempt to lower his voice. . ."Hey Fritz take your clothes off". . .He demonstrated with his hands. . .

"Take kleider ab," grinned the other sergeant practising his German. . .

When the prisoner was naked, they began to search through his clothes and pack. . .He mumbled in protest, ". . . *sechs, das sechste* ". . .

"I think he's trying to say this is the sixth time he's been searched," said the sergeant who knew a little German. . .

"I wouldn't doubt it. Hey Frank, look!" He was peering into an old faded billfold. . .

"French postcards, eh? Let's see 'em". . .

"Whew, not bad". . .

"They aren't supposed to have these are they?". . .

"What for? Give 'em wet dreams!"

"Sorry, chum, verboten," the sergeant told the naked prisoner who began to protest. . .

"Go on, beat it. Next! Next!" The sergeant stuffed the postcards in his pocket. . .

Ahead of me a naive Swabian countryman moved up, stripped, opened his pack. . .A roll of toilet paper fell out, then a battered wallet with photographs of a stiffly posed old couple who were obviously his proud parents, a grinning girl in peasant costume seated on a fence with her legs crossed, the soldier himself in his proud, new uniform with a self-conscious smile, some French money. . .Everything was stained with dirt. . .The last item pulled from the pack was an African *Panzer-Armee* diary, torn, yellowed, the cover decorated with a palm tree rising through the familiar swastika. . With a puzzled frown on his face the sergeant leafed through the pages. . .

How often I'd seen such diaries. . .On the first page next to the familiar stern-jawed Führer with his indomitable will was a statement of Witchdoctor Goebbels: "The homeland greets the soldiers of the African *Panzer-Armee.* The victory, which will at last secure the happy future of our people, will be the best reward for your valiant efforts"...

Throughout the diary mixed oddly together were National Socialist Dates of Honor and Arabic religious holidays:

January 14, 1930--	Murderous attack on Horst Wessel
January 30, 1933--	Adolf Hitler becomes Chancellor
February 4, 1936--	Murder of Wilhelm Gustloff
March 19-------------	Birthday of Mohammed
September 2, 1933-	Reich Party Day, The Triumph of Faith
September 30---------	End of the Monthly Feast (Ramadan)
November 9---------	Memorial Day for Those Who Sacrificed Their Lives for the Movement, 1923. The March to the Feldherrnhalle.
December 11, 1941	Declaration of War against America. Great Beiram-Celebration.
December 25-------	First Christmas Day
December 28------	Islam New Year 1363

Abruptly my Swabian countryman snatched the diary back from the curious sergeant and pointed to several pages as if he were protesting the routine invasion of privacy. . .Under the date of February 13, 1943, I saw scrawled in his almost illiterate hand: *"1st letter home (1)"*. . .On a page covering the dates from March 28 to 31, an intricate doodle of Christian crosses spread down the page to a long series of zeros at the bottom. . .

Under the date of June 18 was scribbled in large letters the joyous--or guilty--acknowledgement: *"1st letter to Marie"* . . .The prisoner continued to protest his claim to the diary with the sergeant who obviously desired it as a souvenir. . . Finally the sergeant shouted, "All right keep your victory," and pushed the contents of the pack over the table. . .

"Ich kann English nicht verstehen," muttered the naked Swabian, clutching his last possessions, a happy smile wreathing his simple face. . .Automatically I moved up and began to strip off my clothes. . .

My first night in the camp I slept only intermittently, jolted awake despite my weariness by fear of Nazis who might recognize me. . .Through the darkness only heavy breathing, the deep sleep of exhaustion, filled the air. . .Early next morning we were ordered into the compound for the count that took place twice daily, morning and evening. . .The American commanding officer, a white-haired, ruddy-faced Colonel with silver eagles shining from the shoulders of his uniform, appeared and spoke to us in English. . .Standing as far as possible behind the rows of prisoners I strained to hear him. . .He spoke in a familiar, official tone: "You are here as honorable prisoners of war, not as criminals. I will not pretend that it will be a pleasant life. I promise you that you will be treated according to the terms of the Geneva Convention which both of our countries have signed. You will be treated firmly but fairly.I trust you will all continue to act as military men with the soldier's respect for discipline. Consequently I will expect due courtesy from each one of you. You will be required to use proper military channels. If you ever need to consult our American authorities about some personal problem, you will get permission through your compound spokesman. That is the correct military procedure according to the Geneva Convention--to go through your own army channels of communication. . .". . .

For a long paralyzed moment I tried to understand. . .*The war is over for us prisoners. . .Why continue this rigorous military discipline?. . .Don't the Americans understand how the Nazis will take advantage of this situation?. . .*That afternoon a General Order, signed by the American camp commander, was posted on all bulletin boards:

GENERAL ORDER NUMBER 1: "All German prisoners who desire to consult the American authorities will go first to their compound spokesman. This is in accordance with the Geneva Convention which states: "In every place where there are prisoners of war, they shall be allowed to appoint agents entrusted with representing them". . .

So the Nazis are to be our "agents". . .Funny how my hands tremble again. . .I thought I had finished with all that process of military communication. . .*The basic law for a National Socialist soldier is that talking to Americans is treason. . .*The unalterable rule. . .Everyone knows it except the Americans. . .

Treason. . .No matter how I try to free myself, the hooks, the swastikas of nationalism, fasten in my skin. . .The camp is being organized. . .The Geneva Convention states that the highest ranking officer will be the spokesman. . .Major Weimann, a General Staff officer, becomes our voice. . .German soldiers are not supposed to have vocal cords. . .Oh, we have a Sergeant-Major in one enlisted men's compound. . .He is our immediate Lord, but the highest Lord is the Major with his distant orders. . .

After the proclamation of *General Order No. 1,* signed by the American Commanding Officer, I wait for an opportunity to contact the Americans. . .Dangerous, impossible. . .Why tell the Americans what's happening if they're too stupid to know?. . .What if they don't believe me?. . .Some stubborn impulse--memories--force me to try. . .After all this is the United States of Revolutionary Freedom. . .Someone will listen to me, believe that this terror is taking place in American camps under the guise of the Geneva Convention. . .

Be honest. . .Admit I'm trying to protect myself, find sanctuary with the Americans. . .I cannot live in this fear of attack again from the Nazis. . .I must find safety by informing the Americans, forcing them to remove me from this camp. . Somewhere is the American who will listen, understand, who will act. . .

Patience. . .Forty of us sleep in one barrack. . .According to the posted sanitary rules, two rows of double-decked bunks are made up so the head of one bunk alternates with the foot of its neighbor. . .This is helpful when the next occupant has a cold, but fails to conceal the stink of closely stacked bodies. . .

During the day the usual military formula for making cots prevails, sharp, tight folds on the bedding, knife creases on the blanket propped at the foot of the cot--"*Knife creases or punishment!*" order the disciplinarians, the non-commissioned officers. . .A daily inspection by the disciplinarians makes certain that the long, dark room, lit dimly at night by light bulbs swaying from cords, conforms to the prescription of orderliness. . .For every two cots there is a clothes rack, a stray piece of wood with bent nails gleaming in it. . .So many prisoners are crowded into the room that two or three men often share one nail, articles of clothing piled on top of each other. . .After my camp experiences it is almost humorous to hear prisoners argue about the confined area of their clothes. . .There are bitter arguments. . .One soldier accuses another of invading the privacy of his shirt or pants. . .

A heavy iron stove squats in the center of the barrack to protect us from the desert cold at night. . .The prisoners who sleep next to it are in constant danger of roasting. . .These undesirable cots are forcibly occupied by the unfortunate, daily losers of card games. . .Although contrary to the rules of American authorities who want the correct prisoner in the correct cot, it's easy enough to change cots rapidly in the event of sudden inspections. . .The ends of the building are also considered undesirable as the limited heat never penetrates there and one freezes. . .Halfway between the stove and door is the ideal location for comfort. . .This area is guarded by the intimates of the barrack leader, Feldwebel Gruber, who commanded an anti-aircraft battery. . .I call him The Man on Stilts. . .His long, thin legs direct his body which displays little torso. . .When he stands at attention proudly during the daily counts, he resembles some curious mechanical stork dominating his preserve. . .

One large latrine building services three barracks. . .Early mornings after the count a long line of cursing men await their turn. . .

"What's your trouble, constipated? You drown in there?"

The calls to hurry grow louder. . .In a vain attempt to quiet the complaints, the latrine orderly appears in the doorway. . . Everyone calls him The Little White Man because, somehow, he has acquired a white American T-shirt. . .The shirt becomes an obsession to him, a mark of prestige. . .It is his only trademark of individuality. . .In the course of time every prisoner acquires at least one object, no matter how small or insignificant, that distinguishes him from other prisoners--a matchbox, book, scarf, handkerchief, a toothpaste, a nude cut from a magazine or newspaper, any object on which to fasten his distinction. . .

When The Little White Man appears in the latrine doorway to calm the line of impatient men, he parades up and down in his white T-shirt. . ."Shut up!" he commands in his high, tinkling voice. "You bastards keep my floor clean when you get in there or else. . ."

Soft derisive cries fill the air. . .The cries cannot be voiced too loudly for fear of arousing the disciplinarians. . .For revenge the prisoners wait until they are inside safe in the steam from ten showers and the flushing of ten busy toilets. . .Then they push The Little White Man into a hissing shower and hold him there. . ."Don't get my shirt dirty, you bastards!" he yells furiously. . .A wet T-shirt he accepts grudgingly, but never a dirty one. . .

In the enforced camp communality the search for privacy assumes a curious ritual. . .Everyone seeks his own method of being alone, even if only for a few minutes. . .One prisoner shuts himself in a closet for ten minutes every evening. . . Another climbs up on the barrack roof to sit alone and watch the moon. . .Others take walks by themselves, deliberately ignoring their friends. . .Some play games alone, games that normally require partners. . .A group of box-sitters form a long row outside of the barrack, far apart from each other, meditating, staring at the distant mountains. . .

In my effort to contact the Americans I make a fatal mistake. . .I inform Major Weimann of my ability in English. . . He assigns me as a clerk in his headquarters office to watch me and mock me. . .Frequently he compliments me sardonically on my English-speaking talents. . .

Major Weimann is young for his rank, thirty-five at most. . Tall, lean, he carries himself stiffly erect. . .His head rises from his collar like the sharp point on a pencil. . .Sparkling blue eyes soften the craggy outline of a prominent nose and high cheekbones. . .When he speaks he never raises his voice. . It is always firm, direct. . .Like most German officers he has a passion for order, though he prefers romantic military action to paperwork. . .He is too aristocratic to be a true Nazi. . .He is proud to be a professional militarist, trained in the old traditions: Germany to rule the world with Bach and Beethoven as well as bayonets and flank movements. . .His fingers are never still. . . Always they drum on whatever surface they happen to be resting, as though he is playing the piano. . .

The nephew of a General, he is a graduate of the General Staff School and a member of Rommel's staff in Africa. . . On special occasions when he wears his full-dress uniform, his chest is covered with medals, including a decoration for hand-to-hand bayonet fighting in the early days of the Russian campaign. . .An officer who plays the role of cultured diplomat, he is personable with the correct austerity. . .In Germany he owns a square stone block house on the Elbe River, two grand pianos, five hunting dogs, horses, a handsome blonde wife with a large bosom, and three children bursting with muscular health. . .These posessions stare at me from his office photographs. . .

After a few weeks of captivity, the power of his authority assured, the Major orders two prisoners, carpenters by trade, to build him some furniture. . .The luxurious chairs, tables and desk that he requests are ingeniously made out of waste lumber. . .Still the Major remains unsatisfied with his colorless, drab office. . .He requisitions paint from the American authorities who are anxious to obtain his cooperation. . .The Major has his walls painted a brilliant emerald green with blue trim. . .What appears incongruous on entering his office is the large picture cut from an American *Esquire* magazine and tacked on the wall. . .The film star Betty Grable's slim legs appear next to nostalgic nineteenth century mist-covered landscapes and a Dürer reproduction showing an aristocratic old man deep in thought. . .On his desk the Major has a pale green blotter and large calendar illustrated with medieval paintings. . .Flypaper hangs from his ceiling, although the prison kitchens are devoid of flypaper. . .

While inspecting compounds with Captain Dampfstoff, the Major is also accompanied by his aide Lieutenant Schimmelwasser, a young, eager submarine officer. . .The Major is fond of small, thin cigars. . .According to German military etiquette the superior officer holds his cigar only when smoking. . .Consequently the honor of conveying the cigar falls to Lieutenant Schimmelwasser who dedicates himself anxiously to this ceremony. . .He holds the cigar clenched in front of him like a torch, regarding it with suspicion lest the ashes drop in the wrong place. . .His signal to rush up with the cigar is a slight pause in the Major's ceremonial progress. .

Lieutenant Schimmelwasser takes two eager steps forward. . . Without looking back the Major plucks the cigar gracefully, out of the air, puffs luxuriously, flicks off the ash carefully, and hands the cigar back to his aide. . .The procession continues. . .

Captain Dampfstoff mocks this cigar ritual as an aristocratic indulgence. . .He cares nothing about manners. . .Dampfstoff has no understanding of how German manners and militarism are connected. . .In civilian life he was a baker. . .His big, white fingers, his carefully cleaned nails seem groomed for kneading dough. . .There is nothing dough-like about his face. . .It observes suspiciously, points like a hunting dog. . . His nostrils twitch nervously adding to his faithful watchdog demeanor. . .

We prisoners discover quickly that Dampfstoff's power and authority brook no interference from anyone, even the Major. . .In the headquarters office I learn that Dampfstoff is not merely Weimann's adjutant. . .He is the most important Nazi party representative in the camp. . .Trained as a Political Education officer, it is his assignment to make all of us prisoners hew to party doctrine. . .

Disguised as Weimann's adjutant he obtains permission from American officials to supervise all work details in a "proper military manner". . .On his "tours of inspection" he stops in every barrack and reads a proclamation, the National Socialist rules of the camp:

1) Every Monday morning there will be a *Kampf* lecture, an explanation (or rather a revelation as it is called) of pertinent parts of the gospel, *Mein Kampf.* All such gatherings will be held under the guise of "recreational" or "educational" meetings.

2) Several radios have already been received from charity organizations. More will be bought in time. A *Pressewalt* has been established to supervise all radio programs and newspapers. A list of suitable radio programs will be drawn up and circulated. It is forbidden to listen to unapproved programs. Special, educational, prepared news bulletins will be read at mealtimes. Because of the importance of these news bulletins

to the Fatherland, complete silence and strict attention are required when they are read.

3) Compulsory physical exercise periods are to be observed strictly. All sports and calisthenics are to be performed with "military spirit and discipline" to keep fit for further "military service to the Fatherland and to the National Socialist cause when you are freed by the superior, dedicated armies of the Third Reich."

4) Education courses are to be organized for "practical use." All anti-aircraft gunners, for example, will enlist in Mathematics for further training in Ballistics. Courses in History--the glorious destiny of the German nation from Frederick the Great through Wagner, Nietzsche and Bismarck to Hitler--are compulsory for everyone.

5) To handle any violations of the national welfare in the camp, a Court of Honor has been created. The Court will mete out appropriate punishments, including the most severe, to those guilty of infringements of camp discipline or traitorous activities. . .

Dampfstoff always concludes his proclamations with a fervent exhortation that transforms his hunting dog face into the capture of destiny: *"Remember, even though you are prisoners in the enemy's country, wherever you are there is Germany! Whatever you do you must always act as Germans. Ein Volk! Ein Reich! Ein Führer! Heil Hitler!"*. . .

All this is only the first layer of hunting instructions. . . Down, down. . .We are forced to attend the "educational" courses. . .Absence results in "Lager-Acht und Bann.". . . Whenever I return from work to the enlisted men's compound, I am isolated in my bunk and have to ask permission every time I leave it. . .I can't talk to anyone without feeling that someone is listening.

The few radio sets that we have are put under the control of party guards who are relieved every two hours. . .We are warned not to use the locked mail boxes in the compounds for our letters. . .All mail home is to be given to the "Postal

Officer," who is supposedly a master in the correction of wrong addresses. . .He is, of course, a censor who throws away letters containing "poor morale" and brings to the attention of the Court of Honor any statements that merit political investigation. . .

Anyone caught reading a forbidden newspaper or listening to a banned radio broadcast is brought before the Court of Honor. . .If the offense is severe enough, the Court will sentence the offender according to the "Rundfunkgesetz von Berlin," which means one month's arrest in quarters and expulsion from the camp community for the same period of time. . .

One day I see this law in action. . .Delivering some papers to one of the officer's barracks, I encounter an elderly captain, a timid, unmilitary-looking reserve officer, who is trying to learn English by listening to the radio. . .Obviously he understands only a few phrases as he listens with a puzzled expression and keeps repeating simple words. . .It is slightly humorous since the broadcast is about increasing Germany defeats. . .A young lieutenant walks in, listens for a moment, then angrily switches off the radio without even a "please". . .Surprised, his mouth gaping, the captain stares at him. Angrily he switches the radio on again. . .The lieutenant glares, shouts, "You're listening to a forbidden program! In the presence of a soldier too!" He points to me. . .

"I'm studying English," the Captain insists doggedly.

The duel of glares continues. . .Finally the Lieutenant stalks out of the room. . .Worried, the Captain asks me if I think the radio program is a corrupting influence. . .No, I try to reassure him, there is little danger of corruption from such a program. . .Several days later, during the reading of the weekly punishment list which grows longer and longer, Dampfstoff announces that the Captain has been summoned before the Court of Honor. . .The Captain has been sentenced to a week's expulsion from the camp community for listening to illegal radio broadcasts. . .

Day after day the discipline strengthens. . .I try to imagine how this organization seems to American officials. . .Do they see only the well-planned, smooth surface movements?. . . Why can't they perceive the shadows underneath? I keep trying to speak to the American authorities, but find no opportunity. . .Every minute I am afraid that some newly arrived prisoner will identify me conclusively as a former concentration camp inmate or a member of the 999th Division. . .

Weimann and Dampfstoff make no secret of their funeral plans for the two murdered officers. . .They call a ban on work in all four compounds until the Americans meet their demands for a spectacular funeral. . .They badger Captain Stevens, the American liaison officer in the compound, with their demands. . .They insist that the guard who killed the officers must be court-martialed with German witnesses in attendance at the trial. . .Also they request permission for every German prisoner of war to attend the funeral. . .4000 soldiers and officers marching in ranks to the designation graveyard outside of the barbed wire fence!. . .Naturally flags, decorations, an appropriate funeral ceremony will be permitted. . .

Captain Stevens, an older, grey-haired, nervous man who can only speak a few words of German that he learned during a brief World War I assignment in Germany, scurries back and forth between the authorities trying to mediate the impasse. . His eyes develop a red, tormenting twitch. . .He complains that he suffers from high blood pressure. . .*"Why should I have been drafted back into the Army at my age?"*. . .He talks longingly about his home in a small town in Wisconsin where he was an insurance executive. . .

How can I talk to Stevens?. . .He relies heavily for all his administrative duties on Sergeant Hochweiler, Weimann's chief clerk in the compound. . .Hochweiler, an approved English speaker and dedicated Nazi bureaucrat from an anti-aircraft unit, prepares all administrative reports for Stevens to sign. . .Hochweiler is dedicated to "the improvement of our administrative efficiency". . .He clings to Stevens as part of the Nazi plan to control key positions. . .Stevens clings to the Sergeant as master of all difficulties. . .

At every chance I linger in the office hoping to catch Stevens alone. . .Usually the room is full of officers confering about the funeral negotiations. . .When I finally catch Stevens alone he tries to excuse himself. . *Don't let him escape.* . .I speak so rapidly that my knowledge of English seems to vanish. . .My eyes scare him. . .He won't look at me. . .I begin at the beginning as if the dawn of memory will save me. . . *Tell him about my wife and her father. . .Then he'll understand my danger.* . .Stevens stares at the top of his desk:

I met her in a cheap Berlin restaurant in 1932. . .She was wearing a faded yellow dress. . .I had just graduated from the university. . .A scarecrow student in a city ruled by unemployment and the rising power of the Nazis, I was seeking a job. . . Jobs didn't appeal to me, but I needed the money. . .Many of us grotesque wanderers haunted the Berlin streets. . .Since there were no jobs we spent our time watching the twisted beggars plead for worthless inflated money. . .

Suddenly Stevens looks up as I speak. . .For the first time he's staring at me directly, his eyes gaping, incredulous. . . I'm telling him a story, a fantasy. . .Desperately I continue, speaking faster, jaggedly:

The lines of her face were set in tranquility. . .Strange word for that time. . .She wasn't one of the grotesques. . .Her hair hung down to her shoulders in a black, curling wave. . .She wasn't beautiful. . .Her face reflected a quiet spirit to calm my restlessness. . .She walked barelegged, with long, graceful legs. . .How many women walked in dignity then?. . .The whore had replaced the Hohenzollerns. . .She took me home that evening. . .I met her father, the educational fanatic. . . Her mother was dead. . .

As we entered the old man was huddled in a chair. . .He didn't look up. . .His thick, grey hair, beard, his restless hands hovered over a battered volume of Spinoza in his lap. . . After she introduced me his eyes lifted slowly. . .He stared at me in silence, a stare with double vision. . .Still deep in the book he muttered a sentence half to himself: *"Thence we shall see how much stronger the wise man is than the ignorant."*. . .After a moment he started at the sound of his voice as if he were hearing an echo. . .He apologized for welcoming a stranger to his house by quoting Spinoza. . .

A Jew, he directed a small, experimental, private school. . . When he discovered that I was an ex-student he couldn't stop talking about his educational theories. . .Education was the discovery of freedom he proclaimed. . .Not in my experience I argued. . .He insisted that you must shock the student out of complacency, force him into ideas foreign to his accustomed patterns. . .Make freedom assume wider and wider boundaries. . .The risk was tremendous, potential chaos, physical battles in the classroom, severe arguments. . .Give up the rigid control, the familiar, sad way of European institutions. . .

How many students did he have in his school?. . .One hundred only he admitted. . .She sat calmly in a corner of the room. . .Through the absurd, idealistic words I stared at her. . Does one find love in calmness?. . .Love is supposed to be a fever, a bloodstream of fire. . .

I came to think she lived in quietude. . .Perhaps that was why I wanted finally to marry her. . .That night in my dingy room I examined myself in the mirror. . .Dark, stringy hair, deep-set eyes, pale complexion, careless, baggy clothes. . My tall, stooped figure leered out of the mirror. . .*That apparition should be a teacher?. . .Don't be a fool. . .*Examine your environment. . .Use your education factually for commercial gain as educations are meant to be used. . .Acquire solid facts to learn the techniques of a growing, technological world and accumulate the luxuries of money. . .

The walls of my attic room sagged with cobwebs spun intricately from the eaves. . .Dirty clothes were flung in a corner on a pile of newspapers sounding the frantic alarms of the day. . .If I went into business, preferably munitions, the aircraft industry, criminal law--then I might earn enough money to marry. . .Why worry about weddings in Berlin?. . .Marry the state, worship Potsdam!. . .Goethe's Weimar was south, fading south, there on the horizon with all great obsolete men and animals, sinking down, gone. . .

He persuaded me. . .The Old Jew persuaded the Gentile Fool. . .*One night I dreamt of myself as a Fool in a jangling cap. . .The old man was an aged, Jewish Lear. . .He was dividing his ridiculously small territory. . .He offered the largest share to his quiet daughter who would say nothing to flatter him. . .In idealistic rage he turned to me, the mocking Fool. . He gave me everything, a vanishing nothing. . .*

I woke from that lost dream to feel her calmness beside me . . .Forget marriage. . .We lived together for several months. .. She came to my room and never complained about the drabness, never urged me to take the job that her father offered in his school. . .Her father knew nothing about our life together. . .Lying together quietly, partaking of the cool world into which our raging bodies entered, we were happy. . We spoke only a few words. . .More than words she believed in signals of assent which baffled me with their love beyond agreement. . .Deliberately I argued with her against her father's folly. . .It angered me to hear her neither deny nor disagree. . .I could feel a different current flowing in her body, a flowing force beyond language that I was unable to understand. . .

Around us the political tension drove the city's face into the twisted lines and colors of a puzzling, satirical cubistic portrait. . .Nothing seemed real, the salutes, the torchlight parades, the grotesque pseudo-Wagnerian mythology, the ceaseless battering words with insistent, attacking rhythms, the growing violent homosexuality, the men with painted faces putting on uniforms. . .We watched a street opera where the meaningful action takes place offstage. . .The curtain rises. . .Abruptly you see the illusion of reality. . .There is the painted backdrop of real houses. . .The chorus sings happily at their daily chores, but the plot develops in the wings. . . An unheard shot offstage, an accident, a political or racial murder, a brief scream. . .One more anonymous man or woman dead. . .Everyone is hypnotized by unseen ghosts manipulated by the passionate, syncopated rhythms of murderers sheltered behind their mystical legends. . .

At home I hid in her touch, the one calm body bending only to a timeless physical rhythm, the pulse of love. . .When the curtain banged down and the inflamed audience surged out to face machine guns and the queer, new figure of power with the toothbrush mustache in the president's seat, the street opera became real. . .

One day, like a sleepwalker, I accompanied her father to his school. . .The crazy old man was talking to a class of ten stupified boys and girls about the image of God. . .*God in the approaching time of Der Führer and his henchmen?*. . .I watched fascinated as he passed out slips of paper. . .A motley group of boys and girls. . .They reminded me of my dog days in school. . .

"I want you to draw on the paper what you think God looks like," the old man was saying. "Then describe him in writing beneath the drawing."...He spoke very calmly...His quick eyes glittered above his silvery pointed beard. . .His blue-veined, thin hands flickered with surprising dexterity as he passed out the papers, pausing briefly to pat a boy on the head or place an affectionate hand on a girl's shoulder by way of encouragement. . .*A teacher should never touch a student!*. . .

"Begin," the old man continued. "Take your time. Draw God exactly as you think he looks."...*Draw God!*...

The children began to take the usual classroom escape routes...Most of them drew time-worn clichēs of an eternally bearded face with long hair. . .Several made frantic attempts at some vague floating conception of a heavenly face and body that came to nothing. . .One girl drew an image half-woman and half-man. . .After long thought one boy put only a dot on the blank page...

Collecting the drawings the old man talked, questioned, illustrated for an hour. . .He began by challenging gently every child who depicted God as a traditionally bearded sentimental ancient...Were they merely imitating what they had heard from their parents or seen in books?...He shook their security by showing them images of many different gods that he had collected all of his life. . .Disturbed I thought: "Why do this in a time when they're insecure enough anyway?"...

"You can see that a people creates the gods it needs. In a desert country beset with warring tribes, the Jews created Jehovah, a frowning patriarchal giant of supreme age, wisdom and morality."...I could hardly believe my eyes...He struck a stance as Jehovah glaring down at his students. . .Instead of laughing the classroom became singularly quiet. . .A real teacher is a good actor, I conceded grudgingly, even if he is a little crazy. . .Trying vainly to contain himself, the boy who had drawn the dot on the page began suddenly to laugh. . . The image of Jehovah vanished. . .The old man pounced on the boy...

"Why did you laugh at me?"

Instead of withdrawing into fear like the usual German student the boy giggled: "You make a funny-looking Jehovah."

In any school I had known such an answer would have earned the smack of a ruler across the hand or a cane against the seat of the pants. . .The old man seized the boy and urged him to explain his vision of god. . .The boy was the kind of brilliant, arrogant mind who must always, at any cost, assert his difference from his fellow students. . ."The dot is only a star spinning in space, an unknown light and energy," the boy began. "That is what God is today, an invisible force. We don't know if he is there.". . .

The old man made no attempt to argue with the brash boy . . .He probed the boy's defenses with seemingly indirect questions and examples. . .As I listened, dazed, to the dialogue, the imagination in that room blazed alive. . . How many dry lectures, sermons, abstract classroom discussions on religion, I had endured!. . .This was the first time that God seemed interesting in a physical way. . .The old man thrust pictures of naked Greek gods at the boy--Zeus and Apollo. . .

"Why did the Greeks show their gods naked?" The old man waved the pictures before the boy's nose. . .

Taken aback the boy muttered, "I don't know,". . .Excited I saw that the boy's natural arrogance was collapsing. . .He was learning, listening in a new way, with a respect for his teacher that I had never seen or felt before in a classroom. . .

Suddenly the girl who had drawn God as a half-man, half-woman, interrupted. . .She asked why God was always depicted as a man. . .Indignantly she said that this was unfair. . . In Germany yet a girl was speaking this way!. . .The old man had all the children eager to listen now. . .He began to tell them stories about the different gods male and female, the Egyptian gods of sun and death; the Teutonic God, Wotan; the Norse God, Thor; the Jewish God Jehovah, the Christian concept of God's son, Jesus Christ. . .Again and again he returned to the Greek gods who seemed to fascinate him more than the others. . .*Why did children wear clothes?. . .Was it just because they lived in a cold climate?. . .My god, I thought, it's turning into a sex lecture. . .The old man even dramatizes sex. . .*

Feverishly he fumbled in his desk. . .After much snorting and shuffling which kept the children's attention riveted on him, he produced an enormous photograph of an Apollo statue with the penis chisled off. . .

"Look!" he patted the picture, "the beautiful God of the sun, Apollo. You see how the ancient Greeks admired man's naked body. Especially in the case of a god, how strong, how powerful that body had to be. But something is wrong. . . What is wrong?". . .

"Somebody chopped off his penis," the arrogant boy observed immediately. . .Giggles sounded through the room. . .

"It was done by the Christian crusaders and their disciples," the old man said sternly. "When they entered Greece with their army and their swords they could not stand the nakedness of the great statues. They destroyed many and chopped off the sexual organs of others. To this day if you visit Athens to see the few remaining statues, the guards will speak to you of the savage Christians.". . .

"Did the Crusaders sleep in their armor at night?" the fresh boy asked. "Were they afraid of their penises? Jesus must have had a penis too.". . .

Some of the girls were blushing, whispering to each other. . The boys were grinning. . .The old man made no effort to stop the commotion. . .He held the children transformed, open to inquiry. . .Eagerly he began to quote Aristotle, Plato, the Greek myths, anything that came to mind to illustrate the way the Greeks loved to train the senses together, to create from strong bodies and inquisitive minds heroic, imaginative actions. . .

"No," I thought, "he's gone too far. They can't understand him. He's lost them.". . .

Perhaps only a few children really understood the old man's historical illuminations. . .Their faces grew increasingly serious, puzzled. . *Had the old man lost control of himself, the risk of a great teacher?*. . .He struggled desperately to pull the children beyond themselves. . .He made no attempt to give them easy answers. . .He wanted to lift them beyond their limited experience into territories of knowledge and vision that they had never entered. . .Beneath their puzzled expressions the children were intent on the old man's mood more than on his words. . .They were flattered that he demanded more, expected more than they had to give. . .At the end the old man transcended himself in his struggle to show the children the joyous faith of the Athenian men and women. . .He chanted reverently Aeschylus's sacred song:

> Joy to you, joy to your justly appointed riches,
> Joy to all the people, blessed
> With the Virgin's love, who sits
> Next beside her father's throne.
> Wisdom you have learned at last;
> Folded under Pallas's wing,
> Yours at last the grace of Zeus.

When he stopped there was a long quiet. . .No sense of urgent time, no clanging bell announced another tiresome session of knowledge. . .The children clustered around to ask questions. . .The cunning old master, his eyes sparkling, reached into his desk and handed out pieces of candy!. . . After religion, philosophy, logic, song, the final touch of sweetness. . .I was worn out, exhausted, amazed. . .The old man had trapped me with his exhibition. . .

That night when his daughter appeared in my room, she brought a bottle of wine. . .I was immediately suspicious. . . .

"What are we celebrating?". . .

"That is for you to decide," she smiled mysteriously. "Must there always be a definite occasion to celebrate?". . .

I calmed down and kissed her. . .That was always the effect she had on me. . .Still I had to bluster my way through her tantalizing mystery. . .After dinner and wine, I paced up and down and gave her a bravura parody of her father's incredible classroom. . .She laughed and laughed. . ."He is so like that. He is so serious and intent on his work that he will teach them anything that comes into his mind, no matter what subject they are supposed to be studying."

Then she became serious. . ."You liked him, didn't you? Are you going to teach there? He needs you." She spoke the last words reluctantly. . .

*He needs me. . .Was I out of my mind?. . .*I stormed on trying to conceal the fact that for the first time in my life

I wanted to be needed. . .What a fool I would be to take such a teaching job!. . .I protested, "How can we live on that if we get married? The salary is almost nothing. There are only a hundred students."

She smiled at me. . .I wanted that smile never to stop. . . Only that smile could cover my fear that I was inadequate to teach. . .I had so much to learn about love, about life, about imagination, about knowledge. . Thank god I was alive in this terrifying nightmare of a city and the Jews, the Jews yet, were willing to love and teach me. . .

Don't you see, Captain Stevens, here in this camp the Nazis are building the same, strict, suspicious channels of authority that I endured in Germany after Hitler came to power. . . One day, without warning, S.A. troops came to the school where I was teaching and locked the doors. . .My father-in-law was seized and deported to an unknown camp. . .That evening, trying frantically to escape, my wife and I were arrested at the bus station. . .For years I've hung suspended between the hope of her survival and the knowledge that such hope is a vicious fantasy. . .I was a pure-blooded Aryan for whom there was a dim promise of re-education, even in a concentration camp. . .But she was a tainted Jew. . .They were going to make an example of us like the Gottshalk case. . .

"The Gottshalk case?" Captain Stevens looks puzzled.

"The famous German film actor, Joachim Gottshalk, the matinee idol. He was married too to a Jewish woman. When Goebbels gave him an ultimatum to divorce his wife they both committed suicide."

"But you weren't famous were you?" Stevens glances at me dubiously. "Why would they want to make an example of you?"

"It was not me. They wanted my wife and her father."

"I'm sorry. What do you want me to do?"

"You must get me out of this camp."

"But you're a prisoner of war. . ."

"Please get me an appointment with your authorities. I will tell them how the Nazis are organizing the camp. . ."

"Do you have any proof of this, any evidence?"

"I can tell them all the details I've seen."

"I'll see what I can do, but I can't promise anything." Stevens focuses his attention on his desk again, as Sergeant Hochweiler enters the room with a file tucked under his arm, pretending not to notice me. . .

Late the next afternoon Captain Stevens calls me to his desk even though Sergeant Hochweiler is sitting in the office working quietly, seemingly absorbed in his work. . .Stevens plays with an eraser before he summons the courage to speak . . .He moistens his lips, twists in his chair. . .Finally he asks abruptly: *"Are you a homosexual?". . .*

My face sags stupidly. . .Rocking back and forth he stares through the window at the mountains. . .

"Who accused me?"

"You can't expect me to reveal my information. . ."

I try again to tell my story. . .Even to me it sounds disjointed, a monstruous dream of the past. . .He listens squirming in doubt. . .Reluctantly he agrees to try and arrange a meeting for me with the American camp commander. . . *He's afraid that some trouble may happen in his domain. . . Better to pass the decision to some higher authority. . .*

"You realize," he cautions, "if you are homosexual you'll probably be segregated. You'd better think it over and tell the truth. I'll try and work out this meeting, but I can't guarantee anything."

*The truth. . .*Is it better if I confess to homosexuality?. . . At least that way I may escape. . .Did Sergeant Hochweiler report me as a "queer" to Weimann?. . .A convenient way to keep prisoners fixed in the correct channels of order. . .Army and prison authorities regard homosexuality as more of a problem than veneral disease--indecent, dangerous gods performing sacreligious rites. . .To allay Hochweiler's suspicions I mention my appeal to Captain Stevens for an appointment with the American camp commander. . .I invent a fictitious sister who has been badly wounded in an air raid, who needs my help. . *Do not mention my marriage despite the accusation of homosexuality. . .*

"We can arrange to contact your sister for you," Hochweiler's eyes inform me that I'm a liar. . ."No German soldier is permitted to contact the enemy for personal arrangements.". . .*The tone of his voice. . .*I struggle vainly to clarify my life. . .Hochweiler cuts me off coldly, saying that he'll investigate the matter. . .He leaves me with the knowledge that I'll be watched even more closely. . .Is it best to give up my futile attempts to contact the American authorities?. . .

Slowly the impasse about the funeral arrangements is resolved. . .An American "undertaker" appears in his black limousine from Trinidad. . .Weimann and Dampfstoff refuse to give up the bodies of the murdered officers. . .They place them upright in the huge kitchen refrigerator "for the preservation of their honor and their sacred burial according to their military rights". . .Captain Stevens is only a frantic messenger, his nerves visibly exploding against his tight flesh. . *.He has forgotten me.* . .He brings Weimann the camp commander's promise that the American guard who fired the incredible shot will be court-martialed and punished. . .Weimann confers with Dampfstoff and a proclamation is issued: "We demand that the charges and details of the court-martial for the murder of two German officers be published in a written order". . .The written order is promised. . .

The Americans grant permission for the entire German officers' compound and a select delegation of soldiers to attend the funeral. . .Weimann and Dampfstoff demand an equivalent number of soliders to officers. . .*One thousand to one thousand.* . .White-faced, Stevens returns with an agreement for one thousand soldiers to match the officers. . .The question of flags, decorations, speeches, is urged back and forth . . .One morning Stevens is missing. . ."Ill", it is whispered. . . The whispers grow into smiles. . .Sergeant Hochweiler announces to me with ironic satisfaction, "Poor Captain Stevens. Evidently his nerves collapsed. . ."

Prisoners cease talking to me. . .A wall of isolation surrounds me. . .Every morning as I come to work in the officers' compound, every evening as I retreat to my own compound, I notice increasing groups of prisoners squatting beside ant holes. . .Searching for idle recreation during the strike, the long hours of waiting, the prisoners have discovered the voracious strength of the big, red ants that crawl, nest in the hard soil. . .To the casual observer, the way of the ants seems pointless, an insane racing around. . .In my isolation I become fascinated and walk slowly to and from work, watching the ants whenever possible, moving from one group of prisoners to the next whenever I sense that I am tarrying too long. . .

Looking quickly at the ants from above, their activity resembles the frantic network of traffic in a small, overcrowded city. . .Only after close study and observation does the unique teamwork of the ants become apparent. . .They have dark abdomens and yellowish or brownish heads. . . Because of the arid desert soil they have worked out an ingenious method of storing juices in the bodies of young worker-ants. . .These workers swell out like tiny balloons. . How organized the ant colonies seem just like prison camps. . Any young worker-ant may become a living storage tank, inflated, ludicrous, hardly able to move. . *Marked, seized as I have been seized. . .*"Go to the ant, thou sluggard," advises King Solomon in Proverbs, "Consider her ways and be wise". .

Consider their squads of destruction. . .Many ants can go through a maze that contains false turns. . .The prisoners build mazes to prove this. . .The ants march through the mazes toward their prey. . .They form squads of destruction to drag their prey into their underground fortress where the Queen rules. . .There is the difference, a matriarchy, a Queen in charge of her prison colony while her worker-slaves protect her, feed the young, fight her wars, defend her territory. . .

The arena of ants is the apt title for a game that prisoners invent to pass the time. . .The game spreads throughout the compounds. . .In an idle moment one prisoner kills a fly and throws it into a line of scurrying insects to see what will happen. . .The fly is too big to pull into the hole. . .The frenzied crossing, circling of the ants increases as squad after squad passes the huge body of the fly. . .A clever plan evolves. . . The plan circulates among the ants. . .*The intelligence of the ants is passed from fighters to farmers to workers by means of a "kiss", a mouth-to-mouth exchange of messages stored in their crops. . .*

Carefully platoons form on each side of the fly's body. . . They begin to tear off the wings, slowly, methodically. . . This takes an eternity of time, a minute of time for such dedicated predators. . .When the wings are off and the naked body lies there like a miniature blimp, reinforcements move in. . .These fresh squads take turns shoving, pulling the body into the hole. . *.Push, pull, push, pull, a steady rhythm. . .*

The prisoners watch, fascinated, removed for a moment from their boredom. . .Soon they bet on the length of time that it takes the ants to remove the wings of the fly and drag him into the hole. . .The rules are strict to suit a prison camp . . .Every fly must disappear completely into the hole before the elapsed time is officially over. . .I watch myself vanish into the hole. . .I am in *The Arena of Ants. . .*

Why did I write that young American lieutenant a note pleading for help?. . .A desperate, foolish thing to do in this wilderness of ant games. . .No one seemed to notice. . .Still Hochweiler and Dampfstoff keep their vigilant watch on me . . .What made me decide impulsively to trust this new American messenger?. . .What if he, like Stevens, considers me a homosexual?. . .He may even report my note to Weimann. . . Youth is not to be trusted. . .A monstrous indifference to justice rules Europe and America. . .Still something about the young American forced me to act. . .He refused to flatter Dampfstoff and spoke back to him in German. . .Even Major Weimann commented ironically to Dampfstoff about their singular exchange of English and German thrusts. .Dampfstoff reddened. . .He and Weimann lose no chance to criticize each other. . .Yet they cooperate. . .Weimann is afraid of Dampfstoff's political power. . .

They are going ahead with their obscene funeral plans. . . Evidently the Americans have consented to the funeral arrangements. . .At least I will not be forced to participate. . . I will not be permitted into their sacred blood and earth rituals. . .Those poor frozen bodies in the refrigerator will become Nazi martyrs whatever their private dreams may have been. . .

The compound orchestra is rehearsing the Funeral March from Beethoven's *Eroica* symphony. . .An excellent orchestra with several professional musicians. . .Doubtless they will sublimate themselves to Beethoven, ignoring the function for which the music will be used. . .Poor Beethoven. . .He will become an unwilling Nazi witness too. . .In 1804 he inscribed

Napoleon's name proudly on the dedication page of his symphony. . .A few months later, raging when he heard that his ideal republican hero had declared himself Emperor, he scratched out Bonaparte's name. . .Now Beethoven, master of joy and freedom, will be forced to celebrate Der Führer in the American desert. . .From their dark tunnels the ants will listen with amazement. . .

Banners are being made from bedsheets. . .Flaming swastikas are painted on them. . .Flags are cut and sewn from blankets. . .Such ingenious industry. . .An old woodcarver is discovered. . .He sits outside our office window carving wooden standards with a penknife. . .Eagles soar lovingly from the wood carrying swastikas in their mouths. . . *Beautiful craftsmanship,* murmur adoring officers. . .

Funeral catafalques are constructed on which the dead officers may be carried in state. . .As Honor Guard twenty officers rehearse to carry each catafalque. . .The catafalques are built with lumber torn out of the sheds that house the coal supply. . .

An official speech writer works in our office under Dampfstoff's supervision. . .Dampfstoff refers to his precious copy of *Mein Kampf,* discusses favorite passages with the speech writer who is a former newspaper editor. . .Reverently they compare possible quotations. . .

How is Weimann taking these preparations?. . .He concentrates on the solemn, martial aspects of the funeral ceremony. . .He too is writing a speech in which I am certain he will quote Frederick the Great and perhaps that Prussian Field Marshal Gneisenau, master of pursuit at Waterloo. . .Ironic that Gneisenau fought in the War of American Independence on the British side!. . .Weimann wants everything to be in correct military taste. . .Any coarse political details that make him cringe he leaves to Dampfstoff. . .

Caught in the agony of these funeral preparations I dream of my nightmare days in the camp at Fuhlsbüttel. . .I feel the same terrible loneliness, the same threats of punishment. . . True Weimann and the Goose Father are totally different individuals, the would-be gentleman-aristocrat and the peasant turned brutal by the sudden power of his S.S. uniform. . . Was it my third or fourth Christmas in Fuhlsbüttel where I was sent after my arrest?. . .I spent that Christmas with my wrists handcuffed to the sides of a chair. . .Courtesy of the Goose Father who resented my shrill protests when I failed to receive mail from my wife. . .

That camp commander liked to be called *Der Gänsevater* because he had so many geese under his protection. . .Mostly purebred Aryan geese in that camp, political prisoners whom the Nazis wanted isolated, Communists, Social-Democrats, labor union leaders, "Jewish-tainted" traitors who spouted "anarchy and heresy". . .All professions were represented from lawyer and doctor to bricklayer and waiter. . .Among our ranks were sixteen-year olds and white bearded men over seventy. . .

Early on Christmas morning--was it 1937?--I was released from the disciplinary chair, shoved into the snow to line up with other prisoners. . .In his immaculate S.S. uniform, ribbons and medals polished to glare, the Goose Father appeared. . .Naked to the waist columns of prisoners stood at attention before him in rows of eight. . .The air was raw. . . A cold wind slashed our bare flesh. . .The Goose Father walked up and down the line, asking each of us cordially whether we had written home to our wives and mothers. . .

"Ja, Herr Oberführer, wir haben nach Hause geschrieben," our obedient answers rang through the sharp air in blue breath-clouds. . .

What happy letter would she receive if she were still alive?. . ."My darling, this Christmas I am sitting here relaxed after a hearty meal. Don't worry about me as I am perfectly well-treated. I have plenty of food and recreation in this camp. . .". . .

I never heard from her after my arrest. . .Not one word during my years in Fuhlsbüttel or later in the 999th Division in North Africa. . .For a long time I struggled to maintain the illusion of correspondence. . .To my immediate official I asserted my rights to send and receive letters. . .I wrote every day pouring forth my love, my loneliness, in letters that evaporated in the air. . .Was she still in Berlin working at forced labor?. . .Or were she and her father in separate labor camps to the east?. . .The rumor we heard was that Jews were being sent to separate camps when they were not used in factories for war work. . .Once at mail call after a year or two in Fuhlsbüttel, I was handed a small box of candy–presumably from her. . .It was maddening because there was no identification, no return address. . ."Look, stop your complaining," snapped the bored postal official when I protested, "Learn to correct your errors and you may receive better treatment. After all you are a German. You should have known better than to marry a Jewess. Why should you expect to hear from her? A box of candy is better than nothing". . .

I passed out the candy except for one piece to other inmates in my hut. . .Then I threw my one remaining piece as hard as I could against the wall. . .The chocolate spattered, cream dripped down the wall. . .It was hard to clean away in time for the next inspection. . .

At night I dreamt of her calmness. . .Was it an illusion?. . . Why always this stupid, haunting image of her calm?. . .If I confessed my fault in marrying her. . .If I confessed my errors in joining that corrupt old man who was intent on instilling loose moralities in a few misguided children, would they release me?. . .I dreamt on day and night, waking and sleeping, of her calmness and the old man's absurd idealism. .

Will they never stop watching me?. . .The Goose Father, Weimann, Dampfstoff, Hochweiler. . .All times run together in my isolation. . .Standing at attention in the Fuhlsbüttel yard I heard the Goose Father's strident voice pierce through the cold wind. . ."Forward March!". . .Half-naked we struggled forward from our frozen positions. . .Past huts, past the massive administration building with its dirty yellow facade. . Past heavy barred windows, underground isolation cells with damp, fetid floors. . .Past watchtowers with uniformed guards and machine guns. . .A joyous order cracked from the Goose Father's mouth: *"In step, sing!"*. . .We began to sing the prescribed song, *"Die Sonne scheint, dass mir das Herze lacht!" The sun shines and my heart laughs*. . .We marched toward the end of the courtyard where several S.S. guards stood beside a new group of strangers huddled together. . .More recruits destined for political corrections. . .

"Louder, louder, be cheerful!" shouted the Goose Father. .

The words of the song sounded in sharp points. . .My mind drifted as I tried to focus on distant places that always betrayed me, returned me to my present barriers. . .I was swimming naked in a cool summer lake. . .Strange faces watched me, Jews, Negroes, foreign races of all kinds. . .Suddenly I heard the prisoner behind me singing very softly to himself: *"Du Volk aus der Tiefe, du Volk aus der Nacht, vergiss nicht das Feuer, bleib auf der Wacht!" You people from the depths you from the night, forget not the fire, stay on the watch!"*. . The wind blew harder across the courtyard. . .Frantically we swung our arms while we marched, trying to keep our naked flesh from freezing. . .

"Louder, louder, my handsome singers!". . .

We bellowed out, *"Es ist so schön, so schön, ein Jägersmann zu sein. . ." It's so fine, so great to be a huntsman. .* .Far beyond the camp walls the lazy, clear notes of church bells began to ring. . .Christ was about to be born again on Christmas Day. . .Smoke from the camp kitchens swirled in the air. . . Tomorrow a holiday dinner for everyone, guards and prisoners alike if we sang well. . .

"Halt!". . .

We stopped before the small group of strangers. . . *Jews staring at us as if we were weird naked forms swimming in a foreign, bleak aquarium.* . .Behind the little group of Jews with their long beards--was that an apparition?. . .Was the old man there?. . .No, he's not one of these new arrivals. . .These were orthodox Jews by their archaic dress and look. . .Near the new prisoners a cage, in which a large ape was chained, barred the sky. . .The Goose Father motioned to a guard who opened the cage door. . .Gingerly, with a pole, the guard prodded the ape out of the cage. . .

"Attention my handsome singers," shouted the Goose Father joyously. "We present for you a Christmas spectacle. Today we have the privilege of entertaining a small group of orthodox Jews who have paused here en route to their last synagogue."

Ripples of laughter from the S.S. men. . .Lifting his hand the Goose Father continued: "On this day of mercy we permit the ape to choose one Jew to redeem themselves for their crucifixion of Christ. Push the Jews forward!". . .

Silence. . .We prisoners stiffened in our ranks. . .The aged Jews were herded forward. . .As the ape was released from his chain the S.S. men fell back. . .Puzzled the ape sat scratching himself. . .I could hear only a soft, rigid inhaling, exhaling of breath. . .

Impatiently the Goose Father commanded: "Poke that lazy ape! Show him his chosen people!". . .

Picking up his long, pointed pole, the S.S. guard approached the ape carefully and prodded him in his rear. . . Furious the ape turned and sprang at his tormentor, hurling him to the ground, snapping and biting at the guard. . .Uncontrollably I began to laugh. . .Despite my frantic effort to stop the laugh continued. . .Soon the entire column of prisoners was snickering in spasms. . .I was pulled out of ranks, beaten, dragged back to the huts where I was chained again to the chair. . . That night vast sexual dreams raged through my body's pain. . .How many years are required for a prisoner to forget his sex?. . .The jailors know. . .That is essential to the punishment. . .*Never*. . .I masturbated all the time. . .I still do. . .I will never forget her. . .She is there in the night, not a planet, not a star--an eerie, lucid glow, a nocturnal transformation that transcends death and the loss of identity. . .

The ritual preparations for the funeral grow more feverish. . .Companies of officers line up for drill. . .The bearers of the catafalques rehearse their solemn march-steps. . .Uniforms are brushed, repaired. . .Shoes are polished, hair cut, nails cleaned. . .Nature blows up clouds of dust as if to deny the ceremony. . .Curses rage through the desert dust that seeps gleefully into everything like a comic demon. . .Everyone cleans again savagely. . .

In the inner office I hear the solemn echoes of Weimann rehearsing his speech. . .Dampfstoff comes and goes hurriedly, supervising every detail, happy in his fanatic love for precision. . .Sergeant Hochweiler is spurred into feverish energy. . His face glows with a patriotic pride that I've never seen before. . .

One afternoon during the turmoil of funeral activities I'm summoned back suddenly to my compound for a medical appointment. . . Since I am on the list of those with medical problems due to my African hospital stay, no one is unduly concerned about my departure. . .*Wherever I go I will be watched*. . .Sergeant Hochweiler warns me to return as quickly as possible. . .He cautions me there will be speeches to type. . .I must work throughout the evening. . .

In the clinic, as is customary, my fellow prisoners snub me as I wait for my appointment. . .I sit in my chair as if frozen into the center of a glacier. . .The warm outer currents of conversation flow past me with cold scorn. . .When I enter the examination room I wait alone for my familiar medical officer in white to enter. . .The door opens. . .Instead of the doctor the young American lieutenant enters the room. . .

I open my mouth to speak and cannot. . .The lieutenant whispers to me. . .Under the pretext of an extensive X-ray examination, he has arranged to take me to the Station Hospital in the American sector of the camp. . .Waiting behind the clinic is an ambulance. . .Dazed I feel as though I am part of some absurd, exultant abduction. . .As we pass through the compound gate into freedom, I think *it is not true*. . .

On the way to the hospital the lieutenant's manner changes abruptly. . .He assumes the official manner of an interrogator. . .He questions me sharply as if through a transparent wall: "I have arranged an appointment for you with the camp commander, Colonel Williams. You must tell me the truth. . .". . .

The truth?. . .Will he believe such fantasies?. . .Watch his face closely. . .Be careful of the truth or he will never listen. . Should I tell him about the camp at Fuhlsbüttel?. . .No, there are too many camp stories. . .My laughter at the ape would have no relevance. . .Should I tell him my experience with the Berlin shadows after my release from Fuhlsbüttel?. . .Too fantastic. . .Stay as close as possible to political and military facts. . .They will be more believable. . .*Even if I tell him about the 999th Division?*. . .

"You mentioned Fuhlsbüttel. . .Was that one of the early concentration camps?". . .

"Yes.". . .*How can I tell this young, naive American what I really feel?*. . .*I must be cautious with him*. . .

"Don't be afraid to speak. You're safe now," the Lieutenant tries to encourage me stiffly. "You were not a political prisoner at Fuhlsbüttel?". . .

Be careful. . .*What if he fears I'm a Communist?. . .Don't offer too much information. . .*"I was there because I was married to a Jewess.". . .

"Only that? You were not politically active?". . .

"No. As I told Captain Stevens I was only a teacher in a school run by my wife's father.". . .

"That was why you were sent to the camp?" The Lieutenant stares at me sceptically. . .

"I suppose so. They don't bother with formal charges.". . . *Why do I need to educate this American boy?. . .*Try to control my sardonic tone. . .Better to keep silent if I can't control myself. . .At Fuhlsbüttel the guards always tested your ability to keep silent. . .It was a game for them. . .They stole little, unimportant things from you, stepped on your hands or feet, slapped you in the face for nothing. . .Still these were irritating trivialities compared with the psychological and physical torments that the Goose Father delighted to invent. .

"When were you released from Fuhlsbüttel?". . .

"Late in 1937.". . .

"That was well before the war. Why were you released?" The Lieutenant's voice becomes worried like his face. . .

"Who knows? Good behavior, perhaps.". . *.Good behavior. . .That may fit in with naive American thinking about prison existence. . .*

"What did you do then?". . .

"Another teaching job was not permitted to me. The only work I could find in Berlin was an occasional job as dishwasher, janitor, delivery boy. . .I was under constant surveillance, though not in any consistent way.". . .

"Why not 'any consistent way'?" asks the Lieutenant pressing his sceptical tone. . .

"I was not important enough". . *.I humiliate myself deliberately and he catches me. . .*

"If you were not *important enough* why did the Nazis follow you?". . .

Control my stupid pride. . .I am not convincing him, I'm merely damaging my situation. . ."Perhaps they wanted me for the 999th Division". . .How strange the number sounds. . *Why should the American youth believe in a military unit with such a fantastic number?. . .*

"999th Division? Why was it called that?". . .

"Perhaps only because it came after 998.". . .*I do not mean to be ironic, but how can I explain what I do not know?. . . Perhaps there was a secret meeting of high-ranking Nazi officers: "Gentlemen, we must give this new division a distinctive title.". . ."I suggest 999.". . ."Why?". . ."1000 is too large a number, 998 too small, too commonplace. . . 999 is the perfect number for suspicion, for anonymity. . .No one will believe in 999.". . .*

I am retreating inside again. . .The American is drifting away from me. . .The ambulance pulls to a halt in front of the Station Hospital. . .The Lieutenant motions me out. . .I walk in front of him, down a corridor past the first young woman I have seen for several years. . .She is very young, not even twenty, in a short dress, her legs bare and tanned. . .She has long, black hair down to her shoulders. . ."Hello, Lieutenant," she says. . .Turning she smiles inquisitively at me. . *My wife ten feet away, ten worlds away. . .No, she isn't smiling at me. . .I'm accused of being a homosexual. . .A prisoner has no sex. . .*

The Lieutenant motions me into a room. . ."Colonel Williams will be here soon. Let's get your story straight before he arrives."

My story. . .Yes, it is a fiction. . .

"How did you get into the 999th Division?"

"One day I was picked up by the Gestapo in Berlin and inducted," I reply.

"Just like that?"

"Yes. The invasion of Poland succeeded beyond Nazi expectations. The war was no longer an anxiety. It was a triumph. German planes and Panzer units had proved their brilliant technology. The Nazis felt that they could now take risks with certain units of political prisoners. So we entered the jurisdiction of the Pug Dog. . ."

"The Pug Dog?"

Try to clarify the strange names of survival. . ."He was an SS lieutenant, our specially assigned education officer, a former university janitor who was rewarded with a commission for his early party loyalty in reporting dissident students and faculty. A flat nose curving up in the middle of his face under a shaved head made us call him the Pug Dog."

"Why did they assign an S.S. officer to your unit?"

The American's face tries to look patient..."For security. Thirty-five to forty per cent of our unit were political prisoners, Socialists, trade union men, Communists, a scattering of all parties and occupations with sufficient dedication to hold out against the Nazis. They had to be humiliated in a way that would eliminate them. The way to do this was with criminals..."

"Criminals?"

How can an American separate political prisoners and criminals?..."The Pug Dog always explained it like this: 'Look at history! You'll never find such a plan, not even with the masters, Frederick the Great and Napoleon. You must admit it's an intelligent scheme. Take thousands of crooks of all kinds--murderers, rapists, arsonists, queers of every possible sexual deviation, and clap them into army uniforms. Make these crooks the majority of a division. Then sprinkle in your minority of political prisoners. Destroy or change the records. Presto! As easy as baking a cake with unusual ingredients. When the cake emerges from the oven looking like a perfect cake, the political prisoners are revealed in their true light as criminals! Each crook has turned into a true German soldier.' "...When the Pug Dog grinned, his mouth shone with lavish gold fillings. He would question triumphantly, "Have I spoken the truth or not?"..."Yes, Herr Leutnant," we chorused obediantly...

The American is frowning: "With their concentration camps available, it is hard to understand why the Nazis would endanger the safety of their military plans by mixing together criminals and political prisoners. Why would they try such a wild scheme?"

Again the rational questions impossible to answer with the documented facts that he wants..."Who can say? Can you find a rational plan in a demonic world? In the early years of the camps, the authorities decided that prisoners should have distinct identities. They gave the criminals green armbands, the political prisoners red ones to mark them communists, the Jews yellow ones to mark them dogs. However, when the war expanded to many fronts, anonymous manpower was needed and group classification was not so important. So someone hit on the idea of mixing political prisoners together with criminals. *"I am not persuading him. . .*

"Why are there no records for each soldier, let alone this 999th Division you claim to have belonged to? Your army keeps very accurate records."

"Why do you say *my* army?"

"I meant you only as a German."

"I always hated the army.". . .*Why do I say that to an American in uniform?. . .Don't try to justify myself to his ignorance. . .He has brought me here. . .He is rescuing me. . . After all what can a materialistic American know about German conflict?. . .*

"What happened to the records of the 999th Division?" the American asks. . .

"The Pug Dog lectured us happily: 'Since your records have been wiped free of your political crimes, some of you may be worried by the apparent danger of being classified as common criminals. That is not your situation if you behave properly. You are now proud German soldiers, possessors once more of the *Ehrenwort,* the pledge of honor that has always been the keystone of the great German military tradition.' *". . .Can this young American understand how the irony of Ehrenwort took the place of records?. . .*

"If your records were 'wiped free', as you claim, how could they continue to watch those of you who were anti-Nazi?"

"They watched the group, the numbers 999, they didn't bother with individuals. And that made us watch each other with growing suspicion. As the Pug Dog put it: 'You're all crooks now, so you're safe! Only maybe one or two bigshots in Berlin know for sure who are the cut-throat murderers and who are the political murderers. So you can't complain about the fairness of the plan. The politicals are selected from different camps, so you'll have a hard time finding any friends. Maybe you'll be more careful about the company you keep. You'll learn not to spout traitorous political ideas. You'll learn the value of being a good soldier!"

"What happened after you were sent to Africa?"

"At first they used us mainly as supply troops. When the military situation grew worse, they threw us into combat.

That was when we began to build up our organization for survival."

"What organization?" The Lieutenant questions.

"An anti-Nazi organization composed of men we felt sure were political prisoners. Any new person we added to our ranks was questioned closely and voted on unanimously. Our little organization within the 999th Division grew rapidly. We even created our own song, the 999th Division song. . ."

"Can you sing it for me?". . .

Is he really asking me this silly question, to sing while the funeral preparations are going on in the compound?. . .Still Beethoven is being rehearsed for the funeral along with the Horst Wessel song. . .Why shouldn't I sing? . . .I began to croak out the words, pretending a false enthusiasm:

"Immer daran denken, niemals vergessen
Was wir erlebt und geseh'n.
Wir haben in Kerkern und Lagern gesessen,
Doch unser Banner blieb steh'n.
Vorwaerts, vorwaerts! Der Morgen ist unser
Lasst uns're Fahne weh'n!"

"Forward, tomorrow is ours, let our banners wave". . .This is our tomorrow. . .The hope of hopelessness. . .

"Tell me more about how your unit survived, how you organized it."

He is worried about the political implications. . .Try to reassure him. . . "Through humor," I hear myself say. . .

"Humor? You're joking." The American frowns again. . .

*How can I explain the strange humor of survival?. . .*In our unit of the 999th Division I became friendly with a miner, Max Sollberg. Max was an anarchist from the coal-producing area of the Saar. Short, ugly, with a twisted, broken nose, he couldn't reconcile the violent history of the anarchists with the freedom of their social goals. Whipmarks from his years in a concentration camp covered his back. A labor union organizer, he had served in Spain during their Civil War, which had greatly influenced his concept of anarchism. Max taught me about humor. . ."

"He doesn't sound very humorous."

The American thinks I am wandering again. . ."In Spain Sollberg said that he learned the first anarchist was really Cervantes in *Don Quixote.* He claimed that Cervantes showed the necessity of humor for survival. Cervantes hated the strangling qualities of the State and proved in Don Quixote how a man may be ridiculous, laughable in the way he lives, yet somehow triumph with his courage and his crazy spirit. Sollberg would say that we anarchists must develop a sense of humor if we're to change society. When Bakunin states doggedly that the new world will be won only after the last king is strangled in the guts of the last priest, he's just being a sour, didactic Russian. If political values are not kept in persepective by a sense of humor, then violence becomes merely the means to destroy the goal. When the idealistic Don Quixote accuses Sancho Panza of being a clown, Sancho replies: 'As a grandmother of mine used to say, there are only two families in the world, the Haves and the Have Nots, and she stuck to the Haves. To this day, Senor Don Quixote, people would sooner feel the pulse of *Have,* they don't want to *know*--an ass covered with gold looks better than a horse with a pack-saddle.' The comic way Sollberg quoted Sancho Panza, the way we joined him in laughter because we were all Have-Nots, revealed the wisdom of Cervantes' humor. . ."

"This Sollberg sounds more like a literary critic than an anarchist. . ."

"You don't understand how he survived. When the Spanish Civil War ended, he barely escaped to France only to be imprisoned in various French camps when the Vichy government turned him finally over to the Nazis. . .". . .*How can one explain the survival of the Have-Nots to the Haves?. . .*

"I can understand how you feel about him, but what do his experiences have to do with your survival in the 999th Division?". . .

Facts, facts, facts, where are they hiding, that's what he means. . . "Please wait a minute, Lieutenant. I know you are impatient. . ."

"We don't have much time. Colonel Williams will be here in a moment. You must explain your situation clearly to him, don't you understand?". . .

Time. . .Colonel Williams. . .Explain clearly. . ."You see, Lieutenant, Sollberg taught us how to survive by laughter, how to stick together by joking in the 999th Division. It was the only way we could survive and outwit the Pug Dog. We must survive, Sollberg told us, like a Jewish doctor with whom he had lived in a camp. The Jewish doctor, with his white, medical hands, had been assigned to scrub out toilets. Forced to shine those bowls, his nose deep in the stink, he had turned into a laugher, a storyteller of toilet jokes which he invented, dirtier and dirtier. Those jokes were the salvation of a Have-Not, Sollberg said, We must learn to laugh inside and survive.". . .

"I see. That's what you mean by the Have-Nots surviving through humor," the Lieutenant's voice is suddenly thoughtful as though he 's thinking of someone, something far away. "What happened to Sollberg in Africa?". . .

He wants me to produce Sollberg out of a magical hat. . . If only I could. . ."He surrendered with the rest of us. I never saw him again. He must be in one of your camps somewhere, wherever you Americans distributed us.". . .*That sounds too much like an accusation again, when I was beginning to make him understand. . .*

"Tell me about the details of your surrender in Africa. Perhaps we can confirm them. . ."

Back to the suspicion of facts, the details of my religious confirmation. . .Search them out, find them to survive. . . "As out anti-Nazi group grew stronger, we organized throughout the division, and planned a mass surrender to the Americans. Suddenly we received orders to march into combat positions to meet the Allied tanks that were advancing. . ."

"Why did you want to surrender to the Americans instead of the British?". . .

Because we thought the Americans would believe us. . . "Because the American troops were the closest to our positions. We decided to talk to the Pug Dog, who hadn't counted on being sent to the front lines as a reward for his Nazi loyalties. The brilliant military stategy was to hold a Panzer crops in reserve and attack unexpectedly after sacrificing the criminal 999th Division as decoys. For two days we dug foxholes and strung barbed wire. Suddenly the Pug Dog found himself one of us Have-Nots, as Sollberg jeeringly described him. Somehow as we dug lower and lower the Pug Dog managed always to dig below us. That made us laugh and continue our digging in the midst of intense strafing and artillery fire. When we raised our noses an inch out of our holes to see American tanks advancing, the Pug Dog led our surrender. He stripped off his white shorts and held them high in one hand, waving frantically at the American tanks. We followed him laughing and crying when the Americans held their fire. . ."

"What happened after your surrender?"

"The Americans were suspicious of us. They had no time to listen to our story. Who could blame them? They were deep in combat. Guns still sounded in the distance. Some isolated units, perhaps even in the 999th Division, had refused to surrender. Who knows why? Maybe they were criminals who continued to fire for the love of firing. No matter how hard we tried to make ourselves known as political prisoners, our American interrogators wouldn't believe us. . .Do you believe me?" *Dangerous to challenge this young American, but I must find out where I stand. . .*

"I believe you. Go on. . ."

His belief is short, not deep. . ."Soon we learned to keep our mouths shut. Immediately after our surrender, the Nazis put into effect a longstanding plan they had to take over control of any prisoner-of-war camp where German troops were imprisoned. As I was shuttled through various camps because of my illness, I was separated from my companions in the 999th Division. I lived in fear that some Nazi officer like the Pug Dog would recognize me. . ."

"Tell me more about how the Nazis have organized this camp."

*Still more details. . .Yet he is asking now for facts that I can describe, marvels that he will witness himself when the funeral procession of the officers begins. . .*I tell the young Lieutenant all of the funeral preparations that I've witnessed. . .When I finish I'm uncertain what he thinks of my facts. . .I feel suspended in a world, a space, a time where there is a sudden possibility for escape, but, abruptly, I've lost the humorous courage to endure, to transform the space and time that are slipping away. . .

"Wait here," the Lieutenant tells me, "When Colonel Williams comes, be sure to salute him. Don't talk about the 999th Division. Tell him everything you've said about how the Nazis are running the camp, how they're preparing to use the funeral.". . .The Lieutenant leaves me alone in the room to wait. . .

As I sit, suspended, the time flows interminably. . .No watch, no clock in the small, white room. . .I start to doze and shake myself awake. . .*Don't sleep or you'll dream. . .* Mutilated, naked bodies hurtle before my eyes, castrated men with the letter P for prisoner painted on their backs, women with their breasts cut off. . .Her body waiting for the sacrifice she appears, her soft black hair falling over her shoulders. . .I rush to her, escaping, laughing with joy, running faster, faster . . .I stumble and fall through endless space, space full of jagged obstacles. . .Fully dressed she joins me again. . . Quietly we walk through a Berlin park. . .Yellow and crimson flowerbeds shine in the sun. . .Suddenly the flowers turn into yellow Jewish armbands. . .They blow away. . .My wife vanishes. . .Time darkens into a black, steady flow of days, months, years. . .

*Wake up. . .You're dreaming the dream that began in African prison camps when you became ill. . .*The half-comic image of a prehistoric beast rises before my eyes. . .Its body is shaped like a dinosaur, but it possesses two heads. . .One head resembles the Pug Dog and the other my anarchist friend, Max Sollberg. . .The beast was discovered deep in the Sahara desert. . .Surrounded by barbed wire it is kept in a camp guarded by a group of curious scientists. . .The beast requires enormous amounts of nourishment to live. . .Always its two heads beg for more to eat. . .One head cries its impatient demands and the other laughs. . .One head speaks for the Haves and the other for the Have-Nots. . .The scientists fear and respect the beast which is reputed to have killed many people. . .To requisition food for the monster several younger scientists, the less important ones, are dispatched from door to door in a nearby city. . .The city in which the scientists demand food is slanted with Gothic buildings in ruins from fire bombs. . .Deep in the ruins hide shadows pursuing obscure tasks of survival. . .When the scientists return with meagre rations, the two heads have to be fed separately. . . One head lectures the other while it eats. . .When the process is reversed and the lecturing head eats, the other head laughs heartily as it tells comic stories. . .

The beast fades into space. . .My father-in-law, the fanatic teacher, appears. . .He is seated at a huge medieval writing desk. . .Behind him my wife in a chair knits calmly. . .He is writing his autobiography, "the humorous story of my life". . His hand moves swiftly over the long expanse of the heavy wooden table, but there is no paper. . .He writes words that disappear into the wood as he shapes them, "It is good never to sleep for the rational man must always think and strive to stay awake". . .

"No, no!" I shout in protest. "One must sleep.". . . Without looking up he mutters, "If I sleep I'll never finish the book," and continues to write rapidly, covering the desk top with illegible words. . .

"Stop him and come to bed," I call desperately to my wife. "We must sleep.". . .But she only smiles at me and keeps on knitting. . .

"You'll never finish your book," I warn. "They'll come to take you away". . .*Too late*. . .Soldiers in tall, archaic helmets march in. . .Smiling at the old man they permit him to finish a few final sentences. . .They lead my wife away, strip her naked, place a monkey by her side. . .They escort her and the monkey into a crowded arena where a clown turns handsprings to encourage the crowd's enthusiasm. . .As the crowd shrieks a limping official with a black crayon in his hand moves down the field and draws two marks over my wife's breasts. . .I strain to see, but cannot identify if the marks are numbers or letters. . .

Startled out of my chair in the hospital room, the half-dream vanishes. . .*Stay awake*. . .Why do these waking dreams haunt me, stifle me?. . .If only I could sleep better at night these day-dreams would not be so obsessive. . .Am I in danger of losing my mind?. . .No, in surviving one grows physically stronger. . .But if the dreams continue. . .Soon I'll be free from the Nazis. . .Be careful, though, how I talk to Colonel Williams. . .The Lieutenant warned not to repeat the story of the 999th Division. . .Keep to the details of the Nazi camp organization. . .Remember to salute the Colonel with military respect. . .They're coming. . .Footsteps, voices in the corridor . . .Try to stand. . .

THE AMERICAN RELUCTANT WITNESS

Colonel Williams must be occupied with another emergency. He waves off my signal that Armind is waiting. "I'll be right with you, Lieutenant." *Hurry up and wait. The old Army slogan.* With his familiar resigned expression, the Colonel is listening to another problem, probably about the lack of personnel, from an anxious medical officer.

How much should I tell the Colonel about the 999th Division? There are no records, nothing to prove Armind's story. No one is likely to believe his tale of a division part-criminal, part-political prisoner. If what he says is true why isn't there any report? Why isn't there some rumor in prisoner-of-war camps about the possible existence of anti-Nazi survivors from the 999th Division? Why does he turn up here alone with this incredible story? Still if the Nazis have organized the prison camps all over the country, any anti-Nazi prisoner wouldn't dare come out in the open. Certainly our Limited Service personnel couldn't protect them against Nazi control.

The way Armind tells his story is more like a jagged dream than any possible reality. If he talks that way to Colonel Williams, the Colonel may start wondering again about the homosexual accusations against Armind. Yet, for some reason, I believe most of Armind's story, even though he gets irrational. No, I won't stress the 999th Division to the Colonel. All I have to do is mention the Pug Dog and the Colonel won't believe a word. Stick to the Nazi organization of this camp. That's our immediate danger. It's going to be tough to do anything about the funeral preparations.

Funny why I feel this way about Armind. When I first entered the German officers' compound that game I played in our canyon wilderness with my dead brother, *Enter a silence and find a sound,* echoed in my mind. I was on my own for sure. I had to acknowledge some kind of responsibility that I didn't want to accept. Responsibility for what? My own limitations, my immaturity? I can't blame it on Limited Service. Not that I'm so different. After we've hidden for years in the innocence of American isolation, everybody my age is being compelled to confront the Nazi domination of Europe. In California before my European trip, I was more a-political than most, at the frontier's end where a word like *camp* meant a family outing in the Sierra mountains and family security was taken for granted.

One time I'll never forget. . .After graduating from officers' school I traveled home to California on a week's leave. My parents summoned me to a family conference in the living room. How could a family conference be an emergency when I was on leave? It was the last time I entered that room. Our enormous living room was a palatial dream of Mother's. If she had been born a Queen she would have created splendid, visionary cities. Instead on a professor's salary she was forced to limit her architectural inspiration to rooms. With her regal presence she walked into beloved San Francisco Chinatown stores and immediately they doubled the price. Nevertheless the old, withered store owners would usher her into their private quarters, serve her expensive cakes, tea, hundred year old eggs because they were captivated by her bearing.

Feeling guilty about neglecting my family during my army months, I stared uneasily at the dimensions of the living room. An ancient, gold-leaf statue of Buddha, purchased by Mother on one of her impulsive Chinatown shopping expeditions, smiled engimatically from a niche in the balcony that overhung the long whitewalled room. As a boy I used to hide with my dead brother behind this statue when my parents gave one of their rare dancing parties. Seizing one hobby after another with feverish intensity my mother was a dancing fanatic. She liked to demonstrate her swan-like grace gliding around the gleaming hardwood floor in the arms of different, attractive men. My father, who disliked dancing, was afraid to have his short awkwardness revealed against my mother's sensuous glide. He sat in a chair, smoking a cigar, using his talents as a linguist and storyteller to send his eager audience into fits of laughter. It was a contest that they both appreciated, his storytelling against her dancing. As the years of their long marriage passed, after my brother's sudden death, the dancing parties ceased. The ceremonial living room, which was expensive to maintain with its separate furnace and its green bathroom with circular, sunken tub the size of a small swimming pool for mother's fantasies, was turned into a rental unit.

My father stood in front of the high fireplace, his face suddenly old, lined with anxiety beneath his thatch of distinguished white hair. A great linguist and Professor of Spanish at the University of California, he had earned his Ph. D. in Germany in the 1890s when a degree was still a ritual.

Often he told us laughingly about his appearance for oral examinations at nine o'clock in the morning when he was required to wear full evening dress, top hat, and white gloves. Living on the western frontier, combined with his love for Don Quixote, somehow increased Father's essential romanticism. A strict scholar, he was also a dreamer who delighted in vanishing into his study to search out the details of his legendary visions.

Since I was born when Father was forty-eight, I never thought of his whitehaired dignity as *Dad*. In the evenings I was often puzzled and hurt when he disappeared into his study not with me but with his large, black cat. He called the cat gleefully "The Grand Inquisitor." Purring his enigmatic questions the cat lay on the desk watching Father work late every night on the complete works of Cervantes that he was editing. Father's study was a respected sanctuary to all of us except the cat. Since I was allowed in there only on rare occasions I was envious of The Grand Inquisitor's privileges. Consequently I mistreated the cat and Father would have to chastise me. Only years later, when Father showed me a cat like The Grand Inquisitor in Goya's etching with the famous, bitter inscription, *The Dream of Reason Produces Monsters,* did I begin to understand. Father liked the cat in the study because those glittering yellow eyes peering at him on the desk promised no compromise with historical ghosts, only the mysterious struggle with the eternal puzzle of lost heroes and civilizations that Father loved. The cat reminded Father that this struggle could never be merely rational.

If Father was valley-short for a man, some five feet four inches of Napoleonic dedication to scholarship, Mother was mountain-tall for a woman, close to six feet, a supernatural work of art. When Father emerged from his scholarly mist, you never saw anyone lean so gracefully as Mother. She should have been a swan the way her long neck swayed down to give us a sense of her regal presence. Only her flesh was a little weak. She kept to her bed a lot and left the supervision of us children to an English housekeeper. Her bed was Mother's sanctuary where she pursued her concerns with American Indian mythology and Jungian psychology. Haughtily the Grand Inquisitor never ventured into Mother's room. The gap between Mother and Father was widened by her inability to learn any foreign language despite her constant, desperate efforts. This caused Father to retreat further into his study where he could conjure up any vision of the Romance Languages that possessed him. Yet, despite their isolation in separate rooms, my brother and I grew up with a great respect for our parents, if not an immediate physical love. We convinced ourselves that respect is as strong as love in cementing family relationships, perhaps stronger. It was my brother, Steven, who gave me a sense of physical love, who taught me about birds, insects, animals in our canyon paradise as we played the games that he invented like *Enter a silence and find a sound.* Steven died suddenly at the age of twelve in the influenza epidemic that swept through the country after World War I. No wonder-drugs then. Particularly shattering to Mother was the fact that Steven seemed to be recovering. He was running only a slight fever, sitting up in bed, deep in his books of birds and flowers. None of us in the family had the slightest doubt of Steven's great future career as a Natural Scientist. If I was a little insecure in the limelight of the focus on Steven's destiny, I was happy and young enough to follow along.

Mother never recovered from Steven's abrupt death. He was her favorite, the first-born, and the shattering of genius unfulfilled in childhood caused her to react by living in his memory. Evenings when she put me to bed, she showed me constantly books of pressed flowers and drawings of birds that Steven had made and given to her. Since I was eight when Steven died I had different memories of him. His ghostly presence began to haunt me in another way. All of us in the family were condemned to live with memories of Steven's promise. After his death my parents had his body cremated. They never told me where his ashes were buried. Until this final day. . .

For the first time in that memorable living room I noticed fear in my parents. Neither could speak. Mother had cut her long hair. They fidgeted nervously. Alarmed I asked, "What's the matter?"

"We didn't want to tell you just when you were drafted," Mother answered, "but now you have to know. Your father wants a divorce and I won't give it to him."

Conditioned to family unity I heard myself protesting: "You've been married for twenty-five years."

"That's just it." Mother snapped vindictively. "Your father

thinks he's in love with another woman. She's far too young for him."

"Please try to understand," Father began to apologize. His long series of abject sentences changed my image of him as the incarnation of remote wisdom and scholarly tranquility. He had waited, he said, waited until I was grown up, waited until I had become an officer. . .

This accolade to my maturity as an officer infuriated me and I lashed back: "Neither of you ever trusted me. You didn't have the courage to tell me sooner."

"That's not true," Mother burst into tears. "You know that's not true. We didn't want to hurt you."

"Well, you have hurt me."

"You see what you've done," Mother turned to attack Father. "You're going to make him hate you."

Instinctively I recoiled from Mother's self-righteous appeal for sympathy. I was trapped in an impossible middle-ground where I refused to take sides and was forced to assert my own selfishness. What would happen to *my* house, *my* canyon with its intricate maze of wonders? "There's no point in hating anyone," I said peevishly. "Can't you wait a little while longer until we all try to work things out?" I heard my voice with amazement in its thin seeking of easy evasions.

"I have waited," Father spoke stubbornly through tight, determined lips. "More than a year I've waited until coming to a final decision."

Final decision. . .

"He should go to a psychiatrist," Mother burst out spitefully.

"I went to a psychiatrist. I did that for you. You know that."

Mother snapped back, "You only went for a few visits. Real analyses take a long time. You never gave it a chance. We could try another analyst, even go together if you wish." She struggled sadly to make amends, failing to recognize how they sounded like tag-ends of resentment.

"It's no use, Father insisted. "Love is not a problem that analysts can deal with."

"It's not love, only sex," Mother shouted at him. "You're not young anymore. You should know better!"

They weren't even talking to me now, just covering old, smoking territory, and their customary ignoring of me infuriated me more than anything. Standing up between them suddenly, struggling to break this wasteland dialogue that ignored my presence,I proclaimed. "I won't take sides. Steven wouldn't have taken sides either."

Astonished they gaped at me. "We don't want you to take sides," Father protested feebly.

"I don't want to meet your new woman and Steven wouldn't want to meet her." I couldn't believe that I was dragging in Steven's name, but with pain and satisfaction I saw him wince.

"Some day you'll change your mind."

"No he won't." Mother's voice was deep beyond reason, shaped only by a need for futile attack. "He's right about Steven too."

"Don't mention Steven," Father replied sharply. "It's no good going on like this. You're just being irrational."

"You'll lose everything," Mother shrilled vindictively. "You must realize that. The courts will deprive you of everything. You can't possibly imagine you can live with that bitch in luxury."

With fierce dignity Father replied coldly: "That's unworthy of you."

"Please Mother." I felt her arm shaking under my touch and then it happened.

"Why didn't you make me bury Steven's ashes?" Mother accused Father. Unable to reply he stared at her his face blanching.

Forced to continue she attacked him: "You make me live in Steven's memory. Every night you retreated into your work and I retreated too. If only you had taken those ashes away from me. They put a curse on this house."

"What did you do with the ashes?" I blurted out.

When Mother hesitated, Father answered as if her secret must be exploded. "She couldn't bury the ashes even though I urged her to. Instead she kept them in an urn in the basement."

Suddenly I remembered a secret cardboard box wrapped with paper and string sitting on a shelf in the basement. Playing in and out of that basement as a child, I'd seen that box many times. When friends were with me we speculated on the treasure in the box, but never dared to open it.

Once, consumed with curiosity and pretending a great discovery, I'd even carried it to Mother and questioned her about its contents. She told me merely that it contained "old clothes" and took it away from me, refusing my immediate desire to see the clothes. The box disappeared and I never saw it again. Somewhere in that basement she found a more secure hiding place for the ashes. . .

This agonizing disclosure ended the quarrel. The next day, Mother, Father, and I took the box of ashes into the canyon: For a short time again we united in an act of salvation. It was as though Mother agreed silently to release Father if we all participated in this final burial ritual. As we descended into the canyon on a narrow dirt path under the towering bay tree that dominated our house, the bluejays cawed raucously. Far away in the underbrush a thrush startled the air in a song my brother had learned to imitate perfectly. *Enter a silence and find a sound. . .*The sounds of a lost family searching through a familiar landscape that had once invited us eagerly into its mysteries. . .

Father led the way, carrying the box, the paper and string still tight around it. Mother followed, her face composed as if some invisible force had erased the lines of tension in her body. She carried a red book in her hands. As the rear-guard of that final family procession, I walked apart from them in my army uniform, yet feeling free from the previous day's disaster.

"Let's stop here by the creek," Mother said and Father nodded assent. Deep in the canyon a narrow creek zigzagged, rippled over a rocky streambed through thick clusters of ferns. Besides the creek Mother had built a bench on a wooden platform where she went frequently to read. Often she must have dreamt of this act of exorcism, but could never summon the courage to take along the ashes rather than a book. Instead she returned always to her bedroom haunted by that waiting box in the basement.

Father unwrapped the box and opened it. "Please, wait." You say a few words first," Mother asked him. Father recited his favorite lines from Cervantes' *Persiles and Sigismunda:*

"We cannot call that hope which may be resisted and overthrown by adversity, for as light shines most in the darkness, even so hope must remain unshaken in the midst of toil; for to despair is the act of cowardly hearts, and there is no greater pusillanimity or baseness than to allow the spirit, no matter how beset by difficulties it may be, to yield to discouragement."

As he spoke the lines from memory Mother looked at him with a new sense of recognition. She loved him, if she would never forgive him. After he had finished Mother opened the book she was carrying. True to her tormented, mystical nature, she read nothing from her conventional middle-class, Episcopalian background. For her God had become a changeable myth, a vision of different masks to wear for specific rituals. She read from the Navajo Night Chant that she had learned teaching school in the southwest after her graduation from college. Fascinated with the Navajos she had lived with them for several months to study their art and myths:

"Today, take away your spell for me,
Away from me take your spell.
Far off from me the spell is taken,
Far off you have taken the spell.

Happily I recover,
Happily the water cools me.

My eyes regain their vision, my head cools,
my legs regain their strength, my ears listen
to sounds again.

Happily, the spell disappears from me,
Happily, I walk, released from pain I walk,
joyous I walk. . .

In beauty I walk,
With beauty in front of me I walk,
With beauty behind me I walk,
With beauty above me I walk,
With beauty above and around me I walk,
It is finished in beauty.
It is finished in beauty.

After she had finished she looked gently at Father and he stared at her with admiration and relief. Both were oblivious to my presence. Mother lifted the box and poured the ashes slowly into the stream. When she had finished, she and Father stood side by side, almost touching, staring silently as the ashes dissolved in water and time.

"There's one more thing to do," Mother turned to me. "Would you please dig a hole?"

"For what?"

"For this box," she said, ripping it into little pieces. . .

That evening Father left home forever. I stood at the hallway window looking down at the canyon where the creek bubbled quietly over rocks, through thick-leafed ferns and dense blackberry bushes. The sun was setting through the eucalyptus and bay trees. The image of an old fire flared into my mind. Our wooden firetrap of a house was fated to endure any catastrophe. When I was seven a flash-fire sparked out the faulty wiring in the basement. Early in the morning my brother Steven had woken me up and led me safely out of the house. For some reason the firemen delayed their rescue operations. Enraged by the inability of the firemen to command water, their natural element, Father darted into the basement, chopped out portions of smoking wallboard, and smothered the flames with blankets and his bare hands. In his moment of triumph and pain my mother annointed his burnt hands with victorious oil like a healing priestess. They loved each other then. . .Still they had won respect again in this canyon burial. They had created the sounds of peace if not forgiveness, in that silence. By that exorcism they had put the ghost of Steven to rest. Somehow in the process they had cast me off, if not set me free. There was no house to return to, no canyon, no security, only a property rented to strangers to sustain Mother's needs. If only Steven had lived he might have told me things, fortified me with realities that seemed to be slipping away in a world at war.

Forget Steven. He was lost in his own dreams of isolation, his birds, his trees, his vision of nature that was fast disappearing in the rapid growth of the city around our canyon. Forget this nostalgic sense of the past that haunts me in the midst of a German prisoner-of-war camp. My parents are still alive, they still love me. Only the family is gone forever. Perhaps family is just a dream-environment to which we cling frantically, a favorite time and place whose attractions we enlarge in memory the older we grow, the more isolated we are from youth. Anyway in prison camps there are no more families, only physical connections between guard and prisoner. How can this ant nest of relationships have any connection with family?. . .

Colonel Williams frees himself from the medical officer and motions that he's ready. We walk toward the room where Armind is waiting. Speaking rapidly, too rapidly as I can see by his face, I try to brief the Colonel about how the Nazis have organized the camp. The details are too much for him.

"Let's get this straight later," he snaps at me as he enters the room. He bangs the door shut as if to assert his authority, a decision to act firmly even if the situation turns out to be impossible.

Jesus Christ. . Armind fails to rise and salute the Colonel. . He sits in his chair as if stupified in the midst of a vacancy.

"God damn, what's the matter with him?" Colonel Williams's face flashes with resentment. "Jesus, Lieutenant, he doesn't even know how to salute. How can you trust him? That's no soldier." He turns away impatiently to leave the room.

"Wait, Colonel, he's sick."

An abrupt, strangled denial emerges from the prisoner, *"Nein, ich bin nicht krank."* What the hell, he's forgotten his English. A maze of languages swirls before me. "Get up, salute the Colonel," I tell him in German. Like an automaton he rises, stiffly, clicks his heels and salutes.

"Like a Nazi," mutters the Colonel. "These Krauts are all the same."

"They've learned the same salute, Colonel," I explain lamely. "Please listen to him."

"All right, I'll give him five minutes. Tell him to lay the facts on the line. You know, Lieutenant, he looks a little effeminate to me." The Colonel stares reflectively at Armind who hunches in his chair again.

"Looks can be deceptive, Sir. He says that the Nazis put him in a concentration camp."

"Ask him which one."

"Welche Konzentratsionlager?" I ask Armind. *I've got to make him speak English, not German. . .*

"Fuhlsbüttel. . ."

"Never heard of it," mutters the Colonel impatiently. "You ever hear of it?"

"No, Sir," I'm forced to admit, "but there are lots of camps."

"There's only one important one, Dachau, right?"

"No, Sir, reports say bigger ones are being built in the east, in Poland."

"Well, does he have any proof, any witnesses?"

"Haben Sie Zeugnisse?"

"Speak in English for Christ's sake," Colonel Williams reprimands me sharply. "You said he knows English."

"Sorry, Sir, I'm just trying to get him started . . .Do you have any witnesses?" I ask Armind, knowing the answer before I hear it.

"No. . ." *At least he's speaking English now. . .*

"How are we going to believe him if he doesn't have any witnesses?" asks the Colonel. "We can't just go on air."

Suddenly the prisoner is listening, comprehending something anyway. He stands up and starts to pull off his shirt. "I have a scar," he whispers.

"A what?"

"A scar. From the whip. In Fuhlsbüttel. The Goose Father. . ." He rips his shirt as he tugs at it frantically.

"Relax," says the Colonel. "I'll look at it." The Colonel examines the scar closely. "How the hell can you tell?" he asks me. "How can we be sure? For all we know, he might have cut himself on a milkbottle when he was a kid. It's just a scar."

The prisoner understands *milkbottle.* "No," he cries, *"der Gänsevater. . ."* He starts to apologize with a nervous grimace, a jagged, gurgling rush of words.

Colonel Williams seizes my arm. "I can't understand him."

"He's talking about the Goosefather."

"Who the hell is the Goosefather?"

I try to explain about the German commander of the camp at Fuhlsbüttel, unable to escape from the story, trying to guide Armind back to the concrete details of the Nazi takeover of this prisoner of war camp. Armind is pleading with the Colonel at the same time, a babble of languages, incoherent pleas. In a time of begging there is no question of dignity, pride. . .

"All right, all *right,*" Colonel Williams interrupts, "I haven't got all day. Tell him to stop driveling and talk sense. We'll see that no one hurts him. Ask him simple questions."

Simple questions. . .What a damn fool I am. The Colonel is right. I turn to Armind and ask: "Have the Nazis organized the compounds in this camp?"

"Yes, every compound."

"Are they using force on prisoners?"

"Yes."

"Have they set up their own Courts of Honor?"

"Yes, they have their own laws."

"Are they publishing their own Nazi newspaper?"

"Yes."

Slowly I pull the details out of Armind, trying to make it easy for him to answer simply. For the first time Colonel Williams is impressed. He shifts uneasily in his chair. "Wait a minute, Lieutenant," he frowns. "Let's get this straight. Do you really think this is so dangerous? What do you expect prisoners to do? Sit on their fannies? When I was a prisoner in Germany in World War I, you can be damn sure we organized against the Krauts. We had everything sewed up tight. They've got a right to organize according to the Geneva Convention."

"But Colonel they don't have a right to run this camp by terror. That's not in the Geneva Convention."

"The minute they step out of line we can crack down," the Colonel is almost talking to himself, reflecting about the possibilities. Unnoticed Armind sinks back into his chair drawing his illfitting shirt on like a shroud. "If we have to crack down on the Nazis we will, but how the hell do we do it with our Limited Service personnel against their combat troops?"

"I don't know, Sir."

"If we lost the war in Colorado we'd look pretty stupid wouldn't we, Lieutenant?"

"Yes, Sir."

"Don't forget the Krauts have a lot of American boys as prisoners over there in Germany. You wouldn't want anything to happen to them, would you?"

"But, Colonel what about the funeral procession? What if the Nazi turn it into a propaganda spectacle?"

"Have you got any idea how to stop them?"

"No, Sir." The reluctant admission forces me to realize that I've underrated the Colonel.

"All right, you've made your point. We can't let these Nazi bastards take over the camp. What we need is some proof of this Nazi plan if it really exists.

"That shouldn't be hard to get."

"Maybe, but we'll need this guy's help. You believe what he says about the concentration camp?"

"Yes, Sir."

"Well," Colonel Williams hesitates, "you may be right. Still he could have been put in the camp because he was a homosexual."

"He claims that it was because he was married to a Jewish woman."

"I know that's what you said, but what do you expect him to claim? Lieutenant, don't make the mistake of trustting one of these Krauts." The Colonel stares at me thoughtfully.

Over the desk the light bulb glares down from its naked cord. "It isn't a matter of trust. It's his safety, Sir. I think he's in danger if we put him back in the compound. The Nazis are watching him. They seem to have set up their own kangaroo court. . ."

"That's why we need proof." The Colonel speaks louder, more distinctly, as if to let the prisoner overhear him deliberately. "What if he consents to go back in the compound just for a day or so until after the officers' funeral. Maybe he can dig up some evidence, a copy of this underground Nazi paper or whatever. Then I could use that to press for some reinforcements here to prevent any Nazi troubles."

The prisoner stiffens, the painted letters PW glistening on the back of his shirt. "You want me to return to the compound?"

"Only for a little while." For the first time the Colonel talks to him directly. "Look, Armind, I'm not saying I believe your story. I'm not saying I don't believe it. We need your help to get evidence that the Nazis are trying to run this camp."

"I do not understand *evidence.*" Bewildered Armind stares at the Colonel.

"Evidence is proof of what you say about the Nazis. Written proof of their plans."

"If I bring that to you I am dead. Already they watch me."

"You help us and we'll help you. There's nothing else that I can do." The Colonel is a tough bargainer when he wants something.

"What help is possible? I tell you everything. They do not like to write things down. In their Nazi world they like to keep everything secret." Armind gestures frantically in the air as if trying to explain invisible plans.

"If you can just get us a copy of that underground newspaper, anything like that. We'll keep an eye on you in the compound. As soon as you get us what we need, I'll see that you're taken out of the compound. You won't ever have to return."

Armind twists in his chair, agonizing. When he speaks it is the tone of a man who knows he has no choice. "If I try to find something in writing, you must not delay. The funeral tomorrow will show you the Nazi power."

Colonel Williams answers: "Major Weimann promised me that the funeral will remain a military ceremony at all times."

"The Major is not the political officer in charge of the Nazi rule. This is Captain Dampfstoff."

"That's exactly why we need evidence of the Nazi plan. If Major Weimann, the senior officer, isn't running the camp, then we can prove that they're not following the Geneva Convention."

"What is Geneva Convention to Nazis?"

"I know how you feel, but we're Americans fighting a war," says the Colonel. "The Nazis have got a lot of American prisoners in Germany too. Both sides have agreed to abide by the Geneva Convention. If you get me evidence, proof, that the Nazis here are ignoring the Geneva Convention, then we can do something."

The word *evidence* sinks deep into Armind's body like a wound. His face sags into gloom. "I will try if it is possible. If I find anything you must take me out immediately."

"You get us the stuff, we'll take you out right away."

"The *stuff*?"

"The evidence. . ."

Armind's face grows darker, resigned. He tightens motionless against his chair as if fate had decided against him again. I sit caught between him and the Colonel, powerless, unable to say anything meaningful, feeling like a crab turned over on his back, legs kicking futilely for a grip on reality.

When the Colonel leaves the room nothing I can say to Armind will re-assure him. All I can do is make sure that he returns to his compound alone without a conspicuous American escort. I give him a medical report as proof of his X-rays to show his suspicious supervisors. How the hell will this help him? Probably the Nazis have already decided what to do about him. Still they'll be concentrating on the funeral ceremonies tomorrow. If Armind finds us some evidence maybe we can get him out of the compound in time. . .

That evening I'm assigned to guard duty. I might have known I couldn't escape. I check the first guard tower. Is another triggerhappy One-Eyed Nellie waiting up there? In the compound a group of prisoners huddles by an ant heap playing the game with the fly. One laughs as he throws a fly into the midst of the ants. Beethoven and the ants. . .So appealing and dangerous, the German mind. Too easy just to be sympathetic to Armind. The Colonel is right--at least about my getting too involved with this prisoner. I have to watch my German background. My father's parents had a tougher side to them when they fled from Germany to the United States in search of freedom after the revolution of 1848. They were political idealists. Armind with his stories seems almost a-political. Don't let his sense of experience overawe me. His racial involvement is too easy. Did he ever really act against the Nazis? Come on. How decisive was I in California when the Japanese couple who worked for our family were shipped off to a "re-location camp" after Pearl Harbor? Certainly my parents protested, but that was all. They signed petitions, wrote letters, whispers in the wind. One day they went to visit Naka and Hana at the "re-location center" and returned white and shaken. Never until that final day in the living room had I seen my parents so disturbed.

"Hana wouldn't see me," gasped Mother. In her matriarchal way she felt especially close to the Japanese woman who took complete care of our house while her husband tended the garden. "She's deeply hurt. Why she feels that we betrayed her."

"It's nothing personal," Father tried to convince her and himself. "They had to sell their possessions quickly. They lost everything to the damn speculators. Naka said they got only one hundred dollars for everything they owned. The bastard who bought their stuff probably made a thousand per cent profit. It's a swindle." With horror Father began to describe the camp, the "re-location center," surrounded by guard towers, the thousands of Japanese-Americans imprisoned there, waiting in lines. "You can't imagine," Father muttered, "the feeling of white versus yellow that you get in a camp like that. It's a racial nightmare."

"How can they ever believe that Naka and Hana were potential spies?" I struggled for some definite answers from my parents, trying to convince myself that I was too young to take any responsibility.

"They're not even accusing them of being spies. They claim this detention is only a precaution. None of the camp officials will take any responsibility. 'Write to Washington', that's all they say."

"Isn't there anything you can do?"

"Keep protesting. . .What else? Nothing will happen I'm afraid. Nothing. . ."

Trudging along between guard towers in the lowering light, the collar of my field jacket up against the night air, I feel Armind's isolation in a new way. What if he's really in danger just because he was involved with a Jewish woman and her father? The Colonel evaded this possibility. Racial problems of necessity are secondary to him. "Don't make the mistake of trusting a Kraut." Sound advice for an American commanding officer face to face with arrogant German Africa Corps prisoners still confident of victory. Yet what was the war about if not for the freedom of all races here at home too? Yellowbelly, Yid, Kraut, Spic, Polack, all the varieties of mixed Americans.

What about the racial segregation that still exists in our Army? *El Paso. . .*After graduation from officers' school, as part of my training with prisoners of war, I was assigned to escort a German prisoner, a sergeant dying with tuberculosis, to a prison hospital near Florence, Arizona. Two military policemen in white armbands, all three of us with guns strapped around our waists, accompanied the prisoner who was too ill to stand up for more than a few minutes at a time. He spent most of his time coughing, slumped in his seat, staring hollowly out the train window.

In El Paso we had to change trains. It was evening. We took the prisoner into the restaurant to eat. Enormous plate glass windows in the restaurant faced the train platform. On the train platform small groups of black soldiers in newly issued American uniforms sat on their barracks bags. Probably they had already eaten. . .I pushed out of mind the uncomfortable fact that the army was still officially segregated. The only Army personnel in the restaurant, we relaxed and ordered from a printed menu on a white tablecloth. The luxuries of home.

The meal came hot and steaming. Suddenly I noticed a thick, broad-lipped face pressed against the glass, staring in at us. Just curiosity. I turned toward the sick German prisoner who was eating his soup with difficulty. The face at the window disappeared. Nose and fingerprints remained comically on the glass. A train whistle howled.

The next course arrived. A sumptuous chicken wing flanked by an island of mashed potatoes with a gravy lake in the middle. I was drinking a beer. A sharp rap sounded on the window. Again the black, broadlipped, grinning face appeared as if in a cartoon. His grin was so wide that it seemed almost a rage of laughter. Another black face appeared beside him. Then another. A vaudeville trio, a song and dance act. One of the MP's was annoyed. He hurried to the window, gestured impatiently as if chasing away some bothersome flies. The faces disappeared. Snorting the MP returned to the table and muttered to me, "Just another curious nigger."

*Nigger. . .*I looked at the sick German prisoner to see how he reacted. He was absorbed in the problem of eating without appetite. Was *Jude* inflected that way in Germany? The waiter brought a large salad bowl with thick slices of avocado on the top. Puzzled the German prisoner awoke from his lethargy and asked, "Please, what is that fruit? I have never seen it before."

*A-vo-ca-do. . .*Abruptly the row of black faces re-appeared, rapping harder on the window, black knuckles knocking rhythmically on the glass. Startled white civilian diners looked up from their meals. In the midst of the blacks leading the rapping, loomed the broadlipped face with the enormous grin. Why are they knocking in this insistent way? Suddenly I realized they had never seen a German soldier before. *Black Americans outside of a whites-only restaurant looking at a German prisoner who's permitted inside. . .*I couldn't eat any more.

Enraged at the voice and worried about his shining window, the tall, greyhaired manager of the restaurant rushed out. He gesticulated frantically as if signalling to children to remove their unwelcome presence from his white sanctuary. The faces would not vanish. It had become a game. The grin of the chorus leader expanded in delight as he urged more black knuckles to rap out the rhythm. A soaring percussive rhapsody threatened to shatter the window. Desperately the manager shrieked across the room at me, "Stop them!"

Reluctantly I arose, futile revolver dangling from my hips. I felt as if I were in a brightly lit acquarium tank, a pilot fish, with many dark, semi-visible spectators gaping in at me, rapping with applause at our peculiar movements. As I moved toward the window, whistles sounded outside. I was saved by several MP's on duty in the station. They started to peel the faces away from the window. Only the gigantic black grin would not move. He pounded doggedly on the window until he was dragged away by force. The manager turned to me and apologized, "I'm sorry, Lieutenant. I didn't mean to yell at you. I know it's not your job."

"What did they want? Why did they keep pounding on the window?"

"Who knows? They're like children. They know they can't eat in here. Signs are posted. Besides, they've already been fed. . ."

That rapping wasn't like children. . .

The manager continued, "I guess they were just curious about your German prisoner here."

"Crazy niggers," said the MP seated next to the German. "You can never tell what they'll do."

"Say, Lieutenant," the manager stared intently at the insignia on the prisoner's uniform. "Can I ask you a favor?" "Do you think he'd sell me that dickybird he's wearing?"

"Dickybird?". . .

"That eagle with the swastika in it. I'll pay you something too."

Stiffly I told the manager it was impossible. The sick German prisoner sat there, impassive over his food. . .

So I must listen to Armind's stories. . .Try to separate the fantasy from the reality. Our racist American society never melted in its vast wilderness pot. What am I? Part German, Irish, English, a touch of French, distant Russian, who knows what else, an eighthbreed more than a halfbreed. Yet it all passes for white. That's the pure color of the spectrum in America or Germany if you're not Black or Jewish.

At the base of the next guard tower the invisible sentry up there in the dark challenges me. I answer quickly to protect myself. God damn it I hope he's not another One-Eyed Nellie. As I climb the ladder into the tower I try to avoid looking down. What's really down there?

A fresco is painted on the wall of a cell or a restaurant-acquarium. Thousands of ants drawn with minute military detail crawl around on the barren desert inside barbed wire. The ants all wear dickybirds. Some have their bellies painted yellow. Major Weimann scurries around serving the Queen Ant, Captain Dampfstoff, trying to disguise his hairy legs in drag. A funeral procession marches up with two flies to be buried. One of the flies reflects Armind's desperate eyes above a sign, Jude, around his neck. My parents flicker in the sky as distant, separated stars. In a guard tower marked Limited Service, a one-eyed American with a pirate's patch over his missing eye aims into the compound. In a second guard tower an officer climbs frantically up the ladder. He's painted all different colors, hands, legs, chest, face, a crazy-quilt of racial colors. He tries to position himself in the desert sky.

Colonel Williams reaches down with a long brush to paint the officer white. With a start I recognize myself. . .

Climbing into the dark guard tower I assume the fake mask of an inspecting officer. . .

THE GERMAN RITUAL FOR THE DEAD

How futile is language. . .The American officers listen to me with scepticism. . .When I speak I freeze in the ice of words. . .After surrendering in Africa, I was so glad to be free from the Nazis that I read all the time. . .I floated in a creative sea of print. . .Language came alive to me, a way of survival. . .I studied eagerly the unique rhythms that space melodic phrases, the action of racing verbs. . .I made catalogues, descriptions in which I recorded all of the extraordinary variations possible on a single image. . .For the first time I even dreamt of becoming a teacher again. . .I believed a way to teach language existed that would not dissect it into meaningless parts, but would reveal it in all of its intricate glory. . .When the American doctors pronounced me well I was almost eager to join the battle of prison life with my companions from the 999th Division. . .Then the Americans separated me and sent me to this camp that the Nazis control. . .A new camp might have permitted me to renew my teaching, to join once more the joyful action of life, not merely to create the fantasies that punish. . .

Consider the barbed wire that guards the arena of ants, how it climbs into the eye to block the center of vision. . . Drink would be an escape, but alcohol is forbidden. . .Sex would be a blessed release. . .Sex is dead. . .Formerly I was alone. . .Now the voices speak to me, the voices that seek out those who live in isolation. . .The voices accuse me, *"You are guilty of hating your own people. We condemn you to your hatred."*

These are not my people. . .Their Court of Honor is meeting to sentence me. . .Perhaps I can get a document of the proceedings to hand to the Americans so they will have their evidence. . .At least the Nazis don't seem to suspect my interview with the American camp commander. . .When I return to the compound, Sergeant Hochweiler says nothing about my journey to the hospital. . .He is too absorbed in preparations for the funeral tomorrow. . .

Evidence. . .What can I find to convince the Americans of this Nazi rule?. . . Like all bureaucrats the Americans expect everything to be resolved on paper. . .The Nazi power is written on flesh, not on paper. . .Still I must find some document or I'll remain here. . .If I steal a copy of the Nazi paper that Captain Dampfstoff edits it will be noticed. . .Only one copy of the paper is tacked to the wall in each barrack. . . Since the paper is printed by typewriter and by pasting, cutting, and altering news items and articles from American newspapers, there are few copies of each issue. . .Yet this paper seems the only possibility of evidence that will satisfy the Americans and gain my release. . .

In the evening as I sit at my desk typing the speech that Major Weimann is to deliver at the funeral ceremonies, an American enlisted man, Sergeant Franklin, enters the office. . He comes every evening to supervise the count of prisoners to make certain that no one has escaped. . .During his visits he and Sergeant Hochweiler exchange observations over my head. . .I am a wall of flesh between German and American suspicion. . .If I want a drink of water to cool my throat, I feel Hochweiler thinking, *where is he going?*. . .If I go to the toilet, *is there anyone inside with him?*. . .To stifle the accusing voices, I develop a category, a judgment for every person and thing I see. . .

The desert landscape with dust blowing through jagged strands of barbed wire is like a broken comb.

Sergeant Hochweiler's rigid, bureaucratic efficiency is like a radiator whose heat cannot be turned off or reduced because it is controlled from a distant, invisible source.

Loneliness has the color of a white flower growing in an imaginary desert oasis.

If voices are the counterpoint of musical instruments, Dampfstoff is a nasal oboe to Weimann's nostaligic English horn.

Men are being taught how to live in camps because they failed to learn how to live in industrial cities.

A prison uniform is a costume for a drama without language.

A prisoner is like an anonymous fish waiting to be hooked by a guard and given an identifying number.

Silence is the fate of confused languages in the Tower of Babel. . .

Sergeant Hochweiler is a short, square man with long brown hair that he pushes back constantly from his forehead. . .He thinks of it as an American gesture he remembers from films. . .In Leipzig he worked for an import-export business that enabled him to travel and speak English with what he believes to be an American accent. . .Hochweiler pretends to Franklin a fascination for all American things. . . He questions Franklin about film stars, automobile factory assembly lines, baseball, politics, the height of the Empire State Building. . .Jokingly Franklin calls him the Leipzig Yankee. . .I cannot help but feel that Hochweiler's American quest is somewhat cynically designed to show me how little I really know about naive Americans. . .Hochweiler learns that Franklin, as a civilian, worked for a popular music company. . .They whistle tunes to each other across my head. . .They speculate on the secondary meanings of the lyrics and how to translate them, mocking sentimental rhymes with the substitution of dirty words. . .

Like most prisoners Sergeant Hochweiler's favorite topic is women. . .Always before the evening count he teases Franklin: "How about taking me into Trinidad tonight for a date?". . .

Franklin laughs, "Aw, you Leipzig Yank, you're no good for an American woman. You're married."

"What do you mean married?" Hochweiler protests. "I'm outside of the limit."

"Outside of the limit?"

"Don't you Americans know the definition of marriage? If you're more than five hundred miles away from your wife, you're outside of the limit, outside of the marriage vows. So take me to Trinidad.". . .

Invisible I hear their laughter. . .*Outside the marriage vows.* . .It is not the marriage vows that bind me, but the memory of truly united flesh, the feeling that I cannot forget of her hair, breasts, legs, mouth, hands. . .Beneath the sergeants' laughter lies another mocking torment. . .When Hochweiler's eager, lewd questions about the sexual capacities of American film stars sound through the office, why does he wink at me?. . .Not directly to be sure. . .He winks at Franklin over my head. . .His pointed questions about the sexuality of these film stars are designed to support the accusation that I am a homosexual. . .Franklin plays along with him. . .Their two laughing voices echo over me like secret messages pulsing along a wire. . .Hochweiler's wink, a sharp, sneering twitch of the eyelid, implies hidden knowledge. . . Their smiles merge into comic masks, distant, inscrutable. . .

I tear myself away from the elevated faces, try to concentrate on my typing of Weimann's speech. . .As expected it is full of solemn quotations--from military authorities such as Gneisenau and Clausewitz to the cultural pinnacles of Goethe and Kleist. . .There is even an excerpt from Sophocles's *Ajax:* "All things does long, innumerable Time bring forth to light, and then again conceal". . .German mysticism seeking to wrap itself in the mysterious clarity of Greek sunlight. . Is that why the German military machine marches into Greece, Herr Major, to possess Sophocles, Aeschylus, and the ruins of the Parthenon?. . .

It is late in the evening before I am finished with the penalty of typing and released to return to my compound. . . When I enter my barrack the clock is approaching midnight. . Everyone seems to be sleeping. . .Doubtless some sentinel has one eye open. . .In the corridor outside of the latrine I notice the one copy of Dampfstoff's Nazi paper tacked to the wall. . Without thinking as I leave the latrine I tear down the paper and hide it in my shirt. . .Insane. . .Someone will notice that I am the last man to enter the barrack and suspect me automatically. . .No matter. . .Time strikes the painful act of necessity. . .Hurriedly I remove my pants and shoes, slide into my bunk. . .Above me my neighbor is snoring. . .In bed I push the Nazi newspaper down under the covers. . .My toes touch it as if the print were hot coals. . .In the morning I will carry it under my shorts, hidden around my waist by the weight of my belt, until I find some way to deliver it to the Americans. . .What if I get a chance to slip it to the American sergeant, Franklin?. . .No, he is too close to Hochweiler even if they only joke over my head. . .Somehow I must get this paper to the young American lieutenant Enders even if I do not trust him. . .*Trust no one in this shadow world. . .*

From my cot as I turn restlessly, unable to sleep, I see at the end of the barrack a huge shadow that the stove casts on the wall. . .How ironic. . .I am in the interior of another shadow world. . .After my release from the camp at Fulsbüttel, I was permitted to live a shadow existence in

Berlin for a brief time. . .The Gestapo watched me closely. . . Still I was a minor shadow and they were not too diligent. . . Since I was theoretically a civilian again, I was able to conduct a furtive, unsuccessful search for my wife. . .One rumor speculated that she might still be somewhere in Berlin undergoing forced labor. . .Impossible to determine the truth of this rumor although I was able indirectly to question several Jews who were forced to work long hours in factories. . .I questioned every shadow with whom I came in contact. . .No one has seen her or they had seen only ghosts who resembled her. . .

To survive in my search for my wife, I began to classify buildings according to their exteriors. . .The interiors were beyond the boundaries of my shadow world. . .Only superior, well-fed Nazi party officials and party members were allowed inside. . .I listed buildings in three categories according to their impressive facades-the facade of money, the facade of pleasure, and the facade of religion. . .If my shadow status forbade me the study of interiors, I would become a master of facades. . .Hitler, the frustrated architect, favored weight and bulk, enormous interiors, gigantic hallways and rooms, impressive staircases down which to descend in the power of uniforms. . .I favored tiny, intricate details high on the exterior walls, almost hidden under the eaves. . .

Hunger sharpened my perception as no one would hire me except for odd, menial jobs. . .If I couldn't beg scraps to eat from the charity houses, one or two remaining friends left occasionally a few inconspicuous items of food on designated benches in different parks. . .They never dared to talk to me. . .If I was lucky I caught a glimpse of their backs as they hurried away. . .I loved their backs. . .

I took great care that my appearance became neither too shabby nor too conspicuous. . .Either extreme might arouse the suspicion of the bored watchers who kept me under surveillance. . .Soon it became apparent that these watchers gave me a measure of freedom because following me furnished them with information of some minor value for their anti-Nazi files. . *.How does a shadow live?. . .On what sort of food does he survive?. . .What stolen clothes does he wear that may identify him?. . .What bench or hidden area of grass is suit-*

able for him to sleep on?. . .How long is it possible for him to live in isolation without betraying friends?. . .

With the arrival of winter I was forced to turn my attention from the external world of facades to the cellars. . .A cellar under National Socialist rule offered the advantages of a pawnshop that does not require a ticket. . .Since the Germans were acknowledged masters of western Europe in plumbing and heating, these advantages ascended from below. . .There were always large pipes to warm us and closets with cleaning materials where a shadow could sleep if necessary. . .Often supplies for dogs and cats were kept in the cellars. . .I found bones with meat on them or, if worst came to worst, some dog food. . .I developed a sixth sense about evading cellars with vicious dogs. . .

The greatest pleasure of the cellars was the chance encounter with other shadows. . .Not that I dared to become too friendly. . .When I met a fellow shadow a prescribed form of conversation ensued. . .You never talked about yourself. . . A shadow might be an informer. . .You learned the language of the cellar. . .This consisted of talking exclusively about the cellar, its particular qualities or dangers, the kind of facilities that it furnished. . .You compared it with other notable cellars in the city. . .

After the classification of cellars, we discussed the unique hobbies of shadows, provided that the hobbies were voiced with objective, impersonal values that did not intrude on the shadow's privacy. . .If mine was the classification of a civilization by architectural exteriors, other hobbies often proved to be more ingenious. . .

Max was a baldheaded, shriveled pea of a man with an enormous pair of ears that protruded from the sides of his head like the handles of a loving cup. . .His hobby was the classification of public latrines. . .He catalogued all the statistics in his mind, the number of standing urinals as opposed to toilets, the problem of pay-toilets as opposed to free toilets, the advantage of paper towels as compared to cloth towels on a roll. . .He could tell you exactly which latrines were watched by the police for sexual deviants and which were not. . .He knew which latrines were well-cleaned, which were dirty, and why. . .The special problem that interested him most was the design of latrines. . .He developed an obsessive theory that if public latrines were larger, better designed, more numerous, people would be friendlier. . .They would learn to get along with each other. . .They would not conceal so many sexual problems. . .

"In a latrine," he speculated, "you learn that concealment is stupidity. You learn to open up. You learn not to be self-conscious about your private parts. Why should your parts be private anyway? If you ever want to love someone other than yourself, you have to learn to make your private parts public! And the best way to do that is in a public latrine. Imagine latrines for a hundred, five hundred people. Think what that would do. People would have to learn to respect each other, to be tolerant of the other person's stink. Imaginations would be liberated from the slavery of private toilets and private parts.". . .

Another shadow-hobbyist, Hermann, differed completely from Max. . .Despite his situation Hermann was an invincible Utopian. . .He refused to concern himself with Max's crude occupation with purely materialistic matters of sexuality and elimination. . .Hermann was big-boned, big-headed, with an enormous quantity of black hair and a pair of eyes that never focused on you, but always up toward the stars. . .Although he admitted that he had never been in a plane, that he was reluctant even to drive a car, that the bicycle was his prefered method of travel, his particular hobby was transportation. . .Utopian transportation. . .He dreamed and planned the time when cities would be extinct and men would live in what he called "city-mobiles.". . .Each city-mobile would be capable of housing between five hundred and a thousand people, would run for an endless period of time on atomic energy, and would be designed for travel on either land or sea. . .Hermann insisted that the growth of stationary, large, industrial cities was the cause of man's difficulties. . .The ideal, small unit of the city-mobile, and its ability to adapt itself to continually change climates and places, would prevent man from putting down the kind of roots and attaining the kind of materialistic power that caused war. . .Also the advantage of the city-mobile was that its freely chosen officials could chart a careful course for the most beneficial environments. . .Areas of potential conflict or exploding nationalistic struggles could be bypassed. . .

George was a thin-faced, hooked-nosed man with a receding chin that he always tried to conceal by holding his hand over his jaw. . .Like all shadows with their obsessive natures, there was something admirable about him in his tenacious courage and concern for details. . .His hobby was public museums, not the collections, but the lecturers. . .The error of society had been to set up the wrong kind of education--the gymnasium, the technological school, the university. . .All of these institutions were run by bureaucrats who were mainly interested in status, promotions, and security. . .It was different with the lecturers in the public museums. . .There the often anonymous lecturers became transformed in the presence of their subjects. . .A lecturer on Egyptian mummies, brooding over those darkly dried corpses, would produce suddenly the most amazing insights into the nature of death and burial practices. . .Paradoxically, specialization, the curse of mankind, was impossible to a museum lecturer. . .A specialist on meteors, while lecturing with one hand caressing the mysterious stone-like objects, would blurt out astonishing revelations about the psychological sources of violence in man's nature. . .As for the lecturer on art, he became a transformed scientist pointing out ecstatically the laws of physics, mathematics, geography, and aerial photography as they flared forth in the genius of painters and sculptors. . .True museum-lecturers were the solution to the disaster of modern education that was at the root of all social problems. . .The major difficulty to overcome, and he, Georg, was devoting most of his time to it, was the problem of bringing the right kind of imaginative lecturer into contact with the right kind of unusual museum material. . .It was not enough that the accidental combination of museum collection and lecturer often produced startling results; surely it was possible to define the sort of lecturers that flourished on particular materials. . . Such a classification would permit again the education of humanity instead of the rigid training of specialists whose range of vision was limited to a few trivial facts and dates. . .

My new friends, the shadow-hobbyists, lifted me into a welcome speculative world that enabled me for several months to suppress my fear of the future. . .Regularly I sent off letters into the abyss where my wife existed in limbo. . .I arranged for impossible answers at a friend's post office box. . . Waiting for letters that never come is a special punishment. . . The mail seems like a sentence to isolation. . .So many letters and packages, none for me. . .Nevertheless she would not die. . .At night in my sexual dreams we rolled together in our lost bed. . .One day in 1939 I snapped back rudely into the world of time, of enforced communality. . .A Gestapo agent, with a soft, black hat and a sabre cut on his cheek, touched me softly on the shoulder. . .The next day the uniform of a Wehrmacht private covered me. . .My new world was a battalion of political prisoners mixed together with criminals, the 999th Division. . .

A whistle at dawn rouses me from my sleepless dream of the shadows. . .After the usual count by the Americans to insure the presence of all prisoners, I make my way to the officers' compound. . .Walking along I feel the Nazi paper bending, rustling softly to the turns of my flesh. . .The rustling seems incredibly loud, although I folded the paper into a long, narrow band to fit under my belt. . .

In Major Weimann's office I hope for a foolish moment that I will be left behind when the funeral procession commences. . .An absurd wish. . .I am given the special task of carrying the written speeches of Major Weimann and Captain Dampfstoff; also the newly sewn swastika banner that is to wave over the speaker's rostrum. . .My punishment is to bear the sacred words and the Nazi standard. . .In this way I am to learn that nationalistic language judges. . .Sergeant Hochweiler grins as he gives me my instructions and designates my place in the rearguard of Headquarters company with my servant props. . .

As the funeral procession lines up it covers the length of the compound road. . .One thousand officers resplendent in a variety of uniforms, even though many of the uniforms are composed of patchwork parts. . .Paratroopers, Panzer Corps, Luftwaffe, Infantry, even a few submariners from the Mediterranean who were captured in an African port. . .Medals dangle from lapels, ribbons shine in the sun. . .The only thing missing is weapons. . .Even though it is early morning the sun promises a scorching day. . .In the midst of the procession are the two catafalques painted black, bearing the dead officers. . .They lie in two open, black coffins decorated with swastikas. . .Their chests are heaped with flowers bought by special permission in the nearby town. . .The four corners of each catafalque have niches in which Nazi pennants are flown. . .At the head of each catafalque an officer holds high a banner on which a portrait of Der Führer has been painted. . .

Major Weimann and Captain Dampfstoff march up and down inspecting the company formations to insure that everything is in order. . .They make their own favorite inspection, Weimann for military appearance and precision of ranks, Dampfstoff for the proper display of Nazi propaganda. . .

Directly in front of the catafalques is grouped the band, no, the *orchestra*. . .Band is too prosaic a term for this collection of instruments. . .Flutes, drums, saxaphone, strings, tuba, clarinets, percussion instruments of all kinds rented, bought, and built through the Red Cross. . .The conductor, formerly employed in a provincial opera house, waves a shining, white baton. . .He gives the orchestra a proud downbeat and the Funeral March from Beethoven's *Eroica* begins. . The honor guard of officers, twenty to each catafalque, their rows of combat medals shining, march with uncanny rhythm--slow, steps, abrupt halt, precise start again. . .*Four steps, halt. . .Four steps, halt. . .*Faces like stone masks carved to endure in time, held stiffly aloft. . .

As the procession passes through the gate into the open desert beneath the mountains that lead to Mexico, we pass the first unit of American guard troops. . .Older men, too fat, too thin, too short, too tall, obviously non-combat soldiers shifting uncomfortably in their ranks, gaping at the rigid German formations. . .The American troops are headed by a middle-aged officer I do not recognize. . .No chance here to pass along the Nazi paper concealed under my belt. . .Will there ever be a chance the way I am surrounded?. . .

As each German formation passes the American company, commands ring out. . .Heads swivel right in perfect timing as if on steel rods. . .Rigid arms shoot up in the Nazi salute. . .

The American officer is forced to salute back continuously, his hand popping up to his cap in amazement. . .When my rigid arm stretches out instinctively, I feel myself a marionette pulled by strings and am able to manage the salute with an inner, grimacing laugh. . .

At the grave site on a slope surrounded by cactus clusters at the edge of the camp, the rest of the American guard forces are drawn up, waiting. . .I see the American camp commander and Lieutenant Enders next to him saluting and receiving the stiff arm as we Germans pass by. . .Oh, not to be a German, but then I would never have met her. . .The Americans seem far away instead of meters close. . .Impossible to reach. . .For a moment I consider breaking out of line, running to the Americans. . .They might reject me again. . .My feet are too conditioned, too numb to respond to my fantasy. . .

Besides two deep holes dug in the hard desert soil we stop. The catafalques approach. . .The columns of German officers are joined by companies of German soldiers, a vast, formal arrangement of defiant troops under the blistering sun. . . . Swastika standards are planted firmly in each grave. . .The rostum decorated with ornate Baroque curlicues is set up to accomodate the memorial speakers. . .At a whispered command from Sergeant Hochweiler, I place my folders of speeches on the rostrum and plant my swastika banner by the stand like a ludicrous flag of greeting to the hawks gliding above in the sky. . .What will the Americans think of me now?. . .They have forced me into this arena. . .

Major Weimann is the first speaker to eulogize the dead. . . He reads solemnly, impressively, from a Gothic-lettered scroll the names and military records of the murdered German officers: "They died for the Fatherland! Far away from their beloved country in this barren desert of an enemy nation, they sacrificed their lives. They were struck down valiantly, as if fighting gallantly on the battlefield. Let their devotion, their dedication to duty, be an example to us who value the great traditions of the German army. Justice will prevail. We have full assurance that their murderer shall be punished. We shall see that their families in Germany are rewarded for their loyal sacrifice. Their reward, even in death, is the knowledge of Germany's inevitable triumph. As Goethe said, "Wer immer strebend sich bemüht, den können wir erlösen". . .The quotation Major Weimann reads burns the air with the false context of history's glory and honor. . ."Whoever strives unceasingly to follow his destiny, he shall be redeemed". . . Who shall be redeemed, Major?. . .The word *redemption* is buried in your mouth. . .

With Captain Dampfstoff the setting alters abruptly. . . Two sergeants goosestep forward with a heavy book wrapped in a scarlet-painted cover, a black swastika gleaming in the center. . *Mein Kampf*. . .Dampfstoff intones fervently his solemn quotations: "When the nations on this planet fight for existence--when the question of destiny, 'to be or not to be', cries out for a solution--then all considerations of humanitarianism or aesthetics crumble into nothingness. . ."

The Führer's words jumble, clash, a buzzing swarm of aggressive bee-language. . .But the fortunate bees dance their communications. . .No joyous dance moves in these words. . . The agony of my listening is concluded by the inevitable "Heil Hitler!" trumpeted three times in rising volume across the desert wasteland. . .After each "Heil Hitler" two thousand voices echo the exuberant pledge to victory, *"Sieg Heil! Sieg Heil! Sieg Heil!"*. . .The belief in German victory is clearer than ever in these fanatically compulsive outcries. . . The Americans have lost respect. . .They have lost control. . . What will the Nazis plan next in this camp?. . .

After the bodies are lifted from the catafalques and placed slowly with due reverence in the graves, we stand at attention saluting death with aching arms. . .The graves are covered over. . .Even in death the officers are not permitted to rest alone. . .Dampfstoff erects a swastika flag over each grave. . .The black swastikas shine darkly in the sunlight. . . As we turn and march back to the compound at a given signal we begin to sing in perfect step the Horst Wessel song, *"Die Fahne hoch, die Reihen fest geschlossen. . ."*. . .

THE GERMAN IN THE GUARD HOUSE

Saluting these stiff-armed Nazis makes me feel like an idiot. All of my miserable Limited Service misfits shift uneasily behind me. Colonel Williams's face is red with anger and embarassment at the precise military humilation he is forced to endure. On the way to the grave site, reluctant to witness the straggling Limited Service march, he ordered those who limped too visibly to remain in their quarters. Shutting his eyes the Colonel drove to the site in his jeep. When I arrived with the ragged remnants of the headquarters company, struggling my best to keep them in some kind of formation, the Colonel winced and refused to look until the pseudo-soldiers were lined up in a presentable unit. "For Christ' sake," he ordered, "Keep 'em standing at ease until the Krauts march up. At attention they look like a bunch of scarecrows. It's unbelievable. You'd think I was commanding the god damn Salvation Army." Shifting uncomfortably from one foot to the other we sweated twenty minutes under blazing sun until the German procession moved in precise lock-step up the road.

The Beethoven funeral march infuriates the Colonel. "Where the hell did they get all those instruments?" he keeps muttering in wonder. "They think none of us ever heard Beethoven before. Those fucking bastards. I've got all the Beethoven symphonies on records played by *American* orchestras.". . .

Is that Armind stepping up with the swastika? He hoists it over the speaker's stand. I can't believe it. I trusted him. What the hell's going on? If the Nazis suspect him as he claims, would they let him play this Honor Guard role? Still he's surrounded by officers. Maybe they're testing him in their cat and mouse way. Wait and see if he's able to get us proof of Nazi coercion. Maybe Colonel Williams is right. Put the burden of proof on Armind. . .

Major Weimann's speech sounds military enough if pompous as expected. No Nazi quotes or threats. The great German cultural tradition, Beethoven to Goethe to Kleist's "Down in the dust with the enemies of Brandenburg!" Even a quote from Sophocles' *Ajax* to insert a touch of classiscism. All for the benefit of the raw Americans. Even though he can't understand German Colonel Williams is livid. Particularly he mumbles with rage when he hears Weimann quote from the military strategists Clausewitz and Gneisenau: "That bastard Gneisenau was a damn mercenary who fought for the British against us during the Revolution. I'll bet he isn't mentioning that is he Lieutenant?"

"No Sir. He's talking about the genius of Gneisenau as a Prussian Field Marshal when he conquered Napoleon and France."

"Bullshit. Anybody who knows anything about military strategy knows it was Wellington and the British who beat the shit out of Napoleon at Waterloo."

Even though Colonel Williams is incensed at the cultural and military one-upmanship, Weimann seems to imply in his eulogy that a greater historical German tradition lies behind the Nazi funeral trappings. Maybe Weimann will keep his word that this will be a military funeral. . .

Wait. . .Here come Dampfstoff and two sergeants. I'll be god-damned. They're carrying a copy of *Mein Kampf* as if it were the Bible. Look at that swastika! Colonel Williams writhes in agony as Dampfstoff starts to read from *Mein Kampf.* The last quote that Dampfstoff recites is a special warning to us mongel Americans. I translate every word to Williams: "Historical experience shows with terrible clarity that every mingling of Aryan blood with that of lower peoples results in the end of the cultured people. North America, whose population consists in by far the largest part of Germanic elements who mixed but little with the lower colored peoples, shows a different humanity and culture from Central and South America, where the predominantly Latin immigrants often mixed with the aborigines on a large scale. By this one example, we can clearly and distinctly recognize, the effect of racial mixture. The Germanic inhabitant of the American continent, who has remained racially pure and unmixed, rose to be master of the continent. He will remain the master as long as he does not fall a victim to defilement of the blood."

As I translate this warning Colonel Williams interjects a rising commentary that threatens to be heard across the desert: "German, hell. Wops, Micks, Polacks, Kikes, you bastards. . .

I should have known you can't trust these Krauts. . .We beat the shit out of 'em in World War I and we'll do it again. . .If only I had some real troops. . ."

After the burial as the German prisoners march back to the compound in perfect formation, singing the Horst Wessel song loud enough to bring rain if there were any clouds, Colonel Williams shakes his head with fury: "Those sons-of-bitches with their Heil Hitlers. They promised me a military funeral and then they pull this. You can bet they'll hear about this in Washington."

"What do you think's going to happen, Sir? What'll we do about Armind?"

"Who the hell knows? They're up to something. They think they've got us on the run. I'll show the sons-of-bitches. . ."

When the Colonel's rage subsides, as the Horst Wessel song echoes in the distance, he says bitterly: "You've got to admit they're well-trained. The bastards can sing. I'm sure as hell going to try and get some healthy soldiers here. We're going to need 'em." He glares over his shoulder at our Limited Service men.

"What about Armind, Sir?"

"Let him sit there until he shows us he's a real anti-Nazi. We can't afford to trust him."

"But , Sir. . ."

The Colonel climbs into his jeep impatiently. He's about to roar off to get on the telephone to Washington, when Major Weimann's aide, Lieutenant Schimmelwasser, marches up to salute and present a message from the German commander. For a moment I think Williams is about to tell Schimmelwasser off. Somehow Williams controls himself and listens. Schimmelwasser extends an invitation to attend a special "musicale" that evening in the officers' compound. Reluctantly Williams accepts the invitation. He replies curtly that, if he is unable to attend, one of his officers will represent him. After the aide departs the Colonel slams the door of his jeep and snaps at me. "I want you to go with me tonight. Probably they'll give us another dose of Nazi Kultur. But as long as we're there, maybe they'll just stick to propaganda and not try anything tough. I don't trust the bastards an inch. I'm going to get on the phone damn fast to Washington to see if there's any chance to change things around." The jeep roars off in a cloud of dust leaving me to march my sweating, disgruntled men back to their barracks. . .

In my room trying to cool off I drink beer after beer, gulping thirstily, wiping the sweat off my face. Now I have the evening to look forward to. No chance to get out of the camp even overnight. I was looking forward to going to Trinidad, escaping even if only for a few hours. A special "musicale!" Trust Weimann to trot out German culture again. Keep us on the run. Also that gives him a chance to feel morally superior to Dampfstoff. Probably there'll be lots of singing, a chorus, soloists, a pianist, the orchestra again. Beethoven to Johann Strauss. If Dampfstoff has his way the Nazis will throw in some propaganda too.

Is it because I'm half-German myself that I admire and hate them? My father's all German and he feels the same way. He loves German poetry and music and hates the German myth of racial superiority. No wonder I've always felt caught in a paradox. How can anyone love Beethoven and listen to *Mein Kampf* at the same time? Yet thousands of German prisoners did just that this morning. To make your peace with the paradox of your blood, you have to understand the conflicts that create the paradox. I know the naked ache for power in *Mein Kampf*, but I go along with Colonel Williams in pigeonholing all the Germans as "enemy". Is that what I'm doing to Armind? Taking the easy way out by classifying him neatly as "enemy."? If I can't deal with him, how can I live with myself? What if I end up just another Limited Service cripple, griping endlessly about the injustice of being drafted? The complaining life of a restricted witness. . .

Witness is the role that's always confined me. Can't I learn by being a witness? Maybe, but there's a point when one shifts to the knowledge of experience and learns to act, isn't there? Or I'm stuck forever amongst the passive spectators who endure without growth, unable to change their lives. I'll never forget my first encounter with the Nazis. It changed my life from a naive American music student in Switzerland who found it easy to ignore the political nature of the world to a horrified witness of German cruelty. *Kristallnacht, October, 1938.* At the age of eighteen my parents sent me to Zürich to study voice with the famous opera singer, Albert Holzreichl, and German with Frau Hedda Simmelstein. I was drifting between high school and college, seeking a music career without any certainty that I had a real ability to sing. One fall day I accompanied an American friend of mine, Cliff Maxfield, who had come to visit me in Zürich, back to the University of Freiburg in southern Germany where he was an exchange student.

When it turned out that Cliff was smuggling some money for an anti-Nazi friend whom he had met in Germany, I was less eager to go. Cliff, always a cocky optimist, laughed and reassured me: "They never search Americans at the border. Once in a while they take a quick look in your suitcase. That's all. You know where I carry the money? I always wear a jockstrap and carry it in there. You'd be surprised how much paper money you can get in a jockstrap. The only trouble is it gives me a sore crotch."

When our train reached the Swiss frontier, we saw huge fires blazing in the night across the border in Germany. Workers were laboring day and night to build "defenses" against the supposedly inpenetrable French Maginot line of fortifications. A uniform clicked heels into our compartment. For the first time I was faced with German military arrogance.

"For Christ's sake," Cliff whispered as I gaped, "Don't let these bastards get you."

Somehow the German uniform concealed the man in it. No meaningful human face was visible. Instead of warm flesh, only a bony head shaved and polished free from a single hair, protruded slightly from the uniform. An anvil-thick neck jutted above immaculately glittering cloth tailored exclusively for the display of insignia, the ultimate exhibit of the swastika. The faceless uniform extended its stubby hand imperiously for my passport. It examined the document suspiciously, carefully, as if all foreign documents were suspect. I began to sweat. Behind me Cliff belched loudly. The uniform stared haughtily at the source of this explosion.

"Sorry," Cliff smiled blandly and handed over his passport.

The uniform studied the document, then relaxed visibly. Another brash, ill-mannered American youth who would be taught better manners as a student in Germany. The uniform handed back our passports with a smile of indulgent scorn. When the door clanged shut I turned to Cliff: "Why the hell did you do that?"

"Relax. It's a game. If he thinks I'm a stupid American student, he won't bother me. Catch?"

When we arrived in Freiburg late in the evening, I began to relax. Despite the Nazis the small university city seemed dedicated to its quiet scholarly, medieval past. After all Heidegger, the famous existentialist philosopher, was chancellor of the university. Students were still coming there from all over the world. Near the train station a Bierstube was crowded with students drinking and singing. The graceful Gothic cathedral soared in the night sky.

"I wanted you to see that first," Cliff pointed. "It's particularly strong at night, the way that spire seems to go up forever into the sky. Imagine me getting to love the Gothic. I used to think Gothic was some kind of professional team."

On the way to the hotel where he had booked a room for me, he walked me past the old university buildings.

"You've got to see these buildings at night to get a real feeling of their age."

"I see what you mean."

"When you walk into these buildings in the day, the petty officials take over, the Herr Doktor Professors and their flunkies. One title isn't enough for them. They have to keep on inventing a string of titles to assure their status. At night the past takes over. . .

"So you haven't learned much from your classes?"

"I've learned more just being here. At first everyone I met seemed to have read three times as many books as I have. Then I began to get over my American inferiority complex and to think about the relationship here between the past and present, between the Nazis and the whole academic scene."

"Have you run into Heidegger?"

"No, he keeps pretty aloof. He's got a cabin up in the Schwarzwald where he goes to hide out and work on his books. I've been trying to read some of his stuff. There's a sentence in one of his works that sticks in my mind: *"Das Nichts nichtet."* Impossible to translate. Something like

"Nothing nothingizes."

"That sounds pretty hopeless."

"Maybe for us optimistic American social-workers type." Cliff grinned. "There must be a curious split in Heidegger. He took over his position from a former half-Jewish professor of his who was thrown out under the racial laws. So why shouldn't he believe that nothing creates nothing? Now he's a bigshot university official under the Nazis. Maybe he had to test his theories of existential existence and action, so he felt compelled to accept public power. The philosopher becomes the administrative politician, the man of action."

"Thats sad."

"Yes, because philosophy rejects the trap. Like the spirit of these ancient Gothic buildings asserting their faith, philosophy always hangs above the social trap of ambition. That's why I smuggle money for my German friend, even though it's only a gesture. I can't stand the university sell-out to the Nazis."

When we reached my hotel in the dingy part of the city it was after midnight. A three-quarters moon glowed on the quiet, narrow streets. Odd talking about Heidegger's relationship to the Nazis in this peaceful town that seemed to hold only memories of the distant religious past. As we entered the hotel clerk was half-asleep behind the desk. He peered up resentfully. Moving in slow motion he led us up to my room, his feet clattering on the steep staircase. More like a shoebox than a room.

"Sorry about this," Cliff looked around the room scornfully. You can come and sleep in my room if you like."

"No, it's all right." I wanted to be alone to absorb my first confused impressions of Germany.

Suddenly his sleepy, lugubrious face alert, the clerk peered out of the window. *"Feuer!"* he shouted and bolted down the stairs. Alarmed we followed him running out into the street. At the end of the block flames flickered against the sky. Windows banged open as people in their night-clothes leaned out to witness the sudden excitement. A line of uniformed men approached. They sealed off the end of the block. Cold, impersonel uniforms and rifles concealing again the reality of faces. . .

"S.S. troops," whispered Cliff pointing to the jagged lightning of their insignia. Finding ourselves directly behind the hotel clerk in the gathering knot of spectators, Cliff asked him about the fire.

The clerk gestured excitedly: "The synagogue is burning. Those Jewish traitors are getting it at last. Look, they're taking away that rabbi and his wife. They must have been hiding money."

Behind the cordon of S.S. uniforms I caught a glimpse of a small bearded man in a hat and coat being bundled into a car with a woman. The S.S. uniforms began to break up the crowd. "The time of judgment is over. Go home!" shouted an officer, pushing us back.

Unable to absorb what we had witnessed Cliff and I stood there frozen. *The time of judgment is over.* I felt as if I had focused on some painful, swift disaster through the wrong end of a telescope. Why didn't I cry out in protest? Why didn't anyone protest? I began to justify my failure to act. I was only a visitor. How could I be sure who was arrested and for what cause? Absurd excuses flooded my mind, but one accusation I could not drive away. *I was a witness, a passive, gaping spectator.*

As the S.S. officer approached again, frowning at us, the hotel clerk tugged at my sleeve. "Sir, you had better return to the hotel." A tone of mockery echoed in the way he called my youth, *Sir.* I felt dizzy, sick to my stomach. Beside me Cliff too seemed unable to move. The S.S. officer, tunnels of eyes piercing us beneath the visor of his cap, motioned to us to depart. Once more the hotel clerk plucked my sleeve nervously: "It's best to return, Sir, before there's trouble.

They don't want anyone here. "*Sir, Sir, Sir. . .*

Initiated as witnesses Cliff and I turned back to the hotel, unable to talk. We made a date to meet in the morning. I tried to reassure myself, "It was only an accident that I saw the synagogue burned down and the rabbi arrested." *Only an accident--the way one witnesses some disaster by chance.* Undressing quickly I climbed into the bed's safety, hoping that rapid sleep would exorcize this nightmare. A coil of broken springs in the cheap mattress poked into my back. I ached to get up, flee from this burning city.

Feet clattered on the steep stairs again. People entering the next room. Paper-thin walls. The clerk's obsequious voice poured through the partition: "A spacious, private room for your pleasure, Herr Leutnant. No one will disturb you." *A Lieutenant.*

Listening eagerly as currents of shame and lustful excitement swept through my aroused flesh I lay rigid in my bed. The officer was a S.S. lieutenant, perhaps even one of the troops assigned to the burning of the synagogue. He had brought a whore to the room. She kept questioning him about the fire. He evaded her questions, finally ordered her to shut up. Sullenly she began to bargain for more money. A long silence. *She's going to leave.* But there was no chance of her leaving. The officer had waited long enough. A loud slap. The girl began to cry, soft tears, almost voluptuous sounds. My ears were enormous listening posts. The sound of cloth ripped harshly. Cries of protest. Another harder slap. More tears. Silence. . .I lay there listening to the sounds as they gathered rhythm, overwhelmed me, creaking, rocking, slapping, scratching. Her muffled pleas of pain and hatred culminated in a resigned gasp of acceptance. When the silence of sleep reigned finally, I masturbated in a sexual fury of guilty visions.

When I met Cliff the next morning he said nothing, only showed me the newspaper. All over Germany Jewish stores and synagogues had been burnt or smashed. Many Jews had been arrested and would be tried in court for various "illegal" acts. "German patience has been tried to the limit," the report said." Finally German honor has struck back against the illegal hoarding of wealth and sinister, anti-Nazi propaganda carried on by Jewish criminals. . .They have been taught a necessary lesson." Cliff and I sat reading in guilty knowledge. *October, 1938. . .Kristallnacht. . .*

Five years later in Colorado I'm a witness again to Nazi terror. Incredible that the American desert should suddenly blaze with more swastikas than medieval Freiburg. I must do something about Armind. For my sake, if only to see whether I can break out of the labyrinth of witnesses. The telephone in the officers' quarters rings sharply through my vision of desert swastikas. Colonel Williams tells me happily that the

Provost Marshal General has promised an immediate investigation of Nazi control in all German prisoner of war camps. Meanwhile, the Colonel continues, we still need all the evidence we can get of Nazi rule in our camp. He asks me to try and contact Armind before the evening musicale. "You go out and take over as officer-in-charge of the evening count in his compound. Try to find a way to contact him without suspicion. At least find out if he's been able to come up with any evidence."

"All right," I agree, "but tomorrow I think we ought to take him out of the compound even if he hasn't found anything. The situation's getting too dangerous."

"Let's see what happens tonight," Colonel Williams replies, "If possible I want more proof that we can trust him. I asked the Provost Marshal if he had any reports on the 999th Division. He said his office had never heard of it. So I don't like being pushed into making a big deal out of Armind. Tell you what. If the Nazis put on another god damn propaganda show tonight, I'll yank him out. Then we can use him as a key witness even if he doesn't come up with any hard evidence."

Armind a witness too? Is that why I'm involved with him? Are we both just witnesses destined to be historical blotters absorbing events without being able to alter them in any significant detail? Maybe the world's being divided into barbed wire fences enclosing anonymous witnesses and executioners only. No prosecutors or defendants any more. No small town courtrooms considering justice impartially. The world in the web of war, flies and ants struggling in the web for power. . .

Don't be a cynical witness. Start thinking how to contact Armind without causing suspicion. Just walk up in the compound with a thousand prisoners staring at you and ask him. The Colonel's request is ridiculous. But maybe I can work out something to at least get a signal from Armind. Then I can put the pressure on the Colonel to yank him out of the compound tonight. Dangerous to wait until morning. These crazy Nazis really think they're going to win the war. What can they really do out here in the desert? Even if they escape it's a long way to Mexico over the mountains. . .

As whistles shriek in the compound for the evening count I sense a new defiance among the prisoners. Watch the American corporal in charge of counting Armind's company. We've worked out a plan. The corporal coordinates medical appointments and Red Cross interviews with prisoners. On the pretext of an appointment the corporal will call Armind out of ranks and try to learn if he's found any evidence to satisfy the Colonel. These appointments are routine and probably the German non-commissioned officers won't suspect anything.

As the prisoners line up in their five deep rows to facilitate counting, they take a long time to assemble. What the hell's going on? Some are grinning. Are they just cocky or are they doing this deliberately? Worried I order the German sergeant in charge of the compound to hurry up the count. "Jawohl, Herr Leutnant," he salutes me mockingly and pretends to speed up. It takes a hell of a long time. Finally each company seems ready to be checked. I warn the American guards to be extra careful.

"Check, Company 1."

"O. K."

"Check, Company 2."

"O. K." *Why in hell is it going so slow?*

"Check, Company 3."

"Wait a minute. . ."

"Anything wrong?" I call anxiously to the Sergeant of the Guard.

"They get different figures. We'd better count again, Sir." I rush over to Company 3. The prisoners snicker, whisper. Their rows of five waver until it's hard to see whether there are four, five or six in a row.

"Damn it, tell the bastards to stand still!" The Sergeant is losing his temper.

The snickering grows into giggles. Suddenly a prisoner stumbles out of line.

"Get back there!" A guard shoves him back. The giggles ripple into laughter. A general milling around like cattle in a stall. Again the prisoner stumbles out. Or is he pushed out?

"What the hell's going on here?" I ask.

A German corporal in charge of the company, built like a boulder, steps forward stiffly: "This man cause dif-*fick*-ul-ty." His heavily accented English gives the *fick* an explosive burst.

"What kind of dif-*fick*-ul-ty?" I can't resist imitating the bastard.

"He Arab. No German. Bad soldier."

Walking over I look at the prisoner. A tall powerfully built man with a swarthy complexion, he stands uneasily in front of the tightly closed ranks as if struggling to decide whether to force his way back into position.

"So what if he's an Arab?" asks the Sergeant of the Guard.

"No like Germans. He talk against Germans."

"Well, what do you want me to do?"

"Take him off."

"What the hell do you mean, take him off. . ."

"Take him out of compound. He cause trouble. No German."

The Sergeant confers with me. "God damn it, how did they get an Arab into the Aryan race? Now what the shit do we do."

The Arab shouts foreign accusations at the closed ranks. German voices curse back at him. The German corporal approaches us gesturing scornfully at the Arab. "See, he speak only Arab curse.He try to curse us. In German he only say word for eat. Eat, eat, eat. He curse us. Take him off before trouble happen."

I step in and address the Corporal in German. "If you don't get your men into formation immediately, we'll restrict your entire company for a week."

The Corporal looks at me with surprise. When he gushes back in German he speaks with a new military caution: "Herr Leutnant, my men are tired of putting up with this Arab. He's like an ape. All he does is eat and he never washes. He curses us in his language."

"You drafted him into your Africa Corps, didn't you? He's your responsibility."

"He can't be trained. He's too stupid," insists the Corporal. "I'm afraid of trouble if he remains."

"All right," I make up my mind. "I'll take him out of your company if you can't handle him."

The Corporal is a little worried by this. "What will you do with him?"

"That's none of your business."

"He's no soldier, only a troublemaker."

"If you're a soldier why can't you line up your own company in proper formation?"

"Yes, Sir." The German corporal salutes, turns, shouts an order. Heals click and the lines become as straight as if drawn by a ruler.

"What are you going to do with this Arab freak, Lieutenant?" asks the Sergeant of the Guard. Completely ignored now by the company the Arab is standing alone, one heavy boot scuffing the ground.

"Take him to headquarters," I hear myself say. "I'll talk to Colonel Williams and see if we can transfer him to another camp for his own safety."

When the count is verified and the prisoners dismissed I remember abruptly about Armind. On the way out of the compound I check with the American corporal. "No problem, Lieutenant," he says. "Everybody was watching the Arab. Armind indicated that he had something to give you. What's it all about anyway?"

When I reach headquarters Colonel Williams is not there. Finally I get him at the officers' club. I expect him to explode, but his voice on the phone sounds worried: "You did the right thing, but it looks like trouble. Where the hell are we going to put this Arab? We can't keep him in headquarters god damn it."

"What about Armind, Sir?" Shall I take him out of the compound?"

"Yes, we'll take him out first thing tomorrow morning. Tonight we'll talk to Major Weimann at this damn musicale and read him the riot act. Otherwise they'll be kicking anybody they don't like out of formation. Wait a minute. I know what to do with the Arab. . ."

"What, Sir?"

"Stick him in the guard house."

"The guard house, Sir?"

"Why the hell not? It's empty at the moment, right?"

"Yes, Sir. The only one in there was One-Eyed Nellie and he's gone."

"Good. Put the Arab in there. Station a guard outside the door just to make sure that he's safe. It would be god damn ironic if the Arab wandered off and was our first escapee. When we take Armind out tomorrow we can stash him in the guard house too for safekeeping. Get some food, Lieutenant, and I'll see you this evening. You did a good job."

*The guard house. . .*Somehow a jail with barred cells seems an ironic hide-out for Armind and the Arab. But they'll be safe there. Where the hell else can they hide? Probably I can persuade the Colonel to leave the cell doors open. That way they can visit back and forth if they wish, spark any secret signals of friendship that may be left. Friendship? They'll need secret signals--an Arab who doesn't understand German and a half-crazy political prisoner. Anyway the Colonel said I did a good job. I feel a little useful for a change. At least I got the Arab out of trouble and the Colonel agreed to take Armind out of the compound tomorrow. I hope nothing happens to Armind before then. If he has some real evidence we can get him transferred to a safer camp. Maybe we can even find some of his anti-Nazi friends from the 999th Division if they exist. Anyway the Provost Marshal General won't need much proof with our eyewitness reports about the funeral ceremony. I'm so tired I'd like to pass out in bed, not go to a damn musicale. Still it'll be a pleasure to hear Colonel Williams read out Weimann. I hope Dampfstoff is there too.

Guard house. . .Maybe we'll develop an anti-Nazi colony there. That's a laugh. Armind and an Arab. Two loners. Still it's a beginning. . .

THE GERMAN   FAUST AT THE MUSICALE

After the Nazi triumph at the funeral Sergeant Hochweiler drops all pretense at concealing his Nazi beliefs. . .When he invites Franklin to the "musicale" he boasts over my head: "You will hear the Golden Throat.". . .

"Who's the Golden Throat?" asks Franklin. . .

"A famous singer who had the privilege of singing for the Führer. It will be a great entertainment of our culture. You will hear excerpts from *Faust* with marvelous actors. You will understand how our culture has triumphed against the international Jewish conspiracy to conquer us.". . .

Again Hochweiler speaks to torment me. . .When Franklin brings up his doubts about the Nazi handling of the "Jewish question". Hochweiler answers quickly: "Well, perhaps Hitler did go too far with the Jews. The way you Americans went too far with the Indians. Hitler had some bad advisers. But you have to understand the Jewish problem that existed in our country. The Jews were everywhere. They controlled the arts, the medical, the legal professions as well as the corporations. And, of course, they dominated education. It was very hard for a real German to advance in these professions. The Jewish teachers. . .". . .

I recoil from the bitter word *teachers* that Hochweiler aims at me. . .Franklin listens to the tirade with resigned patience. . .Hochweiler's monologue switches finally to the theme of Russian Communists. . .He pats his Russian campaign ribbon as he speaks to Franklin in an intimate tone: "It's easy for you Americans to think well of the Russians. You don't know them. You're not their neighbors. Most of your information about Russia comes from Communist Jewish educators. I tell you I've been all over the world. The Russians are the worst barbarians. You should see the filthy way they live. They never wear clean clothes. In all the Russian villages we occupied I never saw one good suit of clothes. We made a big mistake in Germany. Instead of trying to re-educate our fanatical Communists, we should have shipped them all to Russia. Then they could have seen how those peasants live. You have no idea how bestial the Russians are! One time our Company was dug in behind a wall in a village just outside of Leningrad. A squad of Russians approached. We fired at them. Nothing seemed to stop them.

They stood there without moving. 'Idiots!' we called, 'Surrender!' They didn't answer. Evening came. We couldn't attack in the dark. At dawn without sleep we crept around behind them. Slowly we crawled through the ruins toward the motionless figures. When we reached them they were all dead! To fool us they'd propped up the dead bodies with sticks. Barbarians! Did you ever hear of any other country that has such little respect for the dead? Beasts that's what they are. . .But I've talked enough about war. Women, that is a more pleasant subject in this age of growing Jewish homosexuality. I like your American women. They are so independent. They hate homosexuals so much. . .". . .

Hate homosexuals hovers over me. . .Hochweiler continues, "Perhaps you can arrange a date for me this evening at the musicale. I will promise her a fine time. You remember my definition of marriage? Outside the five hundred mile limit I'm a free man. . .". . .

"Aw, you Leipzig Yank," Franklin laughs. . .

If I could only stop listening. . .I understand Hochweiler too well. . .If I could only forget my fellow Germans in their blind worlds. . .The other day I saw a Nazi sergeant checking the license plates of American cars to make sure the numbers were different before he would admit that Americans really owned their own cars. . .Or the kitchen workers, dedicated fanatics of ice cream, who shut themselves in refrigerators on orders to make ice cream until they're blue in the face. . . They stir their alchemist's mixture of ingredients around to achieve the perfect frozen quality even if they suffocate. . . Stop thinking of automatons. . .Think of objects, of how to get the paper I'm carrying to the Americans. . .

After Franklin leaves the office I'm released to my compound for the evening count. . .Hochweiler orders me to return in time to help out with arrangements for the evening musicale. . .Will the American officer attend?. . .Perhaps I can contact Enders there in the dark. . .

During the count a prisoner in another company down the line is pushed out of rank. . .A whisper sounds through our company, "It's an Arab. He's being punished.". . .Since there are no Jews left here an Arab has been selected for racial discipline. . .I see Lieutenant Enders hurrying across the yard to inspect the situation. . .No chance to contact him this time. . .Names are called out for medical and Red Cross appointments. . . *My name*. . .An American corporal whispers to me, "Lieutenant Enders wants to know if you found any evidence.". . .I nod my head afraid to speak. . .The tyrants a few meters away will overhear me. . .Returning to ranks a mixture of joy and fear surge through my body. . .Now the Americans may remove me from the compound. . .Will it be soon enough?. . .They're taking the Arab away. . .Why not me?. . .

At dinner I cannot eat. . .I measure out my evening time before the musicale carefully. . .Afraid to remain alone in the barrack I walk around and around the compound. . .Many prisoners make this promenade. . .They stroll by twos and threes, hands folded behind their backs, conversing leisurely. . I jerk along, twisting constantly backward as if I should be walking in the opposite direction. . .When I come abreast of one of the strolling groups, their conversation stops abruptly as if they met a pariah. . .

Words are forbidden to me. . .I strain to hear music playing from the barracks that I pass. . .Music is friendlier than words. . .The radio has taken the place of sex. . .Prisoners twist the dial furtively in search of a sensuous singer. . .American jazz is officially discredited. . .Insufficiently serious for the mystical dimensions of German culture. . .Yet someone always tunes in a feminine singer, imagining her eyes, lips, body through her teasing, throaty voice. . .If the preoccupied listeners catch sight of me the radio clicks off against my intrusion. . .Anger. . .Rage. . .I walk faster. . .A cunning fear suffuses my veins, an anxious search for impossible places of concealment. . .Last comes a wave of self-pity. . .Why this persecution?. . .Do they really think I am a homosexual?. . .

On with my lonely promenade. . .The time of *the glow* the intense evening light over the prison camp. . .Hypnotized heads stare at the horizon. . .Even though the sun has set the sky glows with a unique violet radiance. . .As I walk I classify in my mind all possible varieties of *the glow* that might occur to susceptible prisoners as the radiant sky fades into darkness. . .*The glow of hate, the glow of eternity, the glow of will, the glow of endless space*. . .I am a shadow again, a master of classification. . .

More music from the next barrack. . .A German classic this time. . .Pure German music. . .Men listening in rapture. . . Pipe and cigarette smoke drift lazily in the air. . .Brahms's *Requiem,* music permitted reluctantly by the Nazis because of its religious nature. . .The strings speak in quietude, then the baritone voice: "Lord, make me to know, know the measure of my days on earth, to discover my frailty. . ." That is all I hear. . .I am afraid to stop and listen. . .*The measure of my days on earth. . .*

At the western end of the yard I stare through the barbed wire fence into the officers' compound where the new theatre has just been finished. . .The musicale will be held there tonight. . .Our heritage of craftsmanship. . .A barrack floor was dug up, sloped so the spectators can see from any seat, a stage was built, electrical equipment rigged from waste materials. . *Heute Abend um sieben Uhr! Variété! Musik! Faust Stücke!*. . . Music, selections from *Faust* at seven o' clock. .. Nothing can happen in a theatre. . .I'll be safer in an audience. . .What time is it now?. . .Six-thirty. . .Time for one more quick trip around the compound, around and around, before I report to the theatre as directed. . .Will they use me as a prop boy again to handle their Nazi banner?. . .

Walk faster. . .How can identical barracks look so different?. . .Each prisoner puts out a small, tentative bloom of color in a window, a plant, a picture, a signal to freedom. . . Wait. . .That group of men sitting on the steps. . .Isn't that Sergeant Hochweiler with them?. . .Are they staring at me?. . . No, they look away. . .Submarine men. . .Why is Hochweiler talking to them?. . .Several weeks ago a U-boat sank off the Atlantic coast. . .The crew members who survived were sent here. . .Mix them all up paratroopers, infantry, Luftwaffe, storm troopers. . .All Germans are the same to Americans. .

Watch out for submarine crews. . .Handpicked for loyalty to the Third Reich. . .Obey, never question. . .As cold as the living honor guards who stand motionless outside of the memorial to the Hitler-Putsch victims in Munich. . .You have to be a fanatic warrior to volunteer for that cage in the dark sea. . .Look back to watch if they're following. . .Almost finished the grand tour again. . .Time to report for duty at the theatre. . .Head through the gate. . .Show my pass authorizing me to attend the performance. . .Safety in numbers. . .I want to hear laughter, laughter. . .

Captain Dampfstoff assigns me to pass out programs. . . At least I don't have to carry the Nazi banner. . .Why does he station me in such a prominent position where everyone can stare at me as he walks in?. . .My wife and I used to watch the workers file into the Volkstheater in Berlin. . .Over the entrance was inscribed *Die Kunst Dem Volke.* . .Art for the people. . .Now the Nazis call it *Theater Am Horst Wessel Platz.* . .In honor of the pimp they have proclaimed a martyr. . .What will Weimann and Dampfstoff call this theatre?. . .The curtain, sewn out of blankets, is decorated with a large, black swastika. . .*Hitler Theater Im Trinidad. . .*

As I stand there exposed with my programs, Colonel Williams and Lieutenant Enders enter with Weimann. . .They are arguing. . .Colonel Williams waves his hands angrily. . . Weimann tries to pacify him. . .Can they be talking about me?. . .No, they do not notice me. . .Probably about the Arab. . .Finally they go to sit down. . .I see Weimann confer with Dampfstoff. . .Are they changing the program?. . .

Standing at the back of the theatre I watch the curtain open. . .Ranks of officers in rigid military formation. . .A master of ritual wearing high, polished black boots and a white scarf marches forward, clicks his heels, bows to Major Weimann and the American officers, and announces: "Company A will begin with *Heidenröslein.*". . .Like expert marionettes the chorus of officers begins to sing without any conductor. . .A singing machine. . .How moving the old sentimental song is in this mechanical setting. . .

After the chorus the ritual master introduces the Golden Throat. . .He is dressed in shorts, sandals, a white, short-sleeved shirt with a golden scarf around his neck. . .Black hair lines his thick legs and arms. . .His voice is hard, metallic, the compelling agent of mass emotions. . .*The Golden Throat!*. . . Steel Throat is more appropriate. . .He sings of devotion to the fatherland, the passionate nation that is always re-born in fire from fiery destruction. . .He sings of the exultant march of the S.S. troops, of the women's proud service to the swastika, of the brownshirted martyrs in Munich who sacrificed their lives for Der Führer and the national honor. . .

He finishes and bows many times to frenzied applause. . .I watch the American officers. . .They do not applaud. . .Instead Colonel Williams and the Lieutenant talk angrily to Weimann. . .Suddenly the Americans leave the theatre. . .I am alone. . .Never get trapped in a building. . .Refer to Military Manual Number Infinity: *"Notice carefully the construction of a building before you seek shelter in it."*. . .Sanctuary. . . In the Middle Ages you were safe if you hid in a church, safe from everyone but God and the priests. . .Control myself. . . Hochweiler and the submarine men are not in the theatre. . . The Americans will rescue me tomorrow. . .

Next on the program, says the ritual master, is Mozart's overture to *The Marriage of Figaro*. . .The conductor taught at the Mozarteum in Salzburg. . .The same conductor who led the Beethoven Funeral March in the morning's ceremonies. . . Why can't I go to him for help if he's an Austrian who loves Mozart?. . .

Hitler is an Austrian, remember?. . .Anyone who loves Mozart, Beethoven, Brahms, how can he be a Nazi?. . .Major Weimann loves Mozart, Beethoven, Brahms. . .Better to stay away from this conductor. . .

Applause. . .The first scene from *Faust* is next on the program. . .German culture is the one culture. . .What was it Goethe said? *"The Roman sense of patriotism! God preserve us from that as from an ogre! We should find no chair to sit on, no bed to sleep in, in that country of the mind!"*. . .

Who's speaking?. . .That isn't what they're saying on stage. . .Even dead men write according to the wishes of Dr. Goebbels. . .

> Habe nun, ach! Philosophie,
> Juristerei und Medizin,
> Und leider auch Theologie!
> Durchaus studiert, mit heissem Bemühn.

Ah, that's Faust. . .I've studied Philosophy, Jurisprudence, Medicine, and even, alas, Theology. . *Alas, Theology*. . . That's suitable to the Nazis. . .They don't need to censor that. . .The actor playing Faust, like a wayward spring, jumps and hops in the air. . .Even German actors can't move quietly anymore. . .

*Wherefore from Magic I seek assistance. . .*My Faust!. . . Magic in this theater, the sweaty smell of prisoners crowded close together. . .Why don't they hear the German who could write, *"No bed to sleep in, in that country of the mind."*. . . Magic in the heart, the sorcery of Mephistopholes. . .

Ich bin der Geist der stets Verneint! I am the spirit that denies everything. . *.Everything?*. . .Wipe the sweat off. . . Too hot in this room. . .Crouch back in the darkness to be inconspicuous. . .Forget the voices. . .

That with the height of Gods Man's dignity may vie!. . . What is dignity?. . .To stand upright, to walk straight forward, straight as the flight of an arrow, straight as a surveyor's line, never to look back and feel that you should be walking in the opposite direction. . .

Loud applause. . .Weimann stands up applauding. . .Would you be a Major, oh Faust, a General Staff Officer who loves Mozart, Beethoven, Goethe, and Brahms?. . .The ritual master announces a minuet by Beethoven, also a party member as witness the symphony of brotherhood in D minor. . .Of course we haven't been able to give him a party number as yet for his spirit soars and is elusive, while ours is more practical, given to the educational policies of camp. . .A minuet. . . Dance of grace. . .Bring on the dancers! . . .Bring on the Golden Throat, the Leipzig Yankee, the Man in the White Shirt, the Hunting Dog, the General Staff Officer!. . .Let them whirl together on stage inside the barbed wire, in the ant shadows under *the glow*. . .

Candles are brought on stage. . .Rococo theatres were lit by thousands of candles. . .How picturesque. . .Sergeant Hochweiler, medals glistening on his chest, brings out a stand, a pulpit really. . .Captain Dampfstoff strides solomnly on stage with a book in his hand. . .Facing the audience he stretches out his arm and cries, "Heil Hitler!". . .The prisoners arise en masse, cry back, "Sieg Heil! Sieg Heil! Sieg Heil!". . . When the echoes die away Dampfstoff begins to read. . *.My first impression of a Jew revolted me. . .Mein Kampf. .* Where did they find it?. . .Doubtless they wrote it out by heart for they are learned scholars, oh lustful learning. . .The reading continues. . .Guards march on, turn simultaneously, stand at attention on either side of the pulpit. . .They carry swastika banners. . .

*Infamous, vile, wretched. . .*Jews, of course, not Germany. . I hear a jumble of words. . .Stop listening. . .Continue with the next lesson. . .Don't shut The Book. . .

My name. . .No, my number. . .Why should Dampfstoff read my name in the sacred company of The Book?. . . *Traitor to the Third Reich. . .Conspiring to overthrow. . .* Overthrow The Book?. . .I am not Goethe. . .Why is everyone turning around, staring at me?. . .The exit. . .Two guards stand there behind me. . .

*According to the judgment of the Court of Honor. . .The sacred duty owed to Der Führer. . .*A roar of approval from the audience. . .Someone is being sentenced. . .*To be exiled from the community. . .In addition, the traitor is to be branded on his back with the swastika. . .*Branded, Mephistopholes?. . .Is that your new science?. . .*Sentence to be executed immediately. . .*Dampfstoff has left. . .The concert continues. . .Why is the orchestra playing so loudly?. . . Gay gypsy music. . .Brahms's *Hungarian Rhapsody. . .*Those men coming toward me. . .Eight of them. . .Why do they wear blankets over their heads?. . .Don't touch me. . .Let me walk by myself. . .Where are you taking me?. . .I will walk in dignity. . .The sound of water, waterfall. . .*The latrine. . . That red-hot wire shaped like a swastika!. . .*

Stuff his head in the toilet!. . .That'll stop his screams!. . .

All the showers are turned on. . .To drown out your screams, fool. . .Don't hit me anymore. . .

Traitor. . .You dirty fairy! You'll learn not to talk to the enemy. . .Hochweiler's voice. . .The Leipzig Yankee. . .I am the spirit that denies. . .Please don't. . .

Brand him. . .

Wherefore, from Magic, the water running from Magic. . .

Don't burn it too deep. . .

Last wash of sound. . .Cool water. . .

THE AMERICAN EXIT TO AMERICA

My dream fades as the hammering on the door wakes me. What was I dreaming of? Graves in the desert. Somehow the graves are mixed up, a canyon landscape tangled with desert clay. With their box of ashes my parents stand staring into the graves where the German officers are to be buried. Just as Father is about to pour the ashes into a grave Mother shrieks, "No!" She seizes the box from him. A stream flows through the desert. "There!" she points, but the sun is too hot, burning. The sun dries up the stream as they search. . .

Bang, bang. . ."Lieutenant, Lieutenant! An emergency. Wake up! The Colonel wants you." I stumble to the door. The Sergeant of the Guard stands there, hand raised in a fist to pound again. "Get dressed, Sir. The Colonel wants you immediately. There's trouble."

"What happened?"

"I'm not sure yet, Sir. Someone cut a hole in the Compound 3 fence near the tower. The Colonel's there already."

Hurriedly I pull on my clothes. We run out to the waiting jeep. As the jeep pulls away I remember *"Compound 3 is where Armind's a prisoner."* Has anything happened to him? Maybe we shouldn't have stalked out of the performance so early last night. Still the Colonel wanted to warn Weimann that the Nazi propaganda had to stop. On the way to Compound 3 we pass the Guard House where the Arab is imprisoned.

"How's the Arab doing?"

"OK. Lieutenant. He just sits in his cell, muttering to himself, as if he were waiting for something. When you ask him something he just looks at you. I don't think he understands a word of English."

Near the Compound 3 fence the Colonel is waiting with a Corporal beneath the shadow of a guard tower. The Corporal wears a black patch over his left eye. For a moment I think One-Eyed Nellie is back on duty. No, it's impossible. The Colonel shipped One-Eyed Nellie out. The Corporal babbles: "I don't see so well, Sir, but something looked wrong from the Guard Tower. I called the Sergeant. . .Then I saw these signs. . ."

Colonel Williams cuts him short. "What the hell do the signs say, Lieutenant?"

Colored black and red the signs are painted on cardboard in intricate Gothic lettering. "The first one reads *The World is Ours!*" I translate.

"They mean the fucking desert is theirs," the Colonel explodes.

"The second sign just says *Exit to America.*"

The Sergeant of the Guard is trying not to laugh.

"Is this their idea of a lousy German joke? Or has anyone escaped?" asks Colonel Williams.

"I don't know, Sir."

"Well, we can't take a chance. Check all the bastards closely at the morning count.

By the time the count is underway the sun is flaming over the horizon. Sleepy prisoners stumble out into the cold morning air. Colonel Williams is checking the roll call himself in the officers' compound. I check Compound 3. This time there is no trouble with the count. The procedure goes quickly. Two prisoners are missing, Armind and a German corporal named Heinkel. Hurrying to the officers' compound I report the news to Colonel Williams. Weimann is standing beside him looking troubled.

"Something's wrong," Colonel Williams takes me aside. "Why would Armind want to escape?"

"I don't think he would escape."

"Where the hell is he then?"

"I don't know, Sir."

"Let's have this out with Weimann."

Weimann shrugs. "I cannot be responsible for the escape of every bored prisoner. You know, Colonel, how many men try to escape from prison camps."

"Are you sure Armind tried to escape?" Colonel Williams asks.

"What else could have happened since he's missing? No one has seen him in his compound."

Weimann seems defensive, nervous. I press him: "Why would Armind and Heinkel try to escape together? Were they friends?" *Armind had no friends.*

"I do not think Armind had many friends."

"Then why would he try to escape with Heinkel?"

"Perhaps there is no connection." Weimann evades me. He addresses his answers directly to Colonel Williams, trying to keep me in my place as a translator.

"Does the disappearance of these two prisoners have anything to do with the Arab?" the Colonel asks.

"There is no connection I assure you. The Arab is merely one of those malcontents we were forced to use in Africa. Actually, they volunteered, for the money you know."

"You mean you permitted Arabs to volunteer for money with the best German troops in the Africa Corps?" I attribute my sarcastic contribution to Colonel Williams.

Weimann drums uncomfortably with his fingers on the table. "Merely an expedient, you understand. You have black supply troops yourselves. This Arab is a troublemaker. He shirks his share of the work in the kitchen. I cannot guarantee the peace of the camp if he is returned to the compound."

"If there are any more escapes," says Colonel Williams firmly. "We'll take away all the camp privileges."

At this Weimann protests. "I assure you, Colonel, I will have this escape investigated thoroughly. Everyone knows prisoners try to escape. You must not penalize the entire camp for what two men have done. That would merely cause more trouble."

Williams turns away and orders me sharply, "Have all of the compounds searched. Begin here in the officers' compound. Then check Compound 3 and the other compounds if necessary. I don't think Armind tried to escape. Weimann is covering up something."

"Maybe we should ask Dampfstoff, Sir."

"It wouldn't do any good at the moment. Dampfstoff would just deny everything."

After we leave the compound a frenzy of activity begins. An alarm is sent out to the police and the county sheriff. The neighboring ranchers are alerted. The Seventh Service Command headquarters is notified. Evidently it is the first time a German prisoner has escaped in the United States. Gloom settles over Colonel Williams's face as he realizes the administrative pressure that he faces if this fact gets to the newspapers. By noon despite an intense search there is no sign of the missing prisoners. Is it possible that Armind did try to escape? I report to Colonel Williams that the compound search is futile. We're sitting in his office when the phone rings. A loud, angry voice sputters over the line.

"Yes, we're missing a prisoner," Colonel Williams says in a low voice. "What? You've got him?"

A long crackling sputter follows as the Colonel's face grows redder. Finally the Colonel asks meekly, "You want us to come and get him?" Another lengthy crackle. The Colonel is strangely silent after he hangs up. Then he looks at me and a slow grin breaks over his face. "Some rancher caught Heinkel. Says he caught him trying to steal some food from his barn. Almost blew his head off with a rifle. Those ranchers are tough sons-of-bitches. He was giving me hell for letting Heinkel escape. Says he'll bring him back personally because he can't trust us."

"What about Armind, Sir?"

"The rancher says Heinkel was alone."

"I'm sure Armind is still in the compound somewhere."

"Maybe you're right. You'd better search Compound 3 and 4 again. Start at the god damn theatre. Tell Weimann and Dampfstoff we'll keep searching until Armind turns up."

This time I take fifty men from Headquarters Company to assist in the search. The theatre in the officers' compound reveals nothing. A script of *Faust* with various speeches underlined, several Nazi banners, some costumes, music. . .Disgusted and frustrated I'm about to cancel the search of the theatre when Sergeant Franklin brings me an envelope with my name on it.

"Where'd this come from?"

"Sergeant Hochweiler gave it to me, Sir."

Inside the envelope is a typed note without any signature: *"Search in latrine closet near theatre behind cleaning equipment."*

"Did Hochweiler type this note, Sergeant?"

"No, he said he found it on his office desk. He doesn't know where it came from."

"The hell he doesn't."

In the latrine behind the theatre we find two closets stacked full with cleaning equipment, cartons of towels, toilet paper. I order everything taken out. Behind a mound of toilet paper in the second closet we discover the bound and gagged body of Armind. Unconscious, badly beaten, he is stripped to the waist, propped up back against the wall. As we pull him out Franklin gasps, "Jesus Christ, the bastards. . ." A swastika is burned in Armind's back.

As Armind slowly regains consciousness on the way to the hospital he begins to struggle against us in fear. Suddenly recognizing me he motions feebly toward his belt. I tell him to be quiet and rest. He resists with a sudden, fierce energy. He reaches inside the waist of his pants and produces a small, wadded-up paper.

"Their newspaper, their Nazi paper," he forces the words out. "Now you have your proof."

The blood from his wound stains the paper. When Armind is rushed into the emergency room, sick to my stomach I hurry into the toilet. As I emerge pale and dizzy, struggling to control myself, I encounter Colonel Williams and give him the bloody newspaper.

"It's time to show the sons-of-bitches," he explodes angrily. "The rancher's just brought Heinkel back. I want you to take Heinkel out to the guard house and shove him in with the Arab."

"But Colonel. . ."

"Look, Lieutenant, do you believe in a kind of frontier justice at times?"

"I guess so, Sir. It depends. . ."

"Don't be a lawyer. It's my responsibility. I'm old enough to believe in an eye for an eye. That rancher who brought Heinkel back is god damn right. We've got to play rough too. If we don't they'll be cutting through the fences in platoons."

When the Sergeant of the Guard and I take Heinkel to the guard house, he doesn't realize that the Arab is inside. Heinkel is still furious, dazed from his ride back to the camp in the rancher's pick-up truck. He claims the rancher's son held a rifle in the back of his neck all the way and the rancher's big German Shepherd bit him. Heinkel keeps protesting bitterly that in Germany "We are not barbarians. Civilians are not permitted to carry dangerous firearms. Also we do not permit savage dogs without muzzles."

Thinking of Armind and the swastika burned in his back I begin to believe in frontier justice too. We put Heinkel in the guard house, shut the door, and wait. A long silence broken by Heinkel's voice shouting in fear, *"The Arab!"* Inside the sounds of a fierce struggle rage up and down the corridor. More shrieks and grunts, the thud of kicks.

"That's enough," I hear myself say. "Let's go in. "

The Arab is kicking Heinkel in the side and jumping on him with his heavy army boots. Heinkel screams in pain. We pull the Arab off. The Sergeant bends over Heinkel and whistles, "Hey, Lieutenant, we better call the ambulance."

THE AMERICAN AFTER THE FUNERAL

In the Guard House the Arab accepts me with joy although he does not speak. . .We are both exiles from the community of prisoners. . .Yet we are still imprisoned. . .Prisons within prisons. . .If Guard House is a military term it is like any other jail. . .A little barred window high in my cell wall admits light. . .I can see only sky outside. . .Waves of sky blow swiftly by. . .High rain clouds gather in the east. . .Jagged streaks of desert lightning strike suddenly. . .I like best the glowing interplay of moon and stars at night. . .Perhaps sky is the freest part of the natural world. . .

The Arab and I seldom talk to each other. . .When I attempt to speak a few words to him in German or English, he grunts only a few syllables in reply that are almost impossible to understand. . .Still his answers are affectionate in tone. . . He seems to understand more than he admits. . .We are captives of isolation where the respect for formal language has ceased to exist. . .We discover new forms of communication when we listen to music. . .Lieutenant Enders brings us a small radio. . .We listen to different programs in amazement. . .Particularly I like a brief program of operatic music that is broadcast in the evening. . .Enders often listens too. . . He tells me that he is a former student of voice in Switzerland. . .I cannot really tell how much the Arab likes the music. . .We make a curious trio, listening silently to these remote operatic excerpts sung by international stars in different languages. . .

The Arab and I are free to roam up and down the corridor, peer in all the unoccupied cells. . .I look into each cell and imagine who may occupy them, the professions, the love lives of these future Guard House residents. . .*The great prisoners of history.* . .What kind of hate did they create in their cells?. . .Dostoyevsky, Galileo, Rosa Luxumburg, Cervantes, Raleigh. . .Did they feel pity for their enemies, compassion?. . No, they felt hate, an intense feeling of revenge. . .At the moment of the crucifixion when pain shot through his body, Christ's thoughts were full of hatred. . .*Oh my God, why have you forsaken me.* . .The tone is unmistakable. . .To confirm my discovery, I take to writing little mottoes on the walls of various cells, far down in the corners where they are almost invisible. . .Messages of salvation must be almost invisible to survive:

Man cannot live by love alone. . .
Death through hatred guarantees survival. . .
The seeker of love is the one sought by hate. . .
Hate is like an apple that survives worms. . .

Often the Arab accompanies me when I write my messages. . .He cannot write, but he enjoys the creation of hidden signs on the walls. . .Twice a day the American guard, who is posted just outside the door of the Guard House, takes the Arab and me for twenty minutes of exercise, walking up and down the dusty road. . .We walk in single file. . .Usually the Arab stalks first, his massive frame sinking into the desert dust as though he were carrying a heavy sack of potatoes. . . I come next, some ten paces behind, hands folded behind my back like a philosopher walking in his garden. . .One day some prisoners on a work detail in the adjacent compound see us and begin to boo, hiss, call insults. . .They pick up rocks and start to throw them. . .The Arab stands there without moving. . .I turn and start to run back to the Guard House. . . The American guard shouts orders, first at us, then at the rock-throwers. . .On the lower, west corner of my cell, I etch in tiny letters: *Where the stones move, there is hatred. . .*

At 10 PM the lights in the cells are turned off automatically. . .After that hour only a light in the corridor burns dimly. . .I cannot sleep any more. . .What I achieve is a kind of half-waking, half-sleeping vision. . .As the hours from ten creep by until sun-rise colors the sky through my cell window, I lie on my back on the hard cot and create the Civilization of Red Ants. . .

The red ants live in a timeless world beyond the earth. . . The exist in a state of unconsciousness, tiny filaments of nervous energy with blank papers for minds. . .They must be taught (teaching is the noblest profession in the world). . . In my cunning in the dark cell, I leave out all the checks and balances of man's most idealistic political systems. . .I teach them only hate, not merely wild, emotional hate, but planned, logical hate. . .

All civilizations are founded on two axes of authority, the secular-political and the sacred-spiritual. . .I design for the ants the two most powerful buildings ever created, a palace and a cathedral. . .To avoid any semblance of light, of love, I erect the buildings underground. . .When these astonishing structures are completed, I instruct the ants in the inaugural ceremony. . .

Sacrificial offerings are the center of civilization . . As victims are an essential sacrifice if the forms of justice are to be maintained, so flies exist as the appropriate sacrifice in ant society. . .All ants hate flies for their ability to fly and buzz in the air. . .The method of trapping flies is to pretend slowness. . .When the flies preen, convinced of their superior speed, let the ants erect nets designed to catch the swiftest and largest flies. . .Select the two finest flies for the ceremony, one for the palace, one for the cathedral. . .

First, the secular ceremony. . .The palace of pleasure and power. . .Enthrone the dead fly as emperor. . .The ants line up in double rows. . .Silence falls over the lines. . .The fly is brought in on jeweled swords laid crosswise. . .The ants stiffen to attention, begin to chant: "Unity in all things. Let One become One, Rich become Rich, Hail to the Emperor of Hate. Hate! Hate! Hate!". . .As the third *Hate* rings out, the ants bearing the swords drop them clanging on the palace floor. . .A battalion of ants begins a perfectly trained and executed flank movement towards the fly. . .*Remove the fly's wings with surgical precision.* . .Place the body on the throne. . .Suspend the wings over the new Emperor, floating wings that hover proudly in conquest of air and light. . .

Next, the sacrifice of the sacred fly in the buried cathedral. . .Remember King Solomon, *"Go to the ants and be wise"*. . .The sacred fly is brought in on a huge tray gleaming with diamonds in the form of a cross. . .Again the ants line up in double rows. . .Sacred ant music, a humming rhythmical chant, swells in volume. . .The ants prostrate themselves before the sacred fly. . .They begin to chant, "We worship hate, Pure becomes Pure, Cold becomes Cold, Hate! Hate! Hate!". .

As the third *Hate* rings out, the tray is dropped on the marble floor of the cathedral. . .The echo of the tray ringing on the floor produces a rising hum of exultation. . .*The intelligence of the ants is passed by means of a "kiss"*. . .In groups of ten (never act alone but always in the mass I drilled into them), the ants move toward the fly and begin the final exalted act of removing the wings. . .When the wings are separated, the body of the fly is elevated to the papal throne. . .The wings are suspended in a cross over the body . .

Now that the secular and divine rulerships of the ant civilization are established, the next step is the burgeoning of a culture to mold suceeding generations of ants. . .*Burn the heretics! Set state against church!*. . No, too commonplace. . Where is hate?. . .In the mind, in haunting night dreams, in fantasies of terror and impossible sexuality. . .Ants have no minds, only blank papers. . .Fill in their blank papers, their nerve filaments. . .Give them nothing but prepared minds. . . Make them incapable of action until they're obsessed by the cold logic of hate. . .

By decree of His Most Elevated Majesty, King Secular Fly (Death is Eternal Life), and with the divine consent of the Supreme Being, Pope Sacred Fly (Life is Eternal Death), all red ants are hereby restricted in movement. . .For a period of fifty years they will be subject to rigorous instructions. . . As Fabre, the great French naturalist, said: "The insect which terrifies us with its extraordinary intelligence, surprises us the next moment with its stupidity.". . .They must be trained. . .They will read only approved books, think only prescribed thoughts, dream only correct, visionary dreams. . . At the end of fifty years what will happen?. . .At first nothing, a long, slow awakening to the world of total law and order. . .Let them perceive a geometry of insects trained so precisely to fit their environment that the relationship between ant and architecture shines with grandeur. . .Perhaps a hint of suspicion at this new hierarchy may emerge at first, nothing significant, easy to suppress by the secret group of ants active in Counter-Intelligence operations. . .Slowly the inevitable revolution of millions of ants occurs. . .They realize with exulation that they are part of a new order beyond intellectual comprehension. . .

Carefully, hoping that its neighbor ant will not notice, eyes begin to stare at the thrones. . .*Insects can never close their eyes; they sleep with them open.* . .The ants' multi-faceted eyes focus on the bodies of the flies enthroned as Pope and Emperor. . .Wait. . .*Why are these black shapes of wingless flies so different from ants?*. . .We have taught the glory of praising, worshiping each other in the perfect equality of law and order, this glory and power of the ant world. . .Surely then, the flies are false rulers of a primitive era. . .

Each ant begins his secret plot to seize power. . .He speaks cautiously to his neighbor, revealing only a few details of his hidden plan. . .As he learned for years, the neighbor considers carefully: "If I help him, am I helping myself?". . . A security alliance of ant groups is formed. . .They approach the throne. . .Suddenly another militant group of twenty ants blocks the way. . .

"Back! You are approaching the Supreme Throne."

"Why shouldn't we approach? You favor the aged rulers, the flies? Can't you see they are dead?"

"If you pass, you must pass by force."

"Make way. We need Lebensraum for the Ant World to grow."

What come to be called "the obstacle wars," the little wars, begin. . .At first they're only path battles, street battles, alley battles. . .Victory to the strongest, most dedicated ants. . .Survival of the fittest ants, true racial stock. . .

Approach the throne. . .Look back with hate. . .The bodies of thousands of ants lie isolated in their little groups, the limited vision of their open eyes staring blindly upward. . . Bury them with praise, an eternal, burning torch of liberation, an honor guard stiff at attention. . .

Look. . .The fly is still enthroned. . .The fly's body is a black desecration against the purity of our new ant society. . . The fly created this false worship of eternal life. . .The fly was crucified and sits there motionless, mocking us. . .*Tear him from the throne!*. . .A squad of ants scales the height and struggles to dispose the dead ruler, but the fly is too heavy, the pressure of time on his wingless shoulders, the weight of dead civilization. . .Sending out coded, secret messages over their new communications systems, the ants summon their followers. . .With great effort, their antennae pulsing with the stored banks of information, the ants tumble the fly's body to the ground and cry out jubilantly: "The King is dead! Long live the King!". . .

The new ant leader prepares to ascend the throne. . .In silence he contemplates his authoritarian mind, preens his ant appearance, justifies his nationalistic ant glory: "Victory to the Ants! Ant Purity is ours. History begins the Ant Era. But wait. . .I am alive. . ."...

Frantically he calls out: "It cannot be. I cannot rule if I am alive!"

His followers crawl over him. . .They tear his arms and legs off, rip the life out of him, the life that cannot bleed. . . Solemnly they place his body on the throne. . .Above the throne, they suspend his antennae in tribute to the new technology of ants that has seized power. . .Again the chant hums, rises in intensity. . ."We worship Hate, Cold becomes Cold, Pure becomes Pure. Hate! Hate! Hate!"

So my Civilization of Red Ants is noted and much admired for its masterful logic of hatred and its triumphant death-worship. . .But I will not die. . .I will not die. . .I will live in the Civilization of Ants. . .

THE AMERICAN   FROM OPERA TO RE-EDUCATION

After Heinkel's futile escape and the brutal attack against Armind an uneasy waiting time possesses the camp. The Nazi takeover under Dampfstoff has established its power, but Dampfstoff seems a little worried. He longs for a resurrection of military triumphs. The German defeat in Africa, the growing sense of enormous casualties in the war with the Soviet Union, are slowly affecting the prisoners. Our American personnel, still limping and peering blindly about, grow visibly in confidence. Colonel Williams sees to that with strict training hours. He starts an educational program to familiarize the men with Nazi plans and objectives. Also Williams is in constant touch with the Provost Marshal General's Office. The possibility for a *Re-Education Program for German Prisoners of War* is being discussed. *Re-education?* We haven't even begun with education. . .

Every evening when possible I visit the Guard House. Armind, the Arab and I listen to a program of operatic excerpts over the radio I've obtained for them. It's a strange form of recreation. The Arab's attraction to opera is almost comic as he listens with a fixed, uncomprehending smile. Is it because of the new brotherhood he feels for Armind? Some deep physical link exists suddenly between the swastika burn and the Arab's outcast state. They don't converse by words. All they do is share their silent, shrunken world. I guess I represent to them only another American ambiguity. In their loneliness they can use a certain sympathetic official contact. Perhaps they still feel too a slight connection to a remote ideal of revolutionary freedom (America the land of the free and the home of the brave) now tangled in the modern prison state's machinery. That the three of us form a habit of listening silently to a program of operatic excerpts is only a surface paradox. The Arab listens because Armind listens. Armind listens because a natural love for vocal music is ingrained in him. He and his wife attended opera frequently. I listen because the confusion of my German-American background is somehow represented in the ambiguous masks of opera . . .

In 1938 in Switzerland I studied voice with the famous opera singer, Albert Holzreichl. I dreamt of an operatic career and had some vocal ability. What really attracted me to opera I began to discover was the variety of dramatic masks, the revelation of unique fantasies provided by the operatic world. Are operatic fantasies so different from prison fantasies?

Holzreichl was my first personal encounter with a great performer, a man accustomed to risk anything. He could assume any mask for any occasion. Viennese by birth, an involuntary German citizen after the Nazi annexation of Austria, he was reluctant to return to Vienna with his family. Well-known in opera houses throughout Europe, he found himself the trapped possessor of a Nazi passport. Often he showed his passport to me with bitter disdain. He held it up by his fingertips as if it somehow polluted him. He could not believe that the swastika was a new symbol that he was forced to carry. His discovery that he required a Nazi passport to further his career in the best European opera houses, which the Germans either ran or controlled increasingly, festered in his mind. Frequently my lesson would be interrupted by a phone call from the Nazi consul in Zürich.

"Herr Holzreichl, if you would return to Vienna, the Intendant has a special part for you. A Mercedes is also waiting for your convenience. . ." Or "Herr Holzreichl, if you will travel to this or that city, we are supporting a Wagner Festival in which you will have a major role. . ."

Holzreichl manufactured elaborate desperate evasions. His wife was sick. His children had fallen from bicycles. His voice was in sad condition. He was suffering from an infected sinus and needed rest. All the time while he was talking to the consul he was mocking the consul's mannerisms to me. Secure in the knowledge that Holzreichl must eventually come to terms, the consul listened patiently to the singer's wild excuses. Sadly Holzreichl sensed the peril of his situation too. When the consul ended the conversation with the inevitable "Heil Hitler!", a convulsion gripped the singer. He repeated the mechanical salutation through locked teeth. His shame and disgust at this enforced greeting caused him to slam down the phone with a gesture of fury. He erupted into a series of curses at the black, silent instrument.

Looking at me slowly with despair his face wrinkled into a clown-mask. Bitterly he spat out Canio's last line in *Pagliacci,* "La commedia é finita!" For a moment only he became Holzreichl, the bald rubber mask of a face that loved its comforts and knew that he would play any role to maintain and assure these comforts. Consequently his self-rage at compromising by echoing the detestable greeting, "Heil Hitler!" Accusingly he pointed his food-and-candy loving hand at eighteen-year-old me and demanded in a pathetic, operatic tone: "Who will save me?"

"Perhaps you can go to New York and sing at the Metropolitan," I suggested lamely.

He pounced on this bait. "You offer me a million dollar contract? What roles?"

"At first I suppose you won't be able to play your own choice of roles. . ." I was in the dunce's seat and he wouldn't release me before I was educated.

"So, my boy, you are a wealthy American manager, pretending to be an operatic impresario! Alas, you want nothing but exquisite sound on your stage, as much volume as possible to overcome your machines. Perhaps you permit your singers to wear unusual costumes for decorative effects. But the only real movement you permit your singers is a step from one position to another, the way a condemned man is forced to move to your electric chair. I am a singing *actor!* What I want is the magic of motion, of gesture, not just the voice. I do my own makeup, build my own costumes, rehearse, rehearse. The real performer must create a character larger than life out of a unity of words and music."

"Couldn't you give a few concerts and work your way gradually into the Metropolitan?"

"My little dramatic innocent, a concert singer compared to an operatic performer is like a pigeon compared to a hawk," his hawk-like contempt swooped at me. "If you could soar and claw in the upper air, would you rather be a little pigeon in the concert hall?"

"A hawk," I agreed hastily.

"The trouble is you stand like a drooping pigeon!" He poked me hard in the diaphragm. "Stand from *there*! Look up at the crazy Nazi world from your stomach. Then you've got the right perspective. The Nazis don't know how to eat. Hitler is a vegetarian. That is their trouble. Feel my diaphragm."

Forty times every lesson I felt his diaphragm and I can still feel it. It was like stone covered by ten gigantic meals from a gourmet restaurant. I developed a theory that only his diaphragm saved him from becoming fat. Of indeterminate height, he had an astonishing ability to shrink or rise depending on the role. If he was to play Sarastro in Mozart's *The Magic Flute,* he grew eight feet tall when teaching me, peering down at me majestically from a holy sanctuary of power. As Wotan in *Die Walküre* he broadened out into what he called "a solid, ancient German tree-trunk."

As Mephistopholes in Gounod's *Faust,* he evolved into a small, weasel-like animal, slithering and peering his sinister way. "Chaliapin was the only great tall Mephistopholes," Holzreichl squinted at me maliciously. "No one else before me saw that Mephistopholes is a satanic weasel. I got the idea one day at the zoo with my children. The weasel is slick and slimy, but also very powerful in his confidence. He is like Dr. Goebbels, although of course the weasel is more majestic. The trick is not to be so obvious as Dr. Goebbels. You must present the vicious majesty of the animal which is impossible for the Propaganda Minister."

Masks. . .I worry about Armind as we listen with the Arab. He rarely talks, grunts short answers when I seek to draw him out by means of some superficial operatic question. He is deep in some memory or fantasy that stuns him. The Arab is becoming almost like a nurse to Armind. We listen increasingly like three men escaping from time and it is pleasant to do so. One evening the radio station plays a program of old records. First several magnificent arias by Caruso. Then several duets by Caruso and Scotti. *Scotti?* . . .

When my face fell as I probed Holzreichl's prodigious diaphragm, he soothed me: "Don't worry, little pigeon. You have a small voice. Perhaps you will find your place in the Mozart operas. You must achieve the support, the hard diaphragm. This I learned from Scotti, the great Italian baritone. You know Scotti's name?"

Did I know Scotti . . . . At home in California, with my

father and mother, I listened to countless recordings of famous singers, especially to the duets of Scotti and Caruso, a marvel of tone and dramatic phrasing that even the hissing, ancient records could not conceal.

Holzreichl beamed with approval. "Perhaps you are not so ignorant after all. Scotti is a mark in your favor. He taught me how to float the tone Bel Canto style as opposed to the Knudelstimme, the throaty, dark voice that Germans fancy. To sing Bel Canto in the mask, bang on pitch, you must have support, support, support!" He punched me again in the diaphragm for emphasis. Suddenly, in a dream of Scotti, he turned away and stalked to the window, leaving behind the always vanishing Holzreichl. Transformed into a hunchback jester, he stared out suspiciously at a streetcar clanging by.

"You should have seen Scotti's Rigoletto. Verdi would have wept. Such a great singing actor . . . He was always perfecting his role. Occasionally he permitted me in his dressing room. Have you ever been in a dressing room?"

"No," I admitted feeling deprived.

"Scotti's dressing room was like a magician's study. He arrived often two hours before curtain time. He rarely talked. As I watched he sank slowly into the character. *Sank* is the only word that describes what I saw. Like a diver he submerged gradually into the character. In that small room I was terrified as the wild, grotesque Rigoletto emerged from the sea of make-up and costumes. Frightened I crouched against the wall, afraid of the sadistic Renaissance jester who loved only one being, his daughter. . ." Remembering Scotti as Rigoletto, Holzreichl permitted a ray of sentimental love to flash briefly through his twisted face and body. The jester's tangled wig seemed to flow from his highbrowed baldness. Then the bland, rubber mask of Holzreichl beamed at me again from the world of illusion. "Pigeon boy, if you want to try your wings as an American eagle, you'd better come backstage with me some night. You must be very quiet though. Usually no visitors are permitted. Would you like to go?"

Would I! We made an appointment for the following week when Holzreichl was scheduled to sing The Grand Inquisitor in Verdi's *Don Carlos.* I arranged to meet him at his apartment.

"I never make love on the day of a performance," he grinned at me, "although I am not like some Italian tenors in that respect. Sometimes before a performance they never make love for three days! That is the difference between tenors and basses. Thank god you are not a tenor. I can't stand teaching tenors. They sing about their desire to make love and most of the time their only worry is their high notes." He snorted in laughter. "Basses and baritones and those throaty mezzo-sopranos make opera into real drama. Yes, the evening *before* my performance I make love--not always to my wife either. Sometimes to a pretty member of the chorus. Or a fan."

He winked at me strongly, watching carefully to see if his education of a provincial American boy was taking effect. Even though I was getting used to his ways, I was a little shocked because of his wife. Always she handed me the bill and received payment for my singing lessons while directing the activities of their two small, energetic children. She was a vivacious, handsome Viennese woman who acted as his stabilizing manager both at home and in the world. I liked her and admired her efficiency in running that frantic household where the father was forever vanishing into strange disguises, disdaining to stoop to the mundane levels of everyday life.

Perceiving that I was a little taken aback, Holzreichl turned into an immediate aristocrat. "Perhaps you should become a tenor!" he sneered. "Then you could dream about love. Do you think love is a silk handcherchief, a romantic doll, a sentimental song from your Hollywood films? Love is a constant search. It may begin at any moment of the day or night, mostly at night. You are still a young daytime pigeon. It is all right--don't look so worried. You are young. Ah, I understand. You think I don't love my wife? What an American boy you are. I love my wife, but marriage is another landscape, a wall behind which to retreat, a sanctuary from disaster. Marriage is safety, not adventure, and a man needs both." He peered at me with disgust. "What am I to do with you? In addition to singing I have to teach you everything!"

This was a classroom that I never encountered in America. But with the stubbornness of youth I thought: "That may be all right for you, a master of many masks, but I'll go on searching for love. Maybe I'll find out that faith is not the main thing, but it will be my discovery, not yours."...

My discovery...What are we searching for here in this prison camp? Three men lost in uniforms far away from women and the world of love. Armind is dreaming of his wife, a dangerous dream that seems to drive him deeper into memory. On the verge of total dissociation from reality he listens to this music like a drug addict. To him the present must be sacrificed for a few moments of transcendence, as if fantasies will make his wife live again. Perhaps the Arab has transferred his sexual dreams to Armind, a love of victim for victim, a familiar possibility in prisons and armies as I'm learning. As for me I've given up the long-range ideal of women. Play it on a day-to-day basis, sex magazines and masturbation in the familiar pattern of American frustration. Look for the sexual encounter and don't expect too much from it. That's what armies are about, why every camp creates its own whore houses nearby despite the hypocrisy of public opinion. Do I really believe this? Somehow, when they're pushed to extremes, men have the capacity to renew their dreams of love by such a simple act as listening to music. When I'm released from this god damn war, the first search I'll make is for a woman to love. Meanwhile, maybe Holzreichl was right...

On the day of his scheduled performance as The Grand Inquisitor when I called for Holzreichl, his wife greeted me at the door with a smile, shielding their two children so the master could have his privacy. "He's been sleeping and eating all day," she warned me, "so don't believe him when he tells you he's hungry. And don't lend him any money!"

Holzreichl bounced out dressed in a handsome brown suit, a yellow bow tie, a dapper hat slanted over his bald head. He kissed his wife goodbye and pinched her bottom affectionately. He chucked his children under their chins. The moment we were on the street, waiting for the streetcar, he asked me for a loan. Fumbling dramatically through his pockets he demanded, "Lend me ten francs. We don't have time to go back. We left my money behind. I'm hungry."

I gave him the money. He darted across the street into a shop and emerged triumphantly with two chocolate ice cream cones. Waving them at me he cried, "An American holiday!" Relishing the role of grand host, he escorted me onto the streetcar, licking and brandishing his cone at the conductor with a gesture that included me as the junior member of his entourage before handing the mesmerized conductor *my* money for the fare. He seemed to have forgotten about the Grand Inquisitor.

En route to the opera house he transformed himself into a tour conductor: "That pile of decorated cement is the new Christian Science church, one of your many undistinguished American exports . . . In that restaurant you get the best oysters in Zurich. You don't like oysters? You haven't eaten them with the right woman. First an oyster, then a kiss, then another oyster, and so on. That way they taste perfect . . . Here's the house where Lenin lived while planning the Russian Revolution. If he had stayed in Switzerland, probably he would have become an opera critic. All opera critics are frustrated ex-revolutionaries. That's why their criticism is so bad . . . In that building lived the mad Irishman, James Joyce. A difficult man, too much language. Still he liked opera . . . See that bank? That's where the Nazis keep the money they steal. They're too smart to destroy the modern paintings and books they hate. So they announce burning or confiscation and in the night they sell the books and paintings to Swiss agents. Naturally the Swiss agents sell them to rich Americans. Then the Nazis put the money in that bank on the corner where Fat Goering can draw on it for his pleasures."

I looked around the streetcar apprehensively. Holzreichl's diction was perfect, his volume an unsubdued *forte*.

"Don't worry," he grinned. "I know a Nazi when I see one. Soon they will have banks like that all over the world. Then I will have to be quiet. Anyone who resists them will be living in camps."

"Camps?"

"You Americans have a lot to learn about camps. Unless I want to end up in a camp, I will probably have to go to Berlin and sing in the opera under Göring's patronage. Even though he knows nothing, he has much power over the arts in Berlin. His wife is an actress and I hear she likes my performances. I will have to sing a lot of Wagner and ruin my voice too soon. You can't imagine the obscene way the Nazis produce Wagner in the dark as if all those crazy northern gods liked to do invisible, dirty things. Some day Wagner must be done with all the lights on to expose those tormented gods in their lust for power."

Visibly depressed by the threat of Göring's yoke he sank back in his seat. As we clattered down the hill toward the lake, I glanced at him to see when he might put on his performing mask. Nothing. Only a despairing Holzreichl thinking of his impossible future. Not until we left the streetcar and crossed the street toward the opera house did I notice a change. Something happened to his walk. He was walking slower, trying out different gaits. I was puzzled. His steps didn't seem to have any relationship to The Grand Inquisitor. Nothing in his experimental pacing resembled an old man. Perhaps it was some mysterious ritual that occurred every time he approached an opera house, some premonition about the strange transformation to which he was forever condemned, some fear that one evening he would become Mr. Hyde for eternity and never be able to return to Dr. Jekyl-Holzreichl. At the threshold of the opera house another transformation invigorated his body. He paused to satisfy his ego by looking at the posters announcing the cast for the evening's performance. A regal smile swept over his face. *"Opera,"* he pronounced the word mysteriously like a benediction. "Now you will see the backstage fantasy . . ."

Again the generous patron, the imperious leader, he ushered me behind the building to the stage door as if guiding me to an incredible destination. As we entered the stage door the guard greeted him with great respect, the respect I learned that backstage personnel give only to unusual performers. The guard handed him some mail. Holzreichl winked at me. "Lady fans." He patted the mail as he put it in his pocket, as if he were patting the ladies on their delightful, feminine posteriors. Backstage he halted me suddenly to observe a visiting Italian tenor talking to a pretty Swiss dancer who obviously didn't understand a word of Italian. "Listen!" Holzreichl commanded.

A bubbling fountain of lyrical language flowed into my ears with that flowing syllabic stress that only a trained singer can produce. "Listen pigeon boy," Holzreichl whispered with satirical delight, "to the tenor's melodies of love. Beneath those surface melodies he is calling her, luring her with every dirty expression he can command. I assure you that Italian tenors command every dirty expression man has ever conceived. It is the way they compensate for their inadequacies. If you don't believe me look behind the girl."

Two stagehands were perched on a platform above and behind the girl. Obviously they understood Italian. They gestured their silent applause and encouragement to the tenor who responded willingly with a fresh torrent of silver-coated lyrical obscenity to the uncomprehending dancer. Resigned she stood in her rehearsal tights, a mute, sacrificial offering . . .

As we listen to the operatic programs in the Guard House, I keep hoping to hear Holzreichl although I know he made few recordings and disappeared early in the war. In any case after the invasion of Poland I never heard from him. Perhaps with his hated German passport he was forced into the army and vanished like so many in the eastern campaign. Still he taught me how to survive. With his ability he may be living somewhere under another mask--the mask of a prisoner of war, even the mask of some officer like me if he found that necessary to survive. Imagine Holzreichl as the Grand Inquisitor of prisoners . . .

Talk ceased abruptly in Holzreichl's dressing room. Unlike the glamorous dressing rooms I imagined in my dreams of opera it was dingy. A few naked light-bulbs glittered savagely over the mirror above the dressing table. One picture frowned down from the bare walls, a photograph of Scotti twisted into Rigoletto with an inscription in a lavish hand: "To my dear colleague and student with the hope for a great career." A closet with a faded blue curtain half-concealed his costumes, parts of which peeped out in a clash of discordant colors and historical styles. Holzreichl pushed me into a corner chair as if it were time to discard the trivial courtesies. Time rushed backward as though the clock were altered counter-clockwise. For the first time I understood what he had told me about Scotti. Staring I watched Holzreichl sink literally into the flesh of The Grand Inquisitor. The process of sinking was frightening. It was like entering a swamp, being forced down into the slime of experience, of corruption, until an ancient knowledge of evil permeated the room. As he etched his face with the dark grease-lines of fanatical old age; as he glued on the whitehaired wig and beard and drew on the majestically simple red robe of The Inquisitor, a shiver constricted my body. For the first time I realized the *danger* of art. I wondered if such a sacrifice was possible for me, if I would ever have the courage to offer myself so nakedly to the inscrutable gods of the imagination who demanded such a transformation.

Glaring at himself in the mirror Holzreichl relaxed a little. He began to vocalize. I seized the opportunity to escape for a moment. Outside the dressing room, in the corridor, I could hear the artists testing their voices, a sound totally different from an orchestra warming up. When an orchestra prepares for a concert you hear a pleasant, mechanical testing of sound. An anonymous group seems prepared at a given signal to burst into the radiance of communal unity. With great singers the effect is the exact opposite. An isolation, a testing of individual courage, occurs. With shattering clarity tenors and sopranos vocalize up and up to those dangerously high pitches they must sound exactly, perfectly, if they are to elicit the ultimate cries of "Bravo" and "Brava" from the voracious audience. As I listened to the testing sounds emerging from the stars' dressing rooms down that long corridor, I seemed to hear the absolute notes of human isolation that are produced only from the lonely depths of performers in search of distant, foreign identities.

When I re-entered Holzreichl's dressing room he failed to notice me. He was walking up and down in a slow, sinister shuffle. Unconsciously he turned and shuffled towards me. He forced me back into my corner chair. His eyes warped to slits, he was blind, staring into immensities beyond place and time. Suddenly a welcome, familiar voice sounded from the ancient menace that threatened me. "Don't worry, little pigeon. This time I will not interrogate your sinful soul."

Half-hidden in the wall over the door a loudspeaker began

to echo: "Half an hour . . . Half an hour . . . Half an hour, please . . . "Holzreichl said gently, "You'd better go. I must get ready." Relieved by his permission to depart I fled haunted by the words "*I must get ready.*" What final preparations remained? What more could he do to lose himself? How could he possibly sink deeper into that old, vicious apparition?

That night, act after act on the edge of my seat, I waited impatiently for Holzreichl to make his appearance. It seemed incredible: "Half an hour before opening curtain he wants to get rid of me, and still he has to wait for long hours alone in his dressing room before he goes on. What is he doing in there?

At last, in the third act, I heard the ominous blare of those deep trombones which Verdi learned to use with such threatening, powerful effects. Led by a page boy, the tall, gaunt, blind figure of The Grand Inquisitor entered the chamber of King Philip. As he entered The Inquisitor's enormous, groping stick hit the floor in a thumping crescendo of agitation. Afraid of The Grand Inquisitor, King Philip and everyone else in the opera house stiffened. Through the shuffling walk and the fanatical, blind inner world of the religious leader, an aura of severity and majesty soared from his richly robed presence.

"A cheap artist creates only easy violence, Holzreichl told me later. It is easy to perform melodrama. What counts is the balance, the contradictions in a man. There lies the real drama."

As the scene continued The Grand Inquisitor's power over the King became more apparent. Weakening in his desire to protect the rebellion of his son, Don Carlos, the King collapsed slowly before the ageless force of The Grand Inquisitor. Like the threatening fist of an avenging God the tyrannical blind leader's hand rose in the air. Then came a miraculous touch. The clenched fingers unfolded to reveal not only a threat, but also the clear promise of divine glory.

"Until the end of the scene I use almost no hand and arm gestures," Holzreichl explained later. "Bad actors always wave their hands as if trying to find some way to escape from their stupid performances. By waiting till the end I wanted to create something like the effect of Rodin's beautiful sculpture, *The Hand of God.* The King is powerful and determined. To conquer the King, The Grand Inquisitor must not only threaten him with the immense social power of the Inquisition, but also reveal the unfolding hand of glory that the King will lose if he fails in his duty to the state and to God."

Triumphing over the King in that magnificent duet, Holzreichl's voice had a dark, cutting edge that I had never heard. For a shattering moment when the King turned away, The Grand Inquisitor sagged back from his divine mission of terror into a feeble, pathetic old man. As the Page Boy rushed to his aid, the King wheeled around to help. Feeling the King observe his weakness, The Grand Inquisitor summoned a final, desperate strength. His authority, his evil genius, his religious dedication returned to dominate the scene as he made his triumphantly thumping, imperious exit. The curtain swished down to a frenzy of applause. As the King and The Grand Inquisitor bowed together, it was obvious which performer had triumphed. Even during the applause and shouts of "Bravo!" that lasted through ten curtain calls, Holzreichl remained deeply involved in his role. He maintained a curiously supreme presence that barely acknowledged the applause. Partly he was still lost in the spiritual complexities of The Grand Inquisitor.

After the performance, although Holzreichl had mentioned an engagement, I wanted to tell him how much his performance had moved me. Backstage the world of opera has a torn, fragmented look as if the ritual participants are dazed because the world of imagination dies so easily. Hastily the stagehands strike the set in their desire to get nome. The electrician reads a newspaper or magazine, tired and eager to escape from the enigma of his darkened spotlights. In front of the dressing rooms cluster small groups of tittering fans, unable to believe that these shabby walls and small cubicles contain the voices and the spectacle that they have just witnessed on stage.

In vain I knocked on the door of Holzreichl's dressing room. Evidently he had left, as quick to depart as he had been slow to prepare. I walked back across the stage, which was now littered with pieces from the broken-down set, down a hall to the stage door exit. Suddenly in front of me I saw Holzreichl emerge from a room. His hat was raked jauntily over his bald head. A polka dot bow tie angled from the soft blue silk collar of his shirt. He was holding the arm of the blond Swiss dancer to whom the Italian tenor had poured out his richest obscenities. Not wanting him to see me, I shrank back into a doorway. Envious and a little bitter, I thought Holzreichl was not so different from the Italian tenor as he showered the girl with gallantries and intimate laughter while escorting her into the night . . .

The operatic world of illusions . . . Too much to hear excerpts from *La Boheme* and *Madame Butterfly* with Armind and the Arab. The Bohemian life in the Guard House. Still I'm beginning to understand why the Nazis can listen to Beethoven one day and burn a swastika in someone's back the next day. Holzreichl and Frau Hedda taught me that the Nazis were conquering Europe by theatrical spectacles, illusions, as much as the reality of industrical and military power. Masks are as necessary in politics as on the operatic stage. Hitler adopted the most singular mask of all, half-clown with dangling forelock and toothbrush mustache, and half-tragedian, the chosen Führer of destiny. Even in this camp the Nazis used the masks of a funeral spectacle to demonstrate their strength. No wonder Armind withdraws increasingly. Lost in his dream world he mutters about "ants." Sometimes it is almost as if ants sing to him rather than performers on the radio. I bring him books to distract him from the voices in his head. One evening I enter the Guard House to hear him reading Emily Dickinson to the Arab. Strange that Emily Dickinson seems almost like a familiar voice in the Guard House . . .

I have no Life but this--
To lead it here--
Nor any Death--but lest
Dispelled from there--

Nor tie to Earths to come--
Nor action new--
Except through this extent--
The Realm of you--

Uncomprehending the Arab nods pleasantly as the words flow through him. These prisoners have almost become my family. Is this crazy? My parents are still alive, although the family is gone forever. Father writes that he's courting another woman, a former student. Mother is deep in her studies of American Indian myths. How far away my parents seem from Guard Houses and prison camps. This place is becoming unreal to all of us. The only way to save Armind is to get him away from this camp into a new situation. Is there any new situation that can escape the pattern of barbed wire and the ants?

One morning Colonel Williams calls me into his office. A Lieutenant-Colonel, Kenneth Jameson, a man with unmilitary posture, grey hair, a red face with bulbous nose, is sitting there. Jameson, a former professor of Political Science at the University of Chicago, has been appointed Director of a new secret, experimental program for the "Re-Education of German Prisoners of War." Williams has recommended me for the program. My head fills with doubts and hopes as Jameson begins to talk. Immediately he warns: "Don't tell me, Lieutenant, you're sceptical about 're-education.' So am I. There's no such thing."

"How can anybody re-educate Nazis?"

"I admit it's an absurd word. Only Americans could think of the word, Re-Education, as if education were an eternally optimistic cycle--educate, then re-educate, educate, then re-educate, etc. forever." He laughs and I like the sound of his scepticism.

"Who named the program then?"

"It was Mrs. Roosevelt's idea I hear."

"What?"

"Why not? Evidently she often puts bugs in her husband's ear. You know what happened as well as anybody. After Rommel surrendered in Africa, several hundred thousands of German prisoners were sent suddenly to camps all over this country. The Nazis put into action their plan to take over the camps. It took months before authorities in Washington realized what was going on. Imagine what the press would do if they discovered that little Nazi dictatorships existed in Colorado, Texas, California, Massachusetts, etc., etc. So you can understand why the Provost Marshal General was finally ordered to do something in the camps."

"What can re-education do to break the Nazi control? How many men do you have on your staff?"

"Ten at the moment," Jameson smiles. "Six officers and four enlisted men. Eleven if you join us."

"Eleven men dealing with 350,000 prisoners . . ."

"I know it sound ridiculous. That's why we need the help of all the anti-Nazi prisoners we can find. What if it's more of a segregation program at first? We use whatever anti-Nazi prisoners we can find to locate other anti-Nazis. Then we try to break the Nazi hold in the camps by segregating and transferring the Nazi spokesmen. . ."

"If you can find them with your eleven men."

Jameson stops grinning and looks at me soberly. "Would you rather just give up, Lieutenant?"

My face flushes red and I answer with instinctive anger. "Look, Colonel, there are four thousand German officers and men in this camp--all of them combat troops. To guard them we have a handful of Limited Service men. How are you going to enforce any break-up of Nazi power even in this one camp, to say nothing of all the other camps?" By the tone of my voice I know I've gone too far.

For a moment Jameson is quiet. He pulls out his pipe and begins to puff up a barrier of smoke between us. "All right, Lieutenant, I'll level with you. You think I'm just another intellectual who was given high rank for some halfbaked program . . ."

"No, Sir, it's just that . . ."

"I don't mind you criticizing, Lieutenant, but you ought to know the facts before you start protesting. Do you know the Nazis have engineered a whole series of escapes in other camps?"

"No, Sir."

"They've been kept secret of course. Still the camp commanders got so nervous that they pressured Washington into doing something. I agree with you the idea of re-education sounds silly. So we don't have enough staff . . . We've got to make this thing work as well as we can. Look, here's the directive for the program from the Secretary of War."

He shows me the directive marked *Top Secret: "An attempt shall be made to impress the German prisoners of War with American, democratic ideals . . ."*

Impress . . . American democratic ideals . . . Isn't that a contradiction in terms? *Impress* is a tough word. Can you stamp out "American democratic ideals" like coins to sell? Still the authorization is from the top. Maybe that means they'll give the program a chance and let it build up. Is there anything wrong with a contest of ideas? Not if it's a real contest. The problem is *impress.* "Colonel," I hear myself say, "I'm sorry if I sounded like a smart-ass sceptic, but . . ."

At this Jameson smiles again. "I hope I was a good-enough teacher to encourage smart-ass sceptics. What's really worrying you?"

"How do you *impress* American democratic ideals? Isn't that like remedial reading and remedial writing in our schools? Maybe this program ought to be called Remedial German."

"That's a good title," Jameson chuckles. "It may well end up Remedial German. You know I don't even speak German. That's why I need people like you in the program."

"My German is not the best. I can read better than I can speak."

"Still Colonel Williams tells me that you've created a little anti-Nazi enclave . . ."

A little anti-Nazi enclave . . . Armind and the Arab . . . "Little is the right word, Sir, a former political prisoner who was married to a Jewish woman and an Arab."

"What if we take those two and transfer them to a special camp that we'll set up. With their help and the help of similar prisoners at other camps, we might be able to set up a group to start out with. We could begin by publishing a newspaper for all the German prisoners of war."

"Who would edit the paper, Sir?"

"The German prisoners themselves if we can find the right ones. What about your political prisoner? How would he be as an editor?"

"He was a teacher, not a journalist." *Maybe he could write about the ants.* "I don't think he knows anything about newspapers."

"We can take care of publishing the paper," Jameson

chides me. "There are some teachers who can write don't you think?"

"I didn't mean . . ."

"I can sit back and point out the problems too, Lieutenant. God knows I've written lots of books and articles attacking politicians and criticizing bureaucratic demons. Do you think I like *impress Democratic ideals* any more than you do? If we make a little dent in the Nazis we'll be lucky."

"Isn't that the problem then, Sir?"

"No, I think we're the problem," Jameson stares at me directly. "The paralysis of people like us in an age of irony."

"I don't get you, Colonel."

"It's easy for us liberals to take defensive, ironic positions. We can criticize, but we find it tough to act when we have to."

I squirm at this, still I know he's right. Limited Service is a category that lends itself to ironic positions. Yet I have to play the role of questioner. "If you set up a special camp, what if a lot of opportunist anti-Nazis come flooding in? Even Nazi informers. In this camp they've got Nazi officers masquerading as enlisted men just to keep everyone in line."

"If we can get enough real anti-Nazis in the camp, don't you think in time they'd be able to weed out most of the Nazis?"

"Maybe if they get the right kind of support."

"Get me right, Lieutenant, I've no illusions that we Americans can do much alone. I don't think we'll ever get enough support, enough staff from the Provost Marshal General to carry out any programs that we decide to do on our own. What we can do maybe is set off a few sparks among the prisoners so they can begin to change things themselves."

"That's going to take a long time, Sir."

"Maybe not so long if the Nazis suffer a few more big defeats."

"How would I fit into the program?"

"I'd like you to be in charge of this special camp for anti-Nazi prisoners."

"*Me?*"

"Don't you think you can handle it?"

"I don't know, Sir."

"I've been looking at a small camp in Rhode Island that might be the right place. It's a former coast guard station."

Rhode Island . . . Still it's a way to get Armind out of the Guard House, away from his obsession with the ants . . .

"Don't look so dazed," Jameson grins. "We'll start out small. I'm thinking of a camp that'll run itself, although that's not the way we'll describe it in Washington."

A camp that'll run itself . . ."How will you describe it?"

"A camp for specially selected anti-Nazi prisoners to assist us in our re-education projects--to put out a newspaper, circulate books that the prisoners have been forbidden to read, start a program of films that the Nazis have banned, and any other projects that might fit under the label re-education."

Put out a newspaper, circulate books and films . . . "It sounds impressive, Sir."

"There you go again, Lieutenant. Leave Washington to me. I may not know German, but I know Washington politics. There are a lot of politicians who will want to axe this program if they get wind of it. They'll call it 'coddling' prisoners, they'll say we're promoting leftist or Red ideas--you can expect every kind of attack against us. We've got to be ready."

I begin to feel a new respect for Jameson. "I still don't understand what I do in this special camp, Colonel. I'm no administrator."

"Your record says you were trained as an administrative officer."

"That's what the record says." I tell him about my Limited Service background.

"I'm not so interested in that," he smiles. "I'm more interested in your family and your European experiences."

He has checked me out . . .

"In this case your youth may even help us out. I don't want an authority figure. I want somebody with a little sympathy and understanding for the plight of anti-Nazi prisoners and you seem to have that. What I want you to do is get the anti-Nazi prisoners to run their own camp. Assure them of our support."

"That'll be a job, Colonel. Most of them have gone

underground if they still exist."

"We've got to find out if they exist. Some of the people I've brought into the program already are German refugees. I plan to send them around to the camps and interrogate German prisoners. Then we'll send the prisoners they select to this special camp in Rhode Island. If we have any luck, in time the anti-Nazis at your camp will screen out any Nazis or opportunists who happen to get there. You may have a rough time for a while."

"I'll do my best, Sir." *That sounds so feeble . . .*

"I know you will. I'll let you in on a little secret, Lieutenant. What I'm really hoping is that we can find a group of anti-Nazis who will help our Military Government in Germany after the war is over."

"That's a long way ahead, Sir."

"I've already spoken to some people in Military Government. I think we have a chance to work in that direction. Maybe we can even take the whole program over to Germany at the end of the war." He's not speaking directly to me any more. He's dreaming. Why not? Even in this god damn army a dreamer starts an infectious dance. Why am I always a doubtful dancer?

Somehow I begin to admire Jameson's stubborn will to change things around. Is it because he has the romantic vision of my father? I've learned to distrust that. Have I really? Jameson seems to be counting on me partly because of my family background. What the hell does that mean? It's only where I come from, nothing that I've done. I want this chance. Even if it's just to get out of this camp and take Armind along. Admit that the lure of taking the program to Germany if it works out is exciting too. Maybe I'll find Holzreichl again. Will he grin through his new mask of survivor? Forget about Germany. The problems of running a secret camp in Rhode Island are peculiar enough to think about.

When Jameson and I part we've agreed on plans. As soon as it's ready for use I'll take Armind and the Arab to the special eastern camp. Eagerly I hurry to the Guard House to tell Armind. In the yard a group of prisoners is playing soccer. Stripped to the waist in shorts, tanned darkly, they look like exultant Greek statues straining for muscular perfection. *Impress American democratic ideals* . . . What do Whitman and Lincoln mean to these Germans? To them Whitman and Lincoln are like a cigar wrapper and a cup of coffee floating on the mainstream of mystical Germanic legends. Jameson is right. The only way to accomplish anything is through the Germans themselves. Play down big slogans like *Re-Education*. Concentrate on our own little experiment in time and place. If I can just do something with Armind that's a start. Face up to it. I thought I didn't need Armind before. I was only sorry for him and myself. Funny how I'm conscious of his name now--Hans Armind. If this special camp is going to work at all I'll need Armind's ability as a teacher. Maybe it'll bring him out of his ant world.

Imagine me as a miniature camp commander in New England. Ralph Waldo Emerson, Henry David Thoreau and Emily Dickinson help me. Dust rises from the rampaging soccer game. Moving toward the Guard House it blazes suddenly in the sun like the burning memory of my childhood canyon house . . .

THE GERMAN   REUNION IN A COAST GUARD CAMP

What will the sentimental Americans think of next? . . . *Re-education program* . . . For Nazis or Germans? . . . *No more teaching, not ever again* . . . Dictate the facts, repeat them, impress them . . . Is that what education has become? . . .*Trust no one* . . . Isn't this a Nazi belief? . . . All of us Germans, admit it, have a little Nazi in us . . . Don't risk losing the little security I've found here in the Guard House . . .*Security in a prison camp?* . . . *In the ant world?* . . . Stop it, you're a true German all right . . . You talk only to your secret self . . .

If I travel east to this new camp will she be waiting? . . . I must go east in search of her although the possibilities of survival are extinct . . . Either she's been killed in an air raid or starved to death in a work camp . . . *Stop it* . . .

Through my cell window the desert sun is hot and forbidding . . . Isn't it enough to face the ant world at night? . . . Keep day and night separate . . . The world outside must be capable of external growth, a world of flowers, love, the sense of wonder when light illuminates familiar objects . . . How do I name this outside world to the Arab? . . . *The Land of Quatsch, I tell him, see that's what it's called* . . . Puzzled he peers through the bars and tries to repeat *quatsch* after me. .That wonderful German word signifying the irony of nothing . . . We're in the Land of Quatsch . . .

When I tell the Arab that we're going east to the Land of Quatsch he laughs . . . He will follow me anywhere . . . It is silly to speak to him of re-education, of change . . . Change is in death, in absence, in the ants . . . In the prison world one merely pretends to assume the mask of change and assents to the demands of force . . . *I am the spirit that denies* . . .

The Arab and I are instructed to pack . . . What do we have to pack? . . . We leave the camp in a truck . . . Lieutenant Enders rides in the front seat with the driver . . . I'm glad that I don't have to talk to Enders . . . The Arab and I sit motionless looking ahead . . . We don't look back at the guard towers, the high barbed wire fences . . .

Another long weary train trip sitting up night and day . . . The train is the best instrument designed for carrying prisoners . . . The pounding on the rails forces us into tranquility . . . America is an endless country like Russia . . . For days we travel . . . Still it is pleasant to journey east in autumn . . . The leaves are barely beginning to turn . . . After the desert one forgets that trees can be so large, so full of shade . . . Mile after mile of rich soil, red barns, acres of thick rows of corn, hogs, cows, sheep, chickens . . . How delightful to see animals instead of ants . . . Animals have always anchored man in society . . . The Arab makes me repeat the name of each animal . . . He delights in animal names as if he were leading them on to Noah's ark in some mythical time . . .

America is the Breadbasket of the World reads a sign in the mid-west . . . A careless boast . . . A gigantic statement of physical greed . . . I keep asking myself where we are going in the Land of Quatsch . . . We are traveling to Re-education . . .

After four days the trip ends in the late afternoon in a Rhode Island city named strangely Providence . . . How the Americans are fixed on destiny, on determination, on process . . . An army truck meets us and drives us through various towns into the country . . . After the desert so much grass seems like a fantasy . . . Many houses are built in enormous, grandiose Victorian styles, as if from a scrapbook of old men's memories . . . These are New England villages I keep reminding myself . . . The ocean must be near . . . Suddenly I'm eager to see water again, the crash of ocean surf, the sound of foghorns, to smell the salt air . . . This time Lieutenant Enders rides with us in the back of the truck . . . He keeps pointing out landmarks as if to stir up our enthusiasm, but we don't answer him . . . I stare at each building as long as I can in the brief instant before the green truck carries us out of sight . . . I am practising my shadow hobby again . . . Through a whirling haze of vision I see intricate, wooden ornaments that often remind me of Germanic woodcarving ability, vivid flower gardens that color my eyes after the barren desert, the flare of women's clothing on laundry lines . . . I see a cat on a porch in an old woman's lap . . . She is rocking, rocking . . . A baby crib covered with netting stands by the old woman . . . Everywhere I look I see her and then, quickly as a reflection on water, she disappears . . .

The truck passes between two small hills covered with luxurious evergreen trees . . . Everything is so green that the color seems unreal . . . *Green is the color of love . . .* On the left side of the road two women are standing by a well . . . One has a white shawl over her head . . . *She seems about the same age* . . . Her dress is blown up by a gust of wind and she holds it down with one hand . . . *She is standing there . . .* No, this woman is ancient . . .

"I'm sorry you haven't heard from your wife". . . What is Enders saying? . . . "I'm going to try through Intelligence next. They may be able to make some contacts . . ."

"What? Oh yes . . ."

A gull whirls into view, white belly shining . . . The power of gliding high over fences . . . We must be close to the ocean . . . It's autumn in Europe now too . . . Soon over the ruins, the rubble smoking from massive bombings, will come the winter wind, snow, points of ice . . . *How will she survive? . . .*

"Are you all right?"

No time for words so I nod . . . Don't think about her and the coming winter . . . Focus on prison camps hot in the sun, burning in wasteland, surrounded by barren desert space . . . The game with the ants . . .

"What'll you do after the war?"

Impossible to answer such absurd questions, although he means well . . . I mumble something to pacify Enders and he turns away. . . *Guard House towers, high stretch of barbed wire, dust blowing in the face, guards, prisoners hiding in closets for a little privacy . . .*

We pass through another village with a square in the center where a huge, bizarre stone building with an imitation Gothic tower is labeled *Town Hall* . . . How ordered everything is like Germany, undisturbed by prison ghosts driving by in an army truck . . . Neat rows of colonial houses with trim lawns, children riding bicycles . . . Soon we're in the midst of fields again with heavy rock walls, bright autumn wild flowers . . .

"We're almost there," says Enders excitedly . . .Even I feel a surge of expectation, a renewal of curiosity . . . *Re-education . . . That old man with the battered volume of Spinoza in his lap . . . Thence we shall see how much stronger the wise man is than the ignorant* . . . How little her father really knew of the new Nazi world when he proclaimed that education is the discovery of freedom . . . *You must shake the student out of complacency. . .The teacher must be willing to take enormous risks* . . . Yet he was talking about education . . . What good is re-education to the ants? . . . If I can forget the ants, this new camp may be one more change, perhaps the last . . . We are all defeated . . . We must begin again with faith, love, and respect . . . *Faith?* . . . Isn't it love, hope, and charity that used to have such hypocritical acceptance? . . . I reach back toward the scar in my back where the swastika was burned . . . The running water of the showers . . . Weimann . . . Dampfstoff . . . The Guard House walls and ceiling . . . The ants in their cathedral and palace, their world of hate . . . *What did she say? . . . Join my father in teaching children. They are the future* . . . But re-education is not involved with children . . . Has this war destroyed the possibilities of teaching? . . .

Will I ever know what happened to her? . . . Death must have some meaning, a shining, a radiance . . . She cannot die without any identity in some camp . . . *Grün des Lebens goldner Baum* . . . The greenness of life, of love . . . Looking at this tranquil New England landscape I can almost believe again that love is green and cannot die . . . I must believe it . . . Look at the three of us in this truck staring inward at ourselves . . . Why can't we look outwards again toward some natural source? . . .

Ewig . . . The end of Mahler's *Song of the Earth* . . . The old eternal, romantic identification with nature is gone forever . . . *Ewig* . . . Lost in time . . . The plant that flames, the tree trembling in wind, the rock worn by riotous sea . . . What happens when man discovers that nature is merely nature? . . . Nature is not freedom . . . How do we deal then with the intricate, superficial ways in which education tries to classify nature, to reduce it to camps and categories? . . . Learn to hate the deception of education, its false, idealistic masks . . . *That crazy old man in his school asking the children to draw God . . . Draw God!* . . . My hand feels paralyzed . . . Where is her touch? . . . I must not lose the illusion of hope . . . If I have loved, I will love again even with an Arab and an American lieutenant . . . *I am the spirit that denies, yes, yes, but also the golden tree of life is green* . . .

The truck climbs another long hill, past elm and birch trees, strange American names floating in the air like *White Wheel Ranch* . . . A prairie wagon wheel painted white is set proudly by a mailbox . . . What does that mean in New England? . . . Bushes growing thickly by the roadside, a land again where climate means variety unlike desert spaces . . . Dairy farms, the settled, peaceful look of grazing cows impossible to imagine in the desert where everything melts or freezes . . . Driving through green woods, the foliage is so thick that it reaches out to embrace you . . . Suddenly over the rise of a hill, the bay opening into the ocean glitters in my eyes, a trace of whitecaps gleaming under blue sky . . . *The special island life* . . . This is the way the world flowers into meaning . . . I'm thirsty . . . My mouth feels parched . . .

"Look!" shouts Enders. "There it is. The old Coast Guard station."

A few hundred yards away a deserted lighthouse, on which a flock of seagulls is clustered, marks the channel . . . We pass a cemetery with a proud sign, *Historical Cemetery* . . . In Germany death has no history, it is always contemporary . . . Only a small fence without barbed wire, simple to climb over, surrounds the Coast Guard station . . . No guard towers, no machine guns . . . Four or five white-painted colonial buildings . . . How can the Coast Guard be so unmilitary? . . .

Enders grins: "This is a little better than Colorado, eh? a new beginning . . ."

I don't answer . . . The Arab and I have no sense of new beginnings . . . Yet a possibility seems to glitter in the gull's wings flying through the air toward the ocean . . . What possibility? . . . That first night I can't sleep . . . Somehow it is not because of my fear of the ant world . . . The Arab doesn't sleep either . . . I hear him stirring restlessly . . . Sitting up we look out the window over the ocean toward Europe and Africa . . . The moon shines on the calm water . . . I sit there a long time watching the glow . . .

The days pass faster in my second American camp . . . Soon we are thirty men who have been screened out of various German prison camps around America . . . To my delight there are four whom I knew in the 999th division in Africa--Fischer, Ingolstadt, Rappberger, Steinert . . . They are changed, subdued . . . No matter, it is a jubilant reunion . . .

Still we must be careful . . . We know nothing about the other prisoners except for reports of the verbal interrogations that Lieutenant Enders has received . . . Several of these new arrivals claim to be from the 999th . . . Since we fail to identify them clearly, who can be certain of their purpose in the camp? . . . The five of us and the Arab take over bunks at the west end of the room commanding the entire space . . . This is our observation post . . .

Re-education passes from our minds . . . During the day our time is spent trying to find ways to create a community out of the misfits who arrive . . . Among the prisoners we receive daily are two Social Democrat labor union leaders whose backs are covered with whipmarks from a concentration camp, a Lutheran minister feverish with the belief that God has betrayed him, a gypsy, two fervent Seventh Day Adventists drafted despite their religious objections, a Communist steel-worker still proclaiming his belief in the "Popular Front," a half-Jewish professor of Russian suffering from the suppression of his Jewish background, and a mentally retarded, mystical cement worker . . . Fischer, a former musician, organizes a small chorus with twelve members . . . Primarily we sing sacred music that Enders locates for us . . . "If God is dead," Fischer smiles, "he still composed the best choral music." . . . Strangely he finds two soprano voices one day in two new arrivals, voices as clear and beautiful as any of the Wiener Sängerknaben . . . These sopranos are two men in their late thirties who were castrated by the Nazis because of suspected "criminal homosexual" activities . . . They claim to have been sent to Africa with the 999th division as cooks . . . They turn out to be excellent chefs, and the morale of our little camp begins to climb . . .

Several of these new arrivals ask me to start a study group in an effort to catch up on the new literature and sciences of which we have been deprived since 1933 . . . At first I refuse because I don't want to teach again. Finally they persuade me to try . . . It is almost an impossibe task . . . Few books or magazines are available . . . Occasionally we receive several old volumes through the Red Cross or some other charity organization . . . These are mostly out-of-date textbooks, sentimental novels, mystery stories, westerns . . . Sometimes the material is mysteriously censored by American authorities outside of the camp . . . When I call this to Enders' attention he is infuriated, but there is nothing he can do . . . As a game I try to discover what the anonymous American censors have eliminated . . . It all seems haphazard depending on the person confined to duty as censor . . . If we are permitted at times to see a picture of a sex queen in a tight bathing suit or to read part of the latest speech of Stalin, at other times similar material seems to have been scissored out leaving puzzling gaps in the page . . . Evidently the primary dangers to us prisoners in the censor's mind are communism and sex . . . We joke about this calling ourselves The New Anti-Communist Society of Sexless Men . . .

At least I hope that we'll have a chance to learn about America and whatever cultural changes are occuring in its vast space . . . Most of the books I manage to obtain are about agriculture and economics, the intricate manipulations of the Stock Market, and the expansive power of corporations . . . When I request work about writers, painters and composers I have little luck . . . I cannot blame Enders who tries his best to get me the materials I request, but my attitude toward the Americans is increasingly haunted by nightmarish images of the ant world . . . A black ant, an American officer, is interrogating a red ant, a German prisoner about a possible transfer to our camp:

Black Ant: "Why should I trust you, a German? Can you blame me for not trusting prison ants who worship a dead fly? I tried to help you, but your civilization of red ants is structured out of hatred. It must be contained in prison camps where re-education can take place.

Red Ant: "Are you so sure that the ant world is only German? Perhaps there is an American ant world too. Look at your chemicals for killing ants and roaches. The label reads: *Kills insects on contact. Kills with residual action--keeps on killing even weeks after it dries.* That is a lot of killing with false promises, with *residual* action that keeps on killing for weeks after your false promises dry in the air."

Black Ant: You red ants are basically the same. You seek to destroy the white wall of love. It begins to crumble . . .

The white wall of love . . . She stretches her arms toward me . . . I rush to her, my skin bleeding from barbed wire, running faster, faster . . . Ants crawl through the white wall . . . The white wall of love is crumbling . . .

I ask the American camp doctor for sleeping pills to escape the nightmares . . . He gives me aspirin the American panacea for all pain . . . I hate the dark, fearing the struggle with my ant visions . . . Waiting, waiting anxiously for the dim light of morning . . .

The security of our observation post at the west end of the barrack increases into a sizable anti-Nazi community . . . It is a community tormented by memories of shattered pasts, a community without a sense of future . . . Several of us work with Lieutenant Enders to formulate plans for an anti-Nazi newspaper . . . We call it *Der Ruf*, a wistful call to freedom . . . It is to circulate to all German prisoner of war camps . . . Still it is difficult to involve our true emotions . . . Such a newspaper should be concerned with present and future plans for Germany . . . We remain too involved with the past . . . The past haunts us in this odd, new camp of re-education . . . Despite preliminary screenings the danger of Nazi sympathizers penetrating our camp becomes apparent one day . . . Fischer and I sit on his cot discussing the surrender of German music to the Nazis and how we can counter this in the newspaper . . . No one seems nearby, but every prisoner knows that walls listen . . . That night a poster lettered in impeccable Gothic script appears on the barrack door:

COMRADES! BEWARE OF FISCHER
A MUSICAL TRAITOR TO THE FATHERLAND!

On the bottom of the poster a swastika is drawn, dripping blood . . . Suddenly the compound assumes the familiar tone of calculated suspicion, the weighing of each word before speech . . . I call the former 999th members to a meeting with the men we have come to trust . . . The next morning sees a new set of posters on walls around the camp:

COMRADES! KNOW YOU A MAN WHO LIVES ONLY
FOR FREEDOM AND HIS COUNTRY? THE GREAT
GERMAN MUSICIAN, FISCHER!

A titter of laughter, muted grins, transform the camp . . .

Tongues wag a little more freely . . .Singular humor is not a German characteristic, but we learn its importance again . . . The sheep begin to discover the confidence of the flock . . . At night we relax our guard without alarm . . . Some nights I am able to sleep for three or four hours at a time . . . Yet the tension in my mind remains, the night world of the ants against the day . . . Goethe's saying that the Nazis distorted in the Trinidad camp springs into my mind with fresh meaning: *Wer immer strebend sich bemüht, den können wir erlösen* . . . He who always struggles we can save . . . I can't sink into apathy . . . I must struggle to find her, to save myself . . . Or I'll end like Schmick . . .

Schmick, the mentally retarded construction worker, is an enormous, strong, impressive figure . . . Evidently he has arrived in this camp for much the same reason as the Arab, a man out of time, out of place with the Nazi theories of racial and physical superiority . . . Schmick is older than most prisoners in his late forties . . . A mass of premature white hair falls over his high, peaked forehead . . . His face is eager, vibrant, with a broad mouth always shining with white teeth . . . He sits all day on a chair outside the barrack door facing the sea . . . In front of him stands a small wooden table he has constructed with great precision and loving craftsmanship . . . It is all hand-fitted without a nail in it . . . The chess set on the table is unique too . . . The large pieces are beautifully carved . . . When I congratulate him on the skill of his work, he nods pleasantly, but doesn't reply . . .

All of his time is spent playing chess . . . Shouting sounds of joy and triumph, he makes his moves with great, sweeping gestures . . . His long, thin fingers dart through the air as if their destiny is inevitable . . . When he wins a game he is incredibly happy . . . He laughs with delight until tears run down his cheeks . . . Prisoners come up, slap him on the back, congratulate him . . .

When he loses, (fortunately this does not happen often), he becomes depressed . . . No one can cheer him up . . . With his head down, he sits in his chair staring bitterly at the frustrating earth . . . When he loses everyone learns to leave him alone . . . Prisoners shake their head when they pass Schmick, although sometimes they like to watch him play since he seems to enjoy the game so much . . ."Poor fellow," they say. "It's too bad he's such a hard loser. Barbed wire fever . . ."

No prisoner ever dares ask to play with Schmick . . . He plays always with himself, with his double whoever that is . . . Hunched forward in his moments of triumph, he sits doggedly alone in his chair . . ."He's harmless," say the passing prisoners . . . It becomes a camp preoccupation, this watching of Schmick's game from a suitable distance to see if he's winning or losing . . . When Schmick shouts in triumph we feel better . . .

The time comes when Schmick begins to lose . . . With increasing agitation his fingers flutter vainly over his lovely chess set as he pursues his feverish contests . . . Day after day he loses his games . . . We no longer dare to watch . . . We stay far away . . . One day Schmick emerges from the barrack, sits down at his table, and refuses to play . . . Stubbornly he squats there . . . He glares at the chess set with defiance . . . For several days this act of refusal continues . . . Everyone is increasingly disturbed . . . It is one thing to play alone with joy . . . To refuse a game is to enter the final world of isolation that we all dread . . . We confer with Lieutenant Enders . . . An ambulance arrives and takes Schmick away to a hospital . . . Before Schmick leaves he does a strange thing . . . He gives his chess set to me and the Arab . . . He requests that we play . . . After Schmick's departure we cannot refuse . . . The Arab and I learn to play chess together . . .

Whenever a new prisoner arrives we plan a series of talks with him . . . If there is something suspicious about him that we wish to test Steinert acts as our spokesman . . . A former coalminer we choose him for his size and strength and his knowledge of Nazi cunning . . . If the new arrival seems a little too proud of the insignia or medals on his uniform, Steinert asks him politely, "Please take the dicky-bird off."

"Dicky-bird?" the puzzled newcomer questions the slang word.

"Ja, der Hoheitsadler." Pretentious word, Hoheitsadler . . . The Nazi insignia, eagle with a swastika . . . How we Germans love compound words that float in the air with mystical double meanings . . .

We are not looking just for hidden Nazi beliefs . . . We have decided to eliminate the militarists and the extreme patriots too . . . They cannot help us if we are to create a new community . . . Consequently if the new arrival requests to retain his *Hoheitsadler,* Steinert insists "Please take it off. Here we are pacifists. No one wears any Nazi or military insignia any more." . . .

Pacifists is misleading . . . Too many of us, including the Arab, are belligerent in our beliefs . . . Yet we have learned our lessons well in American camps where order is preferred to trouble . . . If we can uncover the real mentality of our new arrivals we can deal with them . . .

If a newcomer protests the sanctity of German military honor, we wait patiently knowing from long experience the basic jargon of threats . . . "It is for your own sake, you know, soldier," Steinert continues in his simple, friendly manner, "A few of us here were mistreated by the Nazis." . . .

In rare cases when the newcomer insists on his faith in German victory "despite the Nazis," we recommend his transferral to another camp . . . Occasionally we are threatened with what will happen to us "when we get back to Germany." . . . If we ever return to Germany many debts will be settled one way or another . . . Even revenge seems a lost art requiring too many anonymous deaths . . . The trees, shattered in their images of shelter and fertility, will not be green for a long time . . . Bare winter trees they may remain forever . . . Black skeletons . . . Staring sleeplessly into the darkness from my cot, I come to think that pity, not just love, is green . . . Lost pity . . . There will be no room for pity, for greenness . . .

As the danger from fervent Nazis decreases in the little world of our growing community, we begin to worry more about possible criminals . . . The psychopaths, murderers, rapists, criminally insane who were forced into the 999th Division and mixed together with political prisoners--how to identify them? . . . In the insect world are there criminal ants? . . . In the animal world, if a dog attacks a passing beast, how classify that? . . . Guilty or not guilty? . . . Or the bird world . . . In a blue sky filled with sailing wings if a bird dives suddenly at a human target is that an act of evil?

. . . Hasn't the prisoner always existed suspended between insect and bird worlds? . . . A two-legged unclassifiable prisoner-animal . . . Even though they assent to a common contempt for Nazism, many faceless prisoners in our camp live in silence, morose, anti-social . . .

In the dark I laugh at my dream of criminals . . . My definition of criminal fades rapidly . . . Man assigns sinister shadow-actions to the animal world . . . What if man himself with his strange fantasies of power is the greatest killer? . . . What if a murder in the imagination is just as physical a distortion as a murder in actuality? . . . At night I watch the ant game again . . . Wings are torn off again in that arena created by human eyes . . . The fly's body descends in triumph into . . . *Into what?* . . .

In the morning when I open the door and look out I half-expect to see prisoners kneeling beside that miniature arena of terror . . . The compound is empty except for a few men on garbage detail . . .

Sitting on my bunk I hold my head as tightly as I can between my hands . . . *I'm holding a cold, transparent glass ball* . . . Inside is the mocking ant world, inactive in the daylight suffusing the room . . . The small, dead, ceremonial bodies are fixed in place . . . If I could only talk to a woman . . . A society of isolated men is the greatest torture ever invented . . . *She is outside of my mind if not my memory . . . After World War I ended prisoners were held in camps for as long as three years* . . . If there are no women I must keep on talking to someone . . . The Arab with his silent confidence is not a real companion . . . I must believe in the value of survival . . . Before my prison days I felt a surge of pity when I saw even a bird hurt . . . Now the death of a man is merely another statistic, another number . . . When will I feel again that night is only half of the day? . . . Does some special destiny govern the world of sleep, of dream? . . .

To forget I pour myself into the task of organizing the camp . . . Since it is necessary to know English if we are to solidify our control of the camp, I find myself compelled to teach English . . . My chief pupil is the prisoner, Ingolstadt, with whom I served in the 999th division in Africa . . . There, although we knew little about his background, he was always cooperative and friendly . . . We trusted him as much as we trusted anyone . . . I discover that I need Ingolstadt as a student to jolt me out of my self-tormenting world . . . Remembering my father-in-law's belief in abolishing the classical German distance between teacher and student, at first I simply read American newspapers and articles with Ingolstadt . . . To learn vocabulary and syntax I make him repeat passages after me . . . Then I ask him questions about the contents in English . . . It is a game of chance, this kind of instruction . . .

According to Ingolstadt he was a watchmaker in a Jewish business in Dresden . . . When the Nazis confiscated the business, he tells me, he was offered a share in the new ownership . . . Why didn't he accept? . . . The temptation must have been strong . . . He is reluctant to answer . . . He doesn't want to talk about his background . . . All he wants to do is learn English . . . Can I blame him? . . . Do I want to tell him my experiences with my wife, my Jewish father-in-law, that obsolete idealist? . . . Still I cannot quiet my curiosity about Ingolstadt . . . Is he only a lone wolf who stubbornly refused Nazi bribery? . . . Was he therefore forced into the 999th Division? . . . Is there perhaps some criminal act in his mysterious past? . . .

Tempted deeper into the trap of curiosity that is part of the tangled relationship between teacher and student, I decide to ask Ingolstadt to write short compositions . . . That way he will reveal himself . . . I begin to delight in the role of amateur investigator . . . Another mask for my lost profession of teaching . . .

In the beginning Ingolstadt grumbles at the task and threatens to stop his studies . . . "I am not a writer," he protests . . . "A man who has spent all his time bent over the tiny interiors of watches feels cramped writing on a big, white page." . . .

"Nonsense," I say . . . "It is the only way you can learn, the only way you can be free." . . . *Free* . . . I listen with amazement as it issues from my mouth . . .

His first composition, of course, is quite incorrect, but nevertheless fascinating . . . I instruct him to write about something with which he is intimately familiar, his native city . . . "It's easier to begin in a specific way," I tell him . . .

So the first theme he hands me is labeled like a child's composition, *"The City"*:

"The city is bigger, never too bigger. It rises beyond. It waits into night. Street lights open, then is most glowing. People walk to and from, only at night their faces are vanishing. Their body shadows flash on the walk. They are mass. Nobody is clear enough to be one person. I walk on, all over . . . "

Such language is infectious . . . I begin to think how didactic I have been about grammar . . . How futile and confining it is to conceive of a rigid flow of words strictly aligned in time and space . . . What if language is merely a growth that comes and goes like the leaves on a tree? . . .

"Before theatres can also be seen many lights beating in the blackness. I would like to achieve one drink if there were money, but it is to starve in this city. It is to starve for men, for laughter, for my watch with which I love to make the time. I make the time in a good way. I fasten it on the wrist so it does not speed up and go quick. Before I am owning a collection of watches, but this must disappear also."

"It is a city into night, without women. The women are in death for selling themselves. They cannot have bodies, but ghost faces into these lights. I walk far seeing men who grow into friends . . . "

"Do you mean *seeing* or *seeking*?" I interrupt to ask Ingolstadt . . .

"What is difference?" . . .

I explain . . .

"It should be *seeking* men," he says ponderously pointing at the difficult word with his finger . . . I continue to read, not daring to ask any more pointed questions . . .

" . . . The night makes me too much of myself. The time is speeding too fast and too slow. I walk up to the end of the city, five, ten miles, and return. Where I am seeking to sleep is in the bottom of an apartment dwelling. The floor has sacks and I must forget sleep in the tightness of night . . . "

The *floor* has *sacks* . . . Was he another master of the classification of cellars, another member of the shadow life?

". . . I am afraid what they do if they find out my hiding. My hope is that I know the city night more inside and outside than they do with the swastikas. I did nothing except for men and my watches. The city will hide my friendship. It is free in lights and machines." . . .

After suppressing my old instinct to point out all the grammatical errors, I take care to compliment him on his poetic feeling . . . Using this approach I feel I can focus on the sentence that seems to me most suggestive . . . Trying to act as casual as possible I ask him what he means by "I did nothing except for men and my watches." . . . He smiles and apologizes for his poor English . . . "English, she is a devil." . . .

"American is worse, " I reassure him. "But you don't need to worry as much about the structure of sentences as you do in English. Just try to say things as clearly and directly as you can." . . . The minute I hear myself saying the last sentence I feel uneasy . . .

He apologizes for being such a poor student and then says in a serious voice, "I meant to say that I divorced my wife and felt sorry about it." . . .

I guide him back over the composition . . . Beware of the warning words . . . "It is a city into night." . . . Are his night visions similar to mine? . . . "The time is speeding too fast and too slow." . . . Is there no present time for him too? . . . I force myself not to ask the questions that haunt my mind . . . The tradition of silence among prisoners warns me . . . The only way I can hope to probe his past is as formal teacher to pupil . . . Our surface friendship can never be a deeper relationship . . . Real agony is private, but it is a strange temptation to try and discover it . . .

I find myself spending more and more time with Ingolstadt . . . It is as though some kind of double, some weird mirror image is developing . . . If the Arab is my physical shadow I become obsessed with Ingolstadt as my mental mirror, yet in many ways he does not resemble me at all . . . Studying him day after day, I notice that occasionally his hands shake . . . He tries to hide them in his pocket . . . Nothing he does while he is with me stops the shaking . . . Feeling himself under my eye he goes off into a corner of the latrine for a little privacy . . . I feel him withdrawing . . . I curse my stupidity for increasing the barrier between us . . .

Desperately I tell him one day that I also had a problem of trembling hands after my time in the concentration camp at Fühlsbuttel . . . He does not react to this and volunteers no information of his own . . . But the next composition he writes tells of his being wounded in the Polish invasion:

"I was hit maybe forty miles east from Warsaw. Laying in blood for four, five, six hours. Then medical soldiers are come and take me back, back under the blue, hot sky into night and white doctor tents. Many soldiers are waiting in blood of tents, some waiting to death. In night a much wounded man, face covered with bandage, was brought in next to my body. He cry about water through bandage, and talk about wife. After a long journey of time water comes. We go into half sleep, afraid of battle. In dark, middle night I arouse and feel toward my hurting wound. I also feel towards something on my shoulder. The much wounded man is dead with an open mouth through the bandages on my shoulder. Tomorrow, when I think of dead man, my hands beginning to shake."

So the mystery of the trembling hands is a normal thing, the result of a soldier's familiar encounter with a death that does not want to die . . . Ingolstadt has no special significance in the puzzle that contains the word *prisoner* . . . He is only another number like me fighting to overcome barbed wire through the dangerous medium of memory and imagination . . . Why go on forcing him to write strange compositions? . . . Better to stick to the boring rules of everyday repetitive language training . . . If I probe deeper I will only find a deeper isolation . . . Every prisoner knows that a prison camp drives a man into his dangerous fantasies . . . Most prisoners, like most men, have little imaginative powers . . . Their memories and thoughts run in the usual materialistic and religious channels . . . Yet something about Ingolstadt is different . . . Beneath his stolid, deceptive exterior, why are his thoughts so intense? . . . Why can he only begin to communicate them through the ironic device of compositions written to learn English? . . . I fall into the trap of ignoring the basic rule of prisoner-teacher: *Learn to live in your own privacy or you will destroy the privacy of another person* . . . Under the delusion that I am struggling for my sanity by the charitable act of helping Ingolstadt, I urge him to write about every image and subject that possesses his mind . . . I want selfishly to rejoice in the cruel spectacle of a fellow prisoner trapped with me in the ant world . . . Is my action entirely selfish? . . . I do not know . . . I no longer feel so locked in self-hatred, the self-pity of my destiny . . . The fact that Ingolstadt becomes more and more eager to write convinces me that I've found the key to his delusions . . . In many of his short pieces he seems to be merely working out his hatred of the war, particularly the Russian campaign:

"Bring into your night dream a river of clearest water. Built into the across sides of the river are the two armies, winter between. In the white-colored soldiers are an important thirst, but the one water is below, between. Within the day, great thirst and shooting death. Planes roaring above. Within the night up runs a white flag. Is a peace, why in the black night I cannot understand. No one trusts. But shooting stops, the dying stops, the soldiers of both hating armies climb within the waters to drink cold. Morning comes and shooting death again. It is to completely laugh that only drinking water is night mercy, is between time for enemies." . . .

This kind of ironic meditation makes me impatient . . . I understand it too well . . . Have I not created my own world of red ants? . . . Impatiently I suggest to Ingolstadt that he return in his writings to his past, to his city . . . It becomes tantalizing, imperative, yet almost impossible to follow the hidden web of his thoughts:

"Man is too much woman. That is this German poison that flows into the world. The German, like driftwood, is within mysticism. He seeks for oneness and cannot join the happiness of male and female opposition." . . .

Too close to my own experience . . . Keep him away from killing philosophy, the German disease . . . Prevent him from seeking an impossible solution for the world's agony . . . Yet city, city, Berlin, Dresden, lost love . . .

"City of machines. We are too much fearful of machines. When we kill them, break, smash, we kill the man inside, we make us sterile, no more men. We want to kill the man parts, the woman parts, then we lift up only God, the white abstraction to where we can escape." . . .

God, the white abstraction to where we can escape! ... There are thrones in the ant world too ... I've failed to make him reveal anything significant, any *evidence* of his former city life ... Ironically I congratulate myself on my ability as a teacher in improving his English ... Still he is only withdrawing more and more into his inner world ... He sleeps in the center of the barrack three cots away from me ... I fancy I hear him in the darkness, twisting and turning in his obsessive struggle for what? ... To confront experience? ... Or only to confront the savage compulsion of language? ... Have I discovered another condemned writer? ... The subject of night increasingly shadows his themes and this makes me uneasier:

"Night is the myth, father and lover, lover and loveless. We walk through yellow city lights. We are to be dissolved. The moon shines on top of the night. Children say it is made of cheese. It is not certainly made of man's flesh. It is too cold and far away. The moon is the woman of the night. When we have lost pity we are going into the night." ...

Is the last sentence a hidden reprimand to me? ... Have I lost my initial sense of pity for Ingolstadt? ... Pity is a false luxury in prison camps ... *Night is the myth* ... Early in the morning after reading his childish words about the moon as the woman of the night, I lie awake as usual, staring into the darkness trying to swamp my mind with an assault of disparate images ... I hear Ingolstadt leave his bed ... Raising my head I watch him creep out of the barrack ... Is he sleepwalking? ... He walks as if in the grip of some distant compulsion ... Still every image seems distorted at this time of morning ...

"Anything wrong?" I whisper in a voice that seems terribly loud ... He doesn't answer ... Probably he's just sleepwalking to the toilet ... I lie back on my cot ... 1--2--3--4 --5--seconds, minutes, however the units of time pass ... Numbers, numbers ... 9--9--9 ... This peculiar wheel of fortune .., Count sheep, bayonets, machine guns, swastikas, prisoners, ants ... Ingolstadt can't sleep either ... Is this any satisfaction? ... Do I want him to be like me? ... Do I want everyone to suffer the loss of love? ... Is that why I force him to write something that he distrusts and feels uneasy about? . . . What nonsense . . . *When we have lost pity we are going into the night* . . . Forget about his crazy themes . . . *Crazy?* . . . Is he my double? . . . Think of my wife back in Germany . . . She is waiting, she waits, she will be waiting . . . Teach him the strange forms of American verbs . . . Why don't I hear from her if she is waiting? . . .

Is that a faint scream? . . . Probably a wolf in the desert . . . *There is no desert here* . . . I sit up in bed . . . Nothing moves . . . Everyone in the barrack is sleeping . . . Another grating sound . . . Not an animal this time . . . Something dragging on the ground . . . I get up . . . The night air surges cold on my naked skin . . . I pull on my pants and shoes and creep out quietly . . .

No lights are on in the latrine . . . Suddenly the smell of disinfectant pierces my nose . . . As I enter the door I step into a pool of water . . . One of the showers is leaking again . . . I call his name . . . "Ingolstadt!" . . . No answer . . . Groping my way through the darkness I search toward the urinals . . . I stumble over something on the floor . . . Ingolstadt's body . . . He must have slipped and hit his head on the cement . . . I bend over him and hear him breathing heavily . . . Turning on the light I cup my hands together and pour water from a nearby washbasin over his face . . . Soon he begins to revive . . . He mutters words I don't understand . . .

"Can you get up?" I ask. "I'll help you to the infirmary. What happened? Did you slip?" . . .

"I was attacked," he mumbles, his hand fingering his face where blood trickles down . . . "I didn't slip. Someone attacked me. Look, my pants . . .". . .

His pants are ripped on the right side from waist to knee through the large, white painted letters P.W. . . .

"What'll we do? We'll have to tell . . .". . .

"We can't tell anyone," he protests quickly. "You know what will happen. It will just make the Americans more suspicious of our being criminals." . . .

I want to ask, "Are you a criminal?" . . . Fortunately I cannot speak . . .

Although I tell no one somehow the word circulates among the prisoners that Ingolstadt has been attacked . . .

A closer watch is set up in our barrack . . . We look suspiciously at each other with a new concern for some Nazi or criminal element in our midst . . . As a result Ingolstadt and I become increasingly guarded in our strange relationship . . . He doesn't want to sacrifice me as a teacher . . . I am more determined than ever to extract his secret from him . . .Our contacts grow severely formal like two chess players in a tournament acknowledging each other's presence, testing each other's ability . . . Still I argue with myself there is no reason to doubt Ingolstadt . . . He couldn't have attacked himself . . . Even if he did what difference does it make? . . . Is it so unusual to kill yourself in a prison camp or try, desperately, to attract attention to your particular isolation? . . . I resolve to become more of a formalist in my instruction . . . *All right I will teach him to become a writer* . . . What did she say long ago in Germany? . . . What is it I've been trying to forget? . . . *I want you to teach, I'm proud that you teach* . . . Still I can't convince myself that I'm really helping Ingolstadt in any way . . . I know that I'm searching for time to escape from the ant world, the night world when brilliant points of stars glitter smaller and smaller in the sky, insect-like . . .

Despite my intentions I find myself watching Ingolstadt at night . . . Frequently, unable to sleep, he steals out of the barrack . . . I warn him not to go out alone, but he informs me plainly in a tone of resentment that it is his risk . . . After that we come together as little as possible . . . Only our antagonistic lessons draw us like a magnet . . . A break is inevitable . . . It happens in explosive words . . . At a final session he hands me another theme which I read with growing anger:

"Woman is in the night. Stars, moon of her flesh. Where she is bleeding, there is long, slow blood. She has been killed. See the dark background of always night. Before it is being played her death. It is a gay death, sparkling, because now tomorrow will come. Tomorrow will come with the stare of understanding . . ."

Reading this I grow furious because I feel that he's mocking me with this mystery. . .Behind the outraged mask of teacher I ask the meaning of such sentences. . .

"What meaning do you want?" he asks bitterly . . .

"You must write the truth. If you try to hide something in language, the words rebel and become distorted." . . . In my crude attempt to probe his past, how severely I use the easy maxims of a teacher . . .

"I can't seem to do anything but distort words. Maybe that is my truth." . . .

"You're merely trying to justify your mistakes. You won't learn anything if you don't write out of your deepest experiences. The language will reject you." . . .

He begins to laugh, but his laughter at my indignation is full of resentment . . . "The language has rejected me. I'll never learn. The ideas are my own, yet I can't seem to express them in English. Anyway it's your job to correct the grammatical mistakes and that's all." . . .

Grammatical mistakes . . . "Don't you see?" I shout turning into the guardian of tradition, the haughty schoolmaster, "If the idea is clear and you're not afraid of facing up to it, the grammar will be clear. Anyway I don't like what you write. It's sick." . . .

Like some wounded animal withdrawing into a cave he retreats into silence . . . Suddenly I feel the sick knowledge of guilt . . . *No better than the world of ants* . . . Too late . . . The quarrel begins in earnest . . . "What do you know about sickness, you with your virtuous innocence," he snaps bitterly. "All you have done is teach little boys. You can sleep." . . .

I can sleep . . . It's turning into a farce of surface recriminations . . . Suppress my ironic laughter about my supposed ability to sleep . . . *He'll never let me teach him again* . . . Although he says nothing about stopping instruction he never comes to me again with another composition . . . As far as I know he never writes another word in English . . . *I did that to him* . . .

The suspicion deepens in our compound like a ripple on a lake's surface spreading outward from its center. . . Suspicion of threats, fear of Nazi informers . . . Suspicion of loneliness, isolation, guilt . . . At night the barrack is peculiarly quiet . . . Men sit on their cots saying nothing, waiting for the lights to be extinguished . . . From a corner I hear the beginning of a song, the uneasy question of a melody ending abruptly in melancholy . . . The eternal letter writers work, writing to addresses that have not answered for years, addresses that no longer exist on any map . . . After the lights go out I lie on my back listening to the restless sounds of my neighbors . . . *Neighbors* . . . A stupid, conventional word with the paradoxical meaning that intimacy is often the greatest barrier . . . *The real stranger is the one whom you are forced to live with* . . . Probably they are only counting too . . . Sheep, machine guns, strands of barbed wire, guard towers, 1--2--3--4--5 . . . 9--9--9 . . .

In the morning, the dawn sky still dark through the bleak windows, I watch from my cot to see if the sun will really appear . . . The silence is shattered by a scream . . . Startled I jump up, naked, and flounder toward the direction of the scream . . . Suddenly my foot slips and I fall . . . Pushing out my hand to protect myself I touch something sticky . . . I try to lift myself . . . I'm in a stream of blood . . . I vomit . . .

Ingolstadt lies rigid in his bunk, bedcovers up to his chin, eyes staring at the ceiling . . . As the pale dawnlight seeps into the room I see the brown army blanket suffused with red pools . . . He's dead . . . The terrible scream was from Fischer as he too slipped in the bloody trail . . .

In one sense it's simple to reconstruct this death . . . My analytical eye . . . *Always too late* . . . The futility of logic . . For at least one hundred feet outside of the barrack a path of blood covers the ground . . . Ingolstadt cut his wrists deeply with a razor blade . . . I find the blade near the door sill . . . Then he walked up and down, perhaps even marched up and down grotesquely as a last military gesture of defiance to make his blood spurt out more quickly . . . When he began to feel faint he returned to his cot and pulled the covers over him . . . Why did he want to die inside? . . . Was there some final need for companionship, even though the companionship no longer had any real meaning? . . . Perhaps he wanted only to feel warm at the end, to escape the chilly morning air as his blood continued to flow drenching the blanket, trickling down on the cement floor . . .

We bury him in a brief ceremony with few words . . . Silence seems like a greater measure of respect than military formalities . . . In fact the whole ceremony is strangely more visual than spoken . . . A peculiar thing happens . . . Standing over the simple white cross protruding from the green New England soil, several of us take off our watches . . . We place them on the cross . . . Are they instinctive tributes to Ingolstadt's civilian past as a watchmaker? . . . That is perhaps too sentimental an interpretation . . . As I place my watch on the wooden cross I don't feel I am paying homage to time . . . Instead there is a curious sense of losing time . . . *I'm deliberately losing time* . . . Regret, yes, but more my fury at my failure to discover his lost secrets, his unsolved world of night, war, mysterious cities and landscapes . . .

His burial is by no means the end of Ingolstadt for me . . . The puzzle remains, the night visions, the staring into time . . . One day I reclaim my watch from the cross . . . I discover the other watches have been taken back secretly . . . But this furtive act fails to help . . . *He committed some crime* . . . It's the only answer . . . Perhaps he even killed his wife . . . Doesn't that explain the weird remarks about women in his compositions? . . . Is this the possible meaning when he wrote: "He seeks oneness and cannot join the happiness of male and female opposition," "We want to kill the man parts, the woman parts," and especially "Woman is in the night. She has been killed." . . . In searching through Ingolstadt's few possessions we discover that he kept his English compositions . . . I pour over them trying desperately to discover some meaning that escaped me . . . Ludicrous, as if I'm acting the film role of an American private detective with his analysis of difficult clues . . .

Night is the myth . . . How did he mean that? . . . Was night too powerful in his mind as in mine? . . . One of the Third Reich's proudest achievements is to cloud forever the definition of *criminal* . . . What German can say any longer *I am not a criminal but you are?* . . . The mocking pieces seem to fit together . . . Why did Ingolstadt write only in English? . . . Why didn't he ever explain in German what he meant? . . . He left no writings at all in German, not even a note saying what to do with his possessions at home, if any . . *Stop this analysis* . . . You know the danger of the imagination, the excess to which it can lead . . .

It is a gay death, sparkling, because now tomorrow will

come . . . Death brings a kind of peace then . . . Peace from what? . . . Yes, probably he attacked himself . . . *When we kill them, break, smash, we kill the man inside* . . . It is all so clear and yet it will never be clear . . . Perhaps it is better to believe that Ingolstadt was merely a political prisoner . . . He was in the 999th Division. . . Cling to the superiority of political prisoners . . . Still he showed little interest in politics . . . Why did he write of action in the Polish and Russian campaigns? . . . The 999th served only in Africa if it can be called service . . . So at one time he may have committed a crime which was not even legal enough for the Nazi authorities . . . I will never be certain . . . All that remains of the evidence is a wooden cross on the New England coast marked with his name, rank, serial number in approved military fashion. . .As if the official markings of one more death have any individual significance. . .The world is devoted to indifferent statistical markings of mass casualties. . .

Tomorrow will come with the stare of understanding . . . How many years is it possible to wait before time becomes meaningless? . . . Why did he use that word? . . . There is no tomorrow . . . I've waited through a mass of nights, each longer, heavier than its predecessor . . . How many dawns have I tried to climb into the central world of day, to stare with understanding and compassion into the morning? . . . I failed him . . . I never found sufficient compassion to understand him . . .

It is a gay death, sparkling . . . You bastard, you have escaped from prison, though you may not have escaped from the past . . . If I killed myself I know I would still see her eyes shining at me beyond the grave . . . That is the only meaning of change, transformation . . . It has nothing to do with sentimental resurrection . . . The flow of sunlight becomes the flow of blood. . .The warming aim of the sun's rays becomes the freezing, piercing light of the night sky . . . Ingolstadt's real crime, my crime, was to discover the nightmare visions of the ant world . . . They killed him more than any concealed memories of his past . . . My white wall of love is a wall of barbed wire . . .

When we have lost pity we are going into the night . . . No pity, no compassion . . . Face reality as ant people . . .

Worship the success of pure energy, ambition, movement, power . . . Then I can face your terrible words that I read over and over again seeking to solve their impenetrable mystery . . . They tell me there is no rest, no peace in the imagination . . .

Where is love? . . . By rejecting me, Ingolstadt, you have sentenced me to isolation again in the ant world . . . That was why I wanted to be a teacher, never to be alone . . . You have betrayed me . . . *Where are you, my darling?* . . . Save me from this murderer who is killing me as well as his former victims . . . No, I'm sorry, my love, it is best that you cannot come here into this arena of men and ants . . . I stand at the center of many mirrors of the mind . . . Your beloved, soft feminine skin glitters there in the outermost mirror . . . Love is far away . . . I flash through the mind's thousand images . . . You call to me, "Do not despair. No one can kill love."

But he did, he killed love . . . *Tomorrow will come with the stare of understanding* . . . No, that is Ingolstadt's voice, not yours, my darling . . . He cut the flesh of tomorrow . . . He killed the stare of understanding . . . If I could only die too . . . When will I get the courage to die, smash the mirrors with their mocking images? . . . Slowly they reflect the ant shadows again . . . How small the world is becoming where all flies with their wings torn off are reduced to the scale of ants . . . Tomorrow will come . . . How small we must be to deal with it . . . Love must become tiny in time to survive . . .

THE AMERICAN   THE FOREST OF RE-EDUCATION

Why didn't I listen more to Jameson's warning, *Watch out in the forest of re-education.* Maybe I wouldn't have taken this job as mini-camp commander. I thought I was sceptical enough to deal with the problem of mediating between prisoners and army bureaucrats. Face it, I'm too young. I don't have the experience or the rank. Before Armind became so involved with Ingolstadt a communal feeling was growing in the camp. I encouraged the prisoners to run things themselves--more than I should have perhaps. With Ingolstadt's death we're almost back where we began.

One more incident may be too much for Armind. The Arab's not much help. He's like a magnetic force drawing Armind into a field of silence. The old problem of prisoners in their locked world--Schmick playing chess alone, Ingolstadt with his mysterious background . . .

How can we improve our screening program to bring more stable anti-Nazis into this camp? Too many screening officers seem to think anti-Nazi means anti-Communist. That just brings us negative, self-destructive personalities. You can't run a program on negative policies. We need men who believe in constructive action and still have the will to carry it out.

For Armind's sake I've got to make him work. There's plenty for him to do on Jameson's key projects. The newspaper, *Der Ruf,* is underway and plans to reprint and circulate books that Germans have been forbidden to read for years. Teaching's too personal for Armind. He needs to escape from the past, not get tangled up in it. He doubts his ability to write. I badger him. Finally he consents to try writing an article about Goethe.

After several days he shows me three pages. Sentences are marked through, written over painfully. Paragraphs are crossed out. He seems to think about Goethe like an aristocratic priest rather than a writer relevant to the current situation. How can I get him to face the fact that the newspaper must have a contemporary slant? Otherwise it'll be useless.

"Look, Hans, I like the start of your article, but why the hell do you write about Goethe as if he's totally removed from modern Germany?"

"How do you mean? Goethe is sacred to us."

"That's the trouble," I prod him. "You write about Goethe as if he were on some kind of aristocratic pedestal."

"You want me to compare him with your Walt Whitman?"

"Why not?" *If he's going to be antagonistic let's get it out into the open.* "Compare the difference between Goethe, the aristocratic librarian-cataloguer and Whitman, the journalistic carpenter-cataloguer. Why is the bookish librarian so sensitive to sex? Why is the journalistic carpenter so insecure about women that he has to shout I LOVE YOU in thunderclap capitals every other line?" *At least I force a wry smile on Armind's solemn face.* If only these damn Germans could laugh more . . .

"Your comparison would please only American readers. Goethe may be aristocratic, but he is not a bookish librarian."

"All right, so prove it. Get him into the prison camp world. After all Whitman wrote a lot of his best poems about our Civil War. Mephistopholes ought to be relevant after your experience with *Faust* in Trinidad." *How his face changes . . .*

"I do not want to write about that."

"Then write about the rational, humanistic side of Goethe. Write how at the end of *Faust* his modern scientific spirit pleads for draining the swamps to save mankind."

"You're joking."

"Tell me the truth. Doesn't that end bore the hell out of you compared with the excitement of Mephistopholes in Part I?"

Armind stares at me as if wondering how much I am taunting him deliberately and how much an American really understands about Mephistopholes in Germany. "The first part of *Faust* may be more dramatic, but perhaps we Germans need to be a little more bored and concerned with the rational goals of Part II."

"No one will read your newspaper if you bore them."

"It's better to be bored than to succumb to the false theatricality of the Nazis. In the new age of communication we're entering any extreme politician may conquer a nation if he commands a certain power of personality and controls the communication outlets."

"Maybe but he won't last long unless he has an army behind him. Anyway, Hans, all I want you to do is get some of your own experiences into the damn paper. Get rid of the funeral tone so other prisoners will listen to you."

He shakes his head. I won't give up. Finally he agrees to try again. We plod along struggling to bring the newspaper project to the point of publication, preparing lists of banned books.

To combat Armind's gloomy isolation I have to fight my own. Impossible to avoid loneliness and a sense of futility about our small project in this withdrawn New England camp. When things get tough I try to remember something about education my father always quoted to me from Alexander Meiklejohn's *Education Between Two Worlds:* "Fundamentally education belongs to the world-state. The reasonableness of that institution includes and criticizes all the lesser resemblances of our experience. Every human being, young or old, should be taught, first of all, to be a citizen of the world, a member of the human fellowship."

Citizen of the world? How is that possible when Jameson arrives suddenly and pushes a memorandum at me. His face is full of the angry scorn that he conceals so diplomatically in Washington. The memorandum is signed by an aide to the Provost Marshal General. It describes a meeting with various government officials to approve the contents of the first issue of *Der Ruf.* The final sentence recommends: *"Let's have more of the American way of life in it. Less Thomas Mann and Stefan Zweig and more Herbert Hoover and General Knudsen."*

"Hoover and General Knudsen? Are they kidding?"

"No," Jameson snaps. "They've given me an ultimatum. Put more articles about America and Americans into the paper."

"For Christ' sake, at the moment Thomas Mann lives in California. He's becoming an American citizen. How do I explain to these German prisoners that the American authorities want less Thomas Mann in the paper?"

"Don't mention Thomas Mann. Just try to get them to compromise a little. Get a few more American subjects into the contents."

They won't like Hoover and General Knudsen much either. How can I explain that it's very American to take a big business tycoon, the head of General Motors, and give him a commission as a General to exert the same kind of technological power in the army?"

"Look, Peter, we don't have much choice. Either we compromise a bit or we let the whole program go down the drain. You don't have to focus on Hoover and Knudsen. There are other Americans."

"All right I'll try."

"If that memo is absurd here's another one you'll like even better." With an ironic flourish he shoves another formally typed memorandum across the desk. Addressed to Special War Projects Division, Washington, D.C., it bears the impressive letterhead *House Military Affairs Committee:*

Subject—Undesirable Books

The following books are thought to be unsuitable at the present time for German prisoners of war:

Technics and Civilization	by Lewis Mumford
Story of My Youth	by Ernst Toller
Der Untertan	by Heinrich Mann
Man's Fate	by Andre Malraux
For Whom The Bell Tolls	by Ernest Hemingway

Before I get furious I can't help laughing. "Somebody's got a tight ass, Colonel."

"And a blue nose," Jameson agrees.

"How the hell did they ever come up with a list like that?"

"Weren't they on the list your prisoners submitted for the book project?"

Suddenly I recall the list of fifty or sixty books that Armind and other prisoners drew up as examples of books banned in Nazi Germany that should be reprinted and circulated to all German prisoners of war. I dig the list out of my files. These five books are indeed included. "Why pick on these five books?" I exclaim. "They could have picked lots of other books on the list--Thomas Mann, Schnitzler, Bertolt Brecht..."

"Who knows? I investigated. As you can imagine the guy who signed the memorandum is not much of a reader. But he is trained to write short memoranda. He knows a long list might smell of too much censorship. Five books have a ring of authenticity. . ."

"Come on, Colonel."

"No, really that's the way it is. Now comes the best part. Down the hall from this guy who doesn't read is a German expert, a refugee who's written several unknown books himself . . ."

"You're kidding."

"No, it's this German refugee who prepares your tight-assed list of subversive books."

"I'll be goddamned. He must know that Ernst Toller committed suicide as a refugee in a New York hotel in 1939."

"That doesn't keep him from banning the story of Toller's communist youth. Note he's got an out. He says carefully 'unsuitable at the present time.' "

"Present time, bullshit. Maybe if he's a frustrated refugee writer he may be jealous of his fellow Europeans. But how do you figure him banning Hemingway and Mumford?"

"That's where the non-reader comes in. Evidently he got Hemingway and Mumford from one of those lists of radicals that crackpot anti-communists circulate in Washington. Remember the Un-American Affairs Committee?"

"They were after my father for backing the Loyalist government in the Spanish Civil War."

"The same with Hemingway I guess."

"It's a god damn mess. If we slip this list to some Washington newspaper wouldn't that help to expose this kind of censorship?"

"No, they'd really crucify us then."

"Who are *they?*"

"That's the trouble." Jameson puffs on his pipe. "*They* don't exist. When you look for responsible names and definite orders the bureaucracy becomes anonymous. Oh, individuals can suggest things like these memos, but they never *order* anything. But if we go outside of the system everybody'll be on our necks."

"So what do we do. Ban these five books?"

Jameson stares at me quietly. "I thought you knew me better than that."

"I'm sorry I didn't mean you . . ."

"I showed the list to the Provost Marshal General who turned out to be a Hemingway fan. They've shot ducks together. When he saw Hemingway's name on the list he went through the ceiling and called the chairman of the House Military Affairs Committee. So he gave me approval to go ahead with the book list . . ."

"Good."

"As a result we can expect another problem. The House Military Affairs Committee may get its back up and start investigating us."

"God, Colonel, you have to spend most of your time defending the program. How are we going to get to Europe if you have to fight Washington all the time?"

"Maybe the war in Washington is almost as important. Every military service is building an enormous bureaucracy in the Pentagon. When the war's over it'll be hard to shut them down. Every politician will be forced to agree that America must have the strongest military machine in the world. So any thing we can do to keep a little civilian control of this military power is important."

"We don't look too much like civilians, Colonel."

"Civilians at heart. That's what counts. God help us if we ever get a purely professional army running the Pentagon." Jameson looks at me with a smile. "Peter I've got a little job for you . . ."

"Oh, oh, what is it?"

"The final approvals for *Der Ruf* have to be processed through various offices in the Pentagon."

"Not me, Sir. I've got too much work to do here."

"I need you," Jameson says firmly. "I want you to go back with me to Washington tomorrow and handle the final arrangements. An officer has to hand carry the secret papers around. If anyone brings up any difficult questions you're the one who can answer them."

"Thanks."

"Besides," Jameson waves his pipe at me, "it'll give you a chance to see what the Pentagon is like."

"What if I get lost?"

"Everybody does. You just keep asking the guards where to go."

"Jesus Christ, do I have to go?"

Jameson grins. "You're getting too isolated up here in your little kingdom, Peter."

"Some kingdom."

"How's Armind doing?"

"I'm worried about him again. Ingolstadt's suicide really affected him. He can't sleep."

"Too bad."

"I'm trying to get him to write for *Der Ruf,* but the few words he's written are up in the clouds. No one would ever believe them. He can't or won't write about his own experiences."

"Well, it's not too difficult to understand why," Jameson shakes his head regretfully. "Maybe we can't expect too much from these prisoners until we get them back to Germany. They can't forget how we treated anti-Nazis at first in prisoner of war camps. If we can get them important jobs in Germany through Military Government, they'll justify our whole program."

"You think that Military Government will really accept our program?" *Armind's best chance to recover is in Germany--no doubt of that. I want to go too . . .*

"Don't get your hopes up," Jameson reflects. "Sometimes I think our chances are good, sometimes only fifty-fifty. It depends on which American troops occupy Germany. Every General will have his own political advisor. Those political advisors will want to run their own shows. If they think we're a little too liberal that's the end of our program. So you can see why it's important not to make too many enemies in Washington. Already we've got Counter-Intelligence agents watching us . . ."

"What?"

"Peter, your reactions are about as subtle as an elephant," Jameson laughs. "Don't you know every secret project is bound to be checked by Counter Intelligence?"

"How'd you find out we're being watched?"

"Last week we had a young red-haired lieutenant assigned to our Washington office ostensibly for payrolls and security supervision. One evening my secretary saw him with his feet up on his desk twirling the barrel of his revolver . . ."

"Maybe he was a cowboy."

"Anyway I decided we'd better keep an eye on him. So we started checking the contents of the wastepaperbaskets before burning them every day in accordance with security regulations. Last Friday we discovered a copy of a report that the lieutenant had prepared for the Chief of Counter-Intelligence. In preparing the requisite number of copies the lieutenant had somehow inserted a carbon paper backwards . . ."

"My god, Colonel, a carbon paper backwards?"

"Evidently he was preparing a hell of a lot of copies for all sorts of people and he didn't notice it. One copy came out on the backside of a sheet of paper. He thought it was blank and threw it away."

"It's a farce. He sounds too dumb to be in Conter-Intelligence."

"A dangerous farce if we want to go overseas," says Jameson grimly. "The lieutenant accused us of all kinds of subversive activities."

"You're kidding."

"He listed various subversive organizations we belong to, leftist newspapers and magazines that we read, and suspect books that we've written."

"Did he include your books?"

"I would have been hurt if he didn't. He mentioned my book, *Nationalism, Myth, and Nazism,* as a key work used by communist front organizations to promote their international goals."

"Probably he'd never read it."

"You're right. His information came from *The Red Network,* the book bandied about by the Un-American Activities Committee. Edwin Hall, our man, he confused with Edward Hall. John Porter he somehow identified with Jan Porter. You never read a report so full of blatant errors, thank god . . ."

"What'd you do to him?"

"When the Provost Marshal General saw how ludicrous the report was he called the Chief of Counter-Intelligence and complained. Probably the lieutenant is sitting now on some frozen island off the Alaskan coast. Still you can never tell what a smear-job like that leaves behind . . ."

"I hope it hasn't affected our screening teams in the camps."

"Why do you say that?" Jameson asks surprised.

"Colonel, I'm worried. The screening teams are coming up with too many prisoners who are political or psychological problems."

"What's wrong do you think?"

"I don't know. Sometimes it's just inexperience. Sometimes the screening officers seem to be operating out of a rigid anti-communist mold like your Counter-Intelligence lieutenant. Even if they know something about the Nazis they tend to trust the questionnaires and their own interviews too much. That's why I wanted to use our prisoners, send one of them out with each screening team . . ."

"You can understand why people panicked at the idea of sending prisoners around the country. All the press needs to see at this point is one image of German prisoners fraternizing with Americans and . . ."

"So we've got a worse problem, Colonel. Why the hell do we venerate questionnaires so much? No prisoner will admit he had any Nazi connections. It'll get worse now with the end of the war in sight. There's no way we can check except by personal interviews. If this camp turns into nothing but a screening center we're likely to have some bad encounters."

"It's a risk, but there's nothing we can do. There's no way they'll let us send out prisoners as part of screening teams."

"Get ready then, Colonel. Some socalled anti-Nazis coming in here may cause real trouble."

"That's your job to take care of them, Peter. I've got one more thing to show you even if it is the result of one of your favorite questionnaires. It helps to prove why we need this program." He hands me an envelope marked *Top Secret.*

Inside the envelope is the result of a questionnaire given to twenty thousand German prisoners, a cross-section of prisoners in camps throughout the United States. The first question I read is: "Do you believe that Jews were the cause of Germany's troubles?"

33% answered "No." 49% said "Partly." 8% emphasized "Entirely." 10% evidently had no opinion on the subject.

"How's that hit you?" Jameson asks. "You can expect 8% strong Nazis. It's the 49% that bother me. They're the ones we've got to reach."

"If the statistics are right. The 10% without any opinion

may be a problem too. They may be the ones who conceal their commitment."

"Any way you look at them the figures are pretty scary. You remember what Plato says in *The Republic:* 'No one, if he could help it, would tolerate the presence of untruth in the most vital part of his nature. There is nothing he would fear so much as to harbour falsehood in that quarter.' The vast majority of these Germans don't seem to fear falsehoods too much."

"Maybe we can work your Plato quote into *Der Ruf* if we can find the right context," I say wryly.

"You'll find the appropriate context, Peter, and don't forget a little more American subject matter."

"Hoover and General Knudsen," I groan.

"Leave it up to the prisoners," Jameson suggests. "They'll discover something unusual in America that interests them. It doesn't have to be just nationalistic propaganda."

That evening Jameson and I talk to Armind. As Jameson explains the need for more American subject matter in his most idealistic manner, Armind erupts suddenly, "Emily Dickinson!"

"How do you mean?" I ask surprised. "You'll translate her poems?" *Remember him reading Emily Dickinson to the Arab, "I have no Life but this--"* . . .

"Not only her poems . . . I'll write about her life too, how she wrote her poems when no one wanted them or her."

On the morning plane to Washington Jameson grins at me and says, "Well, at least Emily Dickinson's a start even if they don't take to her in the Pentagon the way they do to Hoover and General Knudsen."

At first sight the Pentagon's not so bad. Set a diamond inside a concrete mixer and you get the idea. Somehow the form got buried in the means. It must have been designed by teams of architects who fought each other with blueprints. So enormous, so ugly in bulk, that it's impressive. A quaint, old-fashioned idea like the French Maginot line except America does it bigger and better. One building is the whole line. A five-sided fortress to defend the U.S.A. Too bad fortresses aren't good military style any more. Visually it ought to be set grandly on top of a mountain. Five hundred years from now it would look good as a ruin if you could ruin it. . .

Anyway it's exciting, admit it. Here I am a secret courier. Not too many of those left in the world. Well, not more than a few hundred in this building. Why don't I carry my briefcase locked to my wrist the way couriers are supposed to carry secret papers? Too easy to notice wrists and cut them off. I carry my briefcase in the tightest five fingers you've ever seen. Let anybody try to snatch it. They'll take my hand first.

Down endless, closed-in corridors . . . I feel like I'm walking through a maze. This place was built by someone who loves the mystery of labyrinths. Everyone walks tensely. No one speaks except to ask directions. The signs are appropriately symbolic. Forget it if you're not a symbolist. The corridors are full of markers that indicate RICD, RR, OCRS, APUT, URRT . . . RR I hope means Rest Room. Or is it railroad? There's a special directory. Also there's a book of instructions on how to read the directory. So this is what Jameson means by bureaucratic growth. Bureaus are too small for this place. You think of men like Samson and Hercules holding up these walls. Hercules had twelve labors to complete to find his place amongst the gods. I have seven offices to visit and get final approval for *Der Ruf.* Of course Hercules had a tough kinsman who kept sending him on impossible tasks like killing the lion of Nemea. Since he found his arrows couldn't penetrate the lion's skin he cut himself a great club that was so heavy nobody else could lift it. That was the only way he could stun the lion. If he took that club and swung it against the wall of this building he wouldn't even make a dent.

Walking in this artificial light gives you a pale complexion. Never thought I'd long for windows so much. After a courier finishes his secret missions here they must put him under a sun lamp. Every time I find an office I have to wait. Several of us couriers sit in the outer room trying to figure some way to improve our position in line. I always seem to be last. My briefcase gets so heavy it's like waiting with a sprained wrist in a doctor's office. This is the way it must have been in medieval fortresses. Knights with their pleas, their poems, and their lutes waiting to get in to see the Baron. Only they didn't have heavy briefcases then . . .

The Baron turns out to be a Colonel, sometimes a Brigadier General. The Brigadier General signs the most secret papers. The couriers waiting for Brigadier Generals have bigger briefcases and heavier locks. When I get in to see the Brigadier General (he runs some kind of Intelligence network that deals with Ground Communications and Domestic Security although I can't figure out what this has to do with German prisoners) he proves to be extremely interested in the newspaper project. In fact he's the one who recommended "More Hoover and General Knudsen." I explain to him that we're working hard to get more American subject matter into the paper. I don't mention Emily Dickinson. Actually he turns out to be quite friendly to the project. "When I was a kid I wanted to be a newspaperman," he says and lectures me on the value of the freedom of the press. He tells me his whole life story and how his family made him give up printer's ink to become a desk general. "Who wants to ride a desk?" he asks with disdain. "You're lucky, kid. You're working on an army paper even if it is in German." By the time I get his signature it's one o'clock. I'm starved. Four more approvals to chase.

Exhausted I stand in a cafeteria line. The cafeteria is as big as an aeroplane hanger. Hundreds of uniforms and civilian employees with identification badges pinned to their chests file through the line with their trays. They collect coffee, soft whitebread chicken or roast beef sandwiches in cellophane, cottage cheese salads with a red cherry on top. The guarded anonymity at the tables makes me feel like bursting into song. Who would join me? When I sit down with my tray at a table of officers, clutching my briefcase between my knees, they focus on the one topic they can discuss freely--*Will the coming baseball season be any good since the best players are in the services?* After all I'm a Limited Service authority. I give them a rundown on baseball ailments that makes them gape. The way everybody sticks to sports reminds me of Werner Jäger's *Paideia:* "The symposium, or drinking party, was for Greek men--through its free friendly companionship and its fine intellectual tradition--the capital of the newly conquered realm of individual liberty." The companionship here is friendly if not free. Alas, the drinking party has been displaced by bad coffee and cottage cheese salads.

After lunch I speed up my pace. I press further into the interior in search of my four missing signatures. Two I get in a hurry. No questions asked. By now I'm so far inside the building I've got a feeling there are no exits. Close to four o'clock. By five most of the offices will shut down. The corridors will be jammed with employees hurrying to be liberated. Still I feel the challenge of a true messenger. I'll solve this god damn labyrinth yet. Through the biggest barriers come the brightest achievements. An absurd true-blue American proposition. Is this why bureaucracies grow? The people in the labyrinth get caught up in the secret search through the maze. As I start half-running nervously, afraid of failing in my quest, *Labyrinthine* and *Pentagonal* seem like strange American words. We've even succeeded in Americanizing classical myths. No wonder I dream of Hercules with his club.

The sixth signature goes quickly once I find the office. I don't even meet the Colonel in his inner sanctum. He's anxious to get home. He signs for some branch connected with the Signal Corps if I read the symbols correctly. At least the Signal Corps runs telephone poles into prisoner of war camps so there must be some German connection. At 4:45 PM with one more signature to go I really panic. I start running down the corridor almost knocking over a couple of secretaries. I shout "Sorry!" and run faster toward an office connected with the Government Printing Service, Military Branch. Evidently this office at the heart of the Pentagon prints all secret documents. That's why it's at the heart, the absolute center secluded from any spying eyes. My heart sinks as I turn the corner. I confront a series of mammoth neon-lighted tunnels full of the high-pitched roar of printing presses. How'll I ever get through these tunnels? The presses rage like Niagara Falls. 4:55 PM my watch warns. I rush from cubbyhole to cubbyhole flinging frantic questions at indifferent secretaries. They're concerned only with lipstick preparations for homeward flights. *Where is the Colonel with my missing signature? Has time expired?* They shrug unconcerned. *What's one more signature in this building of signatures?*

Polishing her nails one secretary says, "It's after five. He's probably gone."

"No," I agonize, "Your watch is fast."

"What's a minute?" she says without looking up.

Another secretary combing her hair points into the noisy turmoil. "Look in there. If he's still around he's usually in the press room. You got clearance?"

"Yes," I fling over my shoulder. In the press room all of the giant machines seem to be running themselves. Enormous claws, rollers, pistons click off magical documents that contain the secrets of the world. How come these secrets are printed in startlingly vivid colors, red, purple, yellow? I always thought the secrets of the world were black. The press room is singularly empty. Despair. Probably this place runs itself at night.

A hand behind me fastens into my shoulder hard. A deep voice shouts over the din: "What're you doing in here? This is a *restricted area!*" This is it. My shoulder feels as if it's under arrest. I swing around squirming to escape. Impossible. I confront an apparition. He's dressed in an enormous scratched leather apron. The apron swings from his waist like an industrial flag over battered army boots. His face is thickly bearded. Grey hair juts like a plow's sharp edge over his forehead. Two black eyes peer angrily at me from under V-shaped eyebrows. His khaki shirtsleeves are rolled up to reveal hairy, muscular forearms. He looks like the blacksmith, Vulcan, forging massive tools for the gods. I've found the real interior of the Pentagon.

"I'm looking for Colonel Atrender," I mutter feebly. "I've got some secret papers for him to sign."

"That's me," he answers suspiciously still holding my wounded shoulder. I stare. This is a Colonel, the Printer of Secrets?

"I was afraid I missed you," I stammer. "It's after five."

"Hell, that's civilian time," he laughs releasing my shoulder. "At five they run like rabbits."

When he sees what the project is an hour passes before I finally get his signature. Ecstatic about the possibility of printing a newspaper in German he tells me proudly his office publishes documents in more than thirty languages. "I can proofread five different languages myself," he grins. As he boasts of the international power of printing he escorts me into his office, opens his desk and pulls out a bottle of Scotch. "Lieutenant, your project sounds damn good. Let's talk about some of the problems you'll get into."

By the time I leave his office I'm reeling with newsprint information, paper stock, layout advice, possible type-faces, and booze. My Pentagon exit beats all records. My briefcase with signatures safely enclosed floats feather-light. I only need to ask directions from two or three guards. My confident walk is almost a strut. The Printer of Secrets remains in my mind. Amazing that a mad individualist rules the center of the Pentagon's labyrinth. I've mastered the labyrinth in one day. It may be a new record. I'm a champion Secret Courier . . .

When I reel into Jameson's apartment he asks in amazement, "How the hell did you get high in the Pentagon?" After telling him the story and absorbing more drinks I'm floating higher. Grinning at me Jameson muses, "Now you know what it's like in Washington. Maybe we'll make you a permanent Secret Courier."

"God forbid, Colonel."

"Did you ever read much Henry Adams?"

"Just *The Education.*"

He goes to a bookshelf, pulls down a book. "Here's what he said in a letter from Washington where he lived. Lewis Mumford was really the first to notice it. The letter was written about 1905 mind you." He reads:

"The assumption of unity, which was the mark of human thought in the Middle Ages, has yielded very slowly to the proofs of complexity. The stupor of science before radium is a proof of it. Yet it is quite sure, according to my score of ratios and curves, that, at the accelerated rate of progression since 1600, it will not need another century or half century to turn thought upside down. Law, in that case, would disappear as theory or *a priori* principle and give place to force. Morality would become police. Explosives would reach cosmic violence. Disintegration would overcome integration."

Stunned by alcohol I listen in amazement. What would the Printer of Secrets say to Adams's prediction, his weird "score of ratios and curves"?

"To predict complexity by complexity itself is typically American wouldn't you say?"

"What's that, Colonel?"

"Never mind. I can see you're still in the Pentagon."

"The funny thing, Sir, is that it seemed like a crazy challenge to get through it in one day."

Jameson's smiling, round face hangs before me like a hazy planet. "Maybe that's what Adams means by 'turn thought upside down.' "

"Read it again to me will you, Sir?"

"Tomorrow," says Jameson gently.

In Rhode Island, nursing a hangover, my journey through the Pentagon remains an ironic, triumphant dream. The feeling of triumph is sobered a little by the Adams paragraph that Jameson has read to me again at breakfast. *It will not need another half century to turn thought upside down . . . Disintegration would overcome integration . . .*

After reporting the good news to Armind and his colleagues about the approval of *Der Ruf* I settle down at my desk to find a pile of official envelopes. I open them to find inner envelopes stamped *Secret*--Chinese puzzles within puzzles. Is this what Adams means by complexity? I pull out more questionnaires with accompanying forms about prisoners who have been selected by screening teams for our special camp. Maybe a hundred forms in this batch. It's going to be some god damn job sorting through them. They all seem to have reliable anti-Nazi, anti-Communist records. Roth, Schmitt, Toth, Warbel, Weimann. . .*Wait. . .Weimann?* I turn to the section where rank is indicated and read, *Major. . .* It isn't possible. There must be some mistake. Clipped to the questionnaire is the recommendation of the American screening officer:

"Major Weimann was associated with members of the German General Staff who are known to have plotted against Hitler. He never belonged to the Nazi Party and comes from an old military-aristocratic family . . . Since 1931 he has a good record of anti-Communist activities. He fought in the Spanish Civil War against the Communists. His record as a devout Catholic is evident. He wears a cross around his neck. He seems to be an extremely well-educated, reliable family man. He stresses that he desires now to cooperate with the western nations, particularly since he fought in Russia and is aware of what the Communistic dictatorship has done there . . ."

I throw down the folder angrily. A highly distinguished record. No trace of Dampfstoff of course. Probably Weimann managed to get Dampfstoff sent away to a camp for "trouble-makers" when the war began to turn with the Russian advance in the east and the invasion of Normandy. Who the hell's the officer who wrote this recommendation? He was snowed by Weimann. What does "associated with members of the German General Staff who plotted against Hitler" mean? "A good record of anti-Communist activities"--as if that's all that counts. Evidently anyone sent by Hitler to fight against the elected Spanish government in the Civil War is "anti-Nazi." "He desires now to cooperate with the western nations." Hail to western civilization fighting against eastern barbarism. Even Hitler sent that message to the surrounded troops at Stalingrad. Above all anyone who's a Catholic is anti-Nazi. It's all so simple to this screening officer. Logic. Reason. Bullshit. Like the idiot American camp commander who ordered that all German prisoners willing to sign the statement "*I promise to cooperate and not to flee*" be classified as anti-Nazi . . .

How can I tell Armind that Weimann is coming? What'll happen when he sees Weimann appear as an officially sanctioned anti-Nazi? The limited privileges Armind has here haven't helped him much. Despite all of my efforts working through various Intelligence agencies no trace of his wife has turned up. Even as strong as he is there's a limit to the stretching of his mind.

I stare at a newsmap on my office wall. The battle lines are marked in red traceries that cover the earth in abstract, spiderweb patterns. *Global War* begins the caption . . . What complex global meaning is there in Armind's twelve years of hangnail survival? Be careful of meaning. There's no room for sentimental good-will in this program. Armind may endanger the whole program if I can't make him understand about Weimann. *Understand?* I rip down the map from the wall. Crumpling it up I throw it in the wastepaperbasket.

That evening I take Armind out for a walk. When I stammer out what's happened he stops and stares at me as if I'd slapped him. "Impossible. I don't believe you." His face hardens into a wall.

"Mistakes happen," I mutter. "It's not my fault. We can take care of Weimann when he gets here."

"Why should he even come here?"

"I told you it's too late to stop him. The orders have been issued and he's on his way."

"I don't believe you." He turns his back against me as if an electric shock had passed between us.

"When Weimann gets here you don't have to see him. I'll try to get him sent away immediately. The officer who screened Weimann simply made a mistake." *Do I really believe it was just a mistake?*

"It makes no difference if it was a mistake or not. You Americans always think that you operate from an infinite well of charity. The fact that other motives of self-interest may be involved never strikes you."

"What self-interest?"

Armind stares at me bitterly. "Anti-Communism to you is like a long, dark tunnel into which a train plunges without any lights. Don't worry, you say, light is not so important. Merely being against something bad will carry you through the tunnel. Anti-Communism will carry you through. You don't need lights."

"We're not all like that believe me."

"I don't believe you anymore." He starts to walk away and I stop him.

I try to keep my temper. "I don't give a damn if you believe me or not. When Weimann gets here I want you to arrange for two or three of your friends to interview him and expose his background. Then I'll confirm what he did at Trinidad and . . ."

Armind points at me accusingly. "What if my friends are then accused by your authorities of being secretly in favor of the communists? You Americans seem to think anyone like Weimann who is anti-Communist can be trusted to save the world for your kind of government. You only pretend to be a democracy."

"I promise nothing will happen to your friends."

"I don't believe you." With that flat repetition he breaks off the impossible dialogue and stalks away. His tone warns that it won't be easy to bridge this new division.

When I manage to get Colonel Jameson on the phone it's almost midnight. "Major Weimann is coming here," I shout impatiently.

"*Who's* coming there?"

"Major Weimann, the German commanding officer at my old camp in Trinidad. I told you about him."

Slowly Jameson's memory begins to churn up the facts. Obviously he's preoccupied with some immediate concern. The damn connection seems bad the way it always is when I talk to Washington. "Are you there? I can't hear you. You remember what I told you about Weimann and Captain Dampfstoff, the Nazi who was running the camp?"

At the other end of the line the distinguished carefully inflected voice begins to curse slowly, steadily. Then his voice cracks and I realize how tired he is. He says in his clipped way, "All right," as if this is just one more difficulty to be faced. "I'll see if I can find out how Weimann passed the screening team. The trouble is we've got too many stupid officers who don't know anything about Nazism. Or democracy for that matter. Be damn careful with Weimann when he arrives. Don't you think you'd better keep him as far away from Armind as possible?"

"I'll try. It's tough to do that here."

"When is Weimann supposed to arrive?"

"Tomorrow."

"Have you told Armind about Weimann?"

"Yes, I may have been wrong. He shut off completely. He just kept repeating 'I don't believe you.'"

"Well, do the best you can. We'll have to justify Weimann's transfer. You know how they worry down here about communism among the prisoners at your camp."

I get edgy, "What the hell has this to do with communists?"

"God damn it, Peter, you don't have to tell me. I'll fix it up. You take care of things when Weimann arrives. I'll get the transfer order. Hopefully you can hustle him out of there day after tomorrow."

"All right . . ."

"It isn't all right. I've got something else to tell you."

"What's up?"

"They've asked me to appear before the House Military Affairs Committee."

The House Military Affairs Committee. "What for?"

"I warned you. Another god damn investigation I guess. They want to be convinced about the purity of our program before they let us go to Germany with our prisoners."

"Do you think we'll be able to go?"

"Let's hope so. Meanwhile you may have to come down here to testify. I trust you more than some others in the program to tell what we're about."

"Me?" *But I'm pleased at Jameson's confidence in me.*

"I might need you. Don't worry I'll let you know in plenty of time." The phone clicks down.

Jesus Christ, what if I have to go to Washington and testify before the House Military Affairs Committee? That's too damn much. This isn't a re-education program. It's some kind of surrealist identity game. Already I can hear Weimann rationalizing his new German-American status when he arrives tomorrow: *"What could I do with a man like Dampfstoff? To accuse me of collaboration is too easy. Errors of judgment, yes. I should have paid more attention to politics in your American fashion. Many of us officers admit that we were wrong about Hitler. He deceived us! Still it's no use crying over what's past. We must learn to work with the western democratic powers. We want to help you Americans, to work with you against the Russians. Remember that Germany will always be the bridge between Russia and America. You Americans will need our help . . ."*

Somehow I must keep Armind and Weimann apart. What is this guarded feeling between Armind and me as if we were probing for some hidden purpose of which neither of us is aware? Admit it. I resent the fact that he's older, wiser because of his experience. Yet there's something dark, concealed about him too. How can one really respect despair? If there were only some way I could get out of this camp for a while, find a woman, forget about prisoners . . .

THE GERMAN INTO THE ARENA OF ANTS

Weimann here at this camp . . . Impossible, it can't be true . . . I trusted this young American despite his naivete . . . For a time this coast guard station, so different from other prison camps, seemed to cure my hatred, my fear of the ant world . . . The radiance of water glowed outside . . . In a momentary spell of tranquility, even though I heard nothing from her, I remembered a sentence of Kant, a sentence that Beethoven liked and copied: *"The moral law in us and the starry heavens above us."* . . . A farce when there will always be new barbed wire fences between us and the starry heavens . . . What a fool I've been with my "privileges" for me and my friends, even the ability to walk outside of the fence for a few minutes if accompanied by a guard . . . The Americans are just trying to use us . . . Weimann's appearance is no accident . . . More German compromisers will appear, all claiming to be anti-Nazi because of their secret anti-communist records . . . *Faust* will be performed again as in the Trinidad prison camp . . . *Ich bin der Geist der stets verneint* . . . The spirit that denies everything . . . Why can't I believe this completely? . . .

Last night my wife walked in the body of Mephistopholes . . . Afraid that I was losing my sex I masturbated . . . Mephistopholes was unsexed . . . How sterile I am, frozen in prison time . . . But I see her white body every night . . . *In my mind* . . . How many years since I've been with her? . . . I struggle on the lost roads back through time . . . They fill with that satanic figure mocking me, threatening me, punishing me with the swastika burned in my back . . . *Er findet sich in einem ew'gen Glanze. Uns hat er in die Finsternis gebracht, Und euch taugt einzig Tag und Nacht* . . . *Faust* again? . . . He thrusts us in darkness out of sight, to you he gives the day and night . . . That's what the Americans want . . . They expect day and night to be given to them free of any indecent communist shadows . . . Weimann was there in Trinidad . . . Don't forget that . . . Of course he had nothing to do with my punishment . . . He merely approved it by his silence . . . The war is almost over . . . Will that bring peace? . . . Peace lies in the mocking future where the hawk circles over a dead tree . . .

I awake screaming . . . My friends at my side shake me. . .

Sweat pours down my face . . . "Are you all right?" . . . I nod my head, but I think of Ingolstadt . . . Why did his life become entangled with mine? . . . My friends are beginning to regard me with strange eyes . . . Now that Weimann has arrived perhaps I will see, see with a blinding clarity . . . Slowly the ants crawl back into my mind, creep over the white points of consciousness, an endless procession over the body of my wife . . . Don't blame Enders . . . He means well . . . Meaning well is meaningless . . .

How can I tell Enders that the ants are returning? . . . This time they have no cathedral, no palace . . . There is no ceremony, no gleaming sword . . . They crawl quietly through the desolate streets of bombed cities dragging the bodies of flies whose wings they have torn off . . . They drag the bodies of men, of countless victims . . . Why can't I communicate with Enders? . . . He has been kind to me . . . He is an idealist of a kind . . . Kindness has no meaning anymore . . .

"You don't know when you're well off," he seems to say. *"What is there for you to go home to except starvation and rubble?" . . .*

"You Americans have never had to live in ruins." . . .

"I know, but there is a job to finish here. I need you to help find anti-Nazis in the prison camps we can trust." . . .

"Like Weimann? . . . I don't believe you" . . .

"All right, go home to the world of ants" . . .

No, the ants will always remain . . . It is our defeat, the defeat of man that is total . . . We must learn to begin anew . . . *I don't believe Enders or any other Americans* . . . I am a German, a part of Germany's defeat . . . It is time to go home, to accept the fact of the ants . . . You Americans think you have never been defeated . . . Victory to you is like some trophy in an athletic contest . . . You have shelves full of trophies . . . You accept the theory of victory as inevitable . . . *Grau, teurer Freund, ist all Theorie, und grün des Lebens goldner Baum* . . . Back through time to Faust again . . . Remeber, Enders? . . . All theory is grey and the golden tree of life is green . . . Words of truth coming from your lips, Mephistopholes, from the ant world . . . Enders may be a grey theorist, but he's so young that he still believes in the golden tree of life . . . How can I believe in any tree growing up through the ruins unless she's waiting? . . . Weimann thinks he'll survive and find his own green tree of life . . . Why should he return before me? . . . He won't return . . . He wasn't bred to be a street fighter, a member of the shadow world, a master of ant hatred . . . He's a General Staff officer trained to that peculiar German mystique: *Out of defeat will come the final triumph* . . . Who but a German could believe that? . . . Have I forgotten the dignity, bearing, conduct of a General Staff officer, that supreme aristocrat of aesthetic warfare, Beethoven, Wagner, aerial bombardments and Panzer thrusts? . . . No, he won't return before me . . .

I tell my friends I'm sick . . . They promise to keep an eye on Weimann . . . "It's better if you stay away from him," they repeat Enders' caution . . . I lie on my cot trying to force the ant world to appear in sunlight . . . I think of the night . . . An idea obsesses my mind . . . Weimann has become the key to the future . . . Somehow he's learned about the arena of the ants . . . He survives, he walks blindly in and out of that arena, he endures. . .I must face him, talk to him . . .*Talk to him?*. . .All languages are talked out unless I translate my new ant language. . .Better to let him disappear in the night . . .

As I lie on my cot almost in a rigid paralysis I imagine what Weimann is doing . . . He too is thinking of the moment of action, of our meeting . . . Yes I'm certain . . . The action has begun. . . All I have to do is lie on my cot and watch it develop . . . Time can't be trapped by barbed wire . . . It flows steadily, slowly, like the inexorable stream of ants undermining the desert soil . . .

Suddenly it is evening . . . I arise and tell my friends I'm feeling better . . . I'm hungry . . . I learn that Weimann has already eaten . . . He is in a room at the far corner of the compound . . . Tomorrow he will be transferred according to Enders . . . I eat a huge dinner . . . My friends are relieved to see my appetite . . . They talk about the continued massive bombings of Berlin with a mixture of fear and hope . . .

"Berlin is being destroyed. Nothing will be left." . . .

"Hitler is mad." . . .

"He's not mad. He's a Wagnerian, creating his latest epic production, his Valhalla in that bunker underneath Berlin". . .

"Who cares as long as it's his last production" . . .

"I care about Berlin. How can it ever be rebuilt?" . . .

The ants will rebuild it . . . Don't worry about that . . . Is there a chance my wife may still be trapped in the ruins of Berlin? . . . No, she's in a camp somewhere if she's still alive . . . Is she safer in a camp than in a burning city? . . . Stupid to think of safety that way . . . The greed with which I'm stuffing food in my mouth . . . I get up and push my chair back . . . A loud grating noise startles me with Berlin teaching memories, a child's fingernail scratching the blackboard . . . *Draw God* . . . I turn to leave the mess hall . . .

"Where are you going?" Fischer asks. "Are you all right?"

"I'm just going for a walk. Don't worry. I'm fine."

"Let me come along . . ."

"No, I'd rather be alone" . . .

They want to spy on me . . . Be careful . . . Walk toward the ocean . . . Wait until it gets dark . . . The sun is setting and the sky stained with colors . . . No trace of wind . . . The calm evening seems to wait in the knowledge that nothing changes . . . But the insect world is alive reflecting its tiny alarms in the water . . . Mosquitoes buzz around me . . .Ants crawl under my heavy military shoes . . . No one seems to be following me . . . At the end of the compound, its roof visible above a clump of trees, is the building where Weimann is quartered . . . He's resting there, planning tomorrow . . .Smoke drifts lazily above the building . . . I walk along the beach . . . At the end of the beach a fence rises between me and Weimann's quarters . . . I laugh . . . I'm outside looking in . . .*This is the way the fly looks into the ant world. . .*

Is he really in there?. . .The building seems strangely deserted. . .A military building is occupied by peculiar distorted objects designed especially for destruction . . . Here there is nothing like that . . . This building is designed for the sea, to reflect man's birth in the water, his crawling development on land . . . The fence is not so high . . . It has no barbed wire . . . I can climb over it as if I were a child again . . .

On the other side of the fence I begin to crawl . . . Enter the crawling world to avoid discovery . . . Crawl very fast . . . Amazing how natural is crawling . . . When I reach the door I hesitate a long time, listening . . . Silence seems to echo everywhere . . . Cross the threshold of the palace . . . No, he's not in there . . . The fly is not in there . . . Have I mistaken the ceremonial nature of this building? . . . A shoe drops on the floor inside . . . Unmistakably a shoe that startles me into the human world again, followed by quiet . . . I am not an ant . . . This is a different unknown ceremony . . . How plain, how mysterious, how essential it is . . .

Enjoy the infinite passing of time . . . Fling open the door . . . It bangs against the wall with a loud report . . . Weimann is moving towards me dressed in a bathrobe and slippers . . . Handsome, erect, that military bearing . . . He hasn't changed at all . . . He will never change . . . He stops, stares at me without any trace of recognition . . . *He doesn't know me* . . . Why should he know me, a number in a numbered world . . . *He is going to take a shower . . . The sound of water, an infinite waterfall cascading its white* . . . He speaks politely, the diction of a gentleman, a General Staff officer . . .

Don't answer . . . He looks at me, puzzled, unworried . . . He steps aside to pass on his way to warm comfort and cleanliness . . . I call to him softly . . .

"You don't remember me?" . . .

He stares intently for a moment, his face almost changing into the half-smile with which someone anticipates an old relationship . . . "No, I'm sorry. Have we met before, perhaps in Africa?"

"My number is . . . " . . . Speak the number slowly as if that will identify me in the ant world . . . *My number* . . .

He tries to laugh . . . "I too have a number. I'm afraid I don't understand. What do you want?"

Numbers, titles, names, ceremonies . . . Forget about the smash of water, talk to him . . .

"I'd like to talk to you a moment, Herr Major . . . " That's better . . . *Herr Major . . . With respect . . . As a private should talk to a Major, a General Staff officer . . .*

Weimann, puzzled, is still looking directly into my eyes . . . How curious is this eye-to-eye clarity that we demand in all forms of life . . . Eyes are like water . . . They reflect eternity . . .

"Have you been here long?"

Be polite . . . Ceremonies have a certain formality that must be enjoyed, adhered to . . .

"Yes, a long time." . . . *As long as the barbed wire coiling around the earth in irredeemable patterns, outlining the architecture of prison camps under the night sky . . .*

"You were brought here by the Americans?" . . . Ah, ant-like suspicion at last . . .

"I was brought here by Lieutenant Enders." . . .

His expression does not change . . . His curiosity probes: "What do you do in this camp?" . . .

I want to laugh and scream at him, *"Re-education . . ."* Instead I say with the ridiculous idealism that ceremony requires, "We are preparing to return and free Germany . . ."

He does not smile . . . "Good. I wish that I could go with you. Now I must go . . . "

"Aren't you coming with us?"

"Later, perhaps. Excuse me. Lieutenant Enders said not to talk to anyone . . . "

I can't hear him . . . He didn't really say that . . . I don't believe Enders . . . Communication in the ant world is essential . . . It's just a matter of the right ceremony . . . *Why is the water running in the distance? . . .*

"You're sure that you don't remember me?" . . .

"We've never met before." . . . His voice sounds impatient now . . . He begins to move away . . .

"Don't you remember a performance of *Faust*?" . . .

He reacts, doubtless recalling all of the loving productions of *Faust* that he has seen, then focusing . . . "You were at that camp?" . . .

"Yes. A remarkable performance. The fountains of water were beautiful . . . "

"Fountains of water? . . .

"You don't remember the water running in the showers?" . . .

"I don't know what you're talking about." . . . He moves to pass me, but I block the way . . .

"I was your Faust in that ceremony. Mephistopholes burned a swastika in my back." . . .

Impossible to re-create ritualistic performances . . . Do I expect fear to shadow his face? . . . There is no fear in the ant world . . .

"I'm sorry. Please believe me, I heard only later what

happened. That evening I left early with the American camp commander. I was not a member of their group. You know how the Nazis planned to control the camps. I was only the senior officer in charge. I tried to work against the Nazis as much as I could . . ."

Herr Major, do not misunderstand me . . . The ceremony does not require verbal arguments . . . We are no longer searching for words . . . It is simply a matter of location in time . . .

"Do you recall the Condor Legion?" . . .

Whatever else he is he is not a liar . . . "Of course. I served in the Condor Legion during the Spanish Civil War. I was very young then. Many Germans who saw the danger of Russian barbarism from the east volunteered to fight in Spain. It was only later that we found out what Hitler was rehearsing us for. We made mistakes. We must try to correct them. It is time to forget the past and work together. Germany must be re-built. German culture . . . "

At last he is speaking about cultural rituals . . . We shall see how justice is composed of pity . . . That is the white truth, isn't it, the pure, naked truth? . . . Remember Ingolstadt's words, "When we lose pity we are going into the night." . . . Draw lines in the night instead of words . . . Do not enter the trap of pity . . .

"Yes, everyone makes mistakes. But how are we to forget the past?". . .

He seizes on this thankfully . . . He even pauses to light a cigarette . . . The smoke curls around his confident face as he begins his instructions, his knowledge of the correct ceremonial procedure . . . "I don't believe in despair. Germany has always had a great destiny, a great future. It has always been able to ignore the devestation of the past. Look at the Thirty Years War. The country was rebuilt. Even if our cities today are smashed to rubble, they can be reconstructed with better planning. The German spirit cannot die. Suffering only makes it stronger. In Germany I think it has always been a little as though we face the necessity of suffering. That will always be our strength . . . "

Ich bin der Geist der stets verneint . . . Suffering makes the spirit stronger . . . But there is a limit to the depth of suffering, a time when the pressure is too great, when the negative spirit denies too often . . .

Weimann nods to me pleasantly as if we will meet again one day for further instruction . . . He swings the towel over his shoulder in an implacably optimistic rhythm . . . He walks to the latrine where the shower waits . . . I stand at the window . . . Dark now . . . The Evening Star hovers at the horizon's edge, flashing its cold light . . . The night is cut with the tension of invisible stars, millions of lifeless worlds . . . Why am I waiting in this building? . . . To hear some particular sound I cannot identify? . . . I can't hear it if I'm caged inside . . . Go out and wait . . .

A sickle moon in the sky invites the fall harvest . . . Time for the ant world to emerge from its tunnels and venerate the moon . . . I stand so quietly, listen so intently, that I feel frozen . . . An eternity of time before I hear it, faint, penetrating clearly through the thin board walls of the latrine a few feet away . . . The hissing sound of water . . .

No one to speak to him . . . Exiled from the community . . . Listen to the chant--"We worship hate, Pure becomes Pure, Cold becomes Cold, Hate! Hate! Hate!" . . .

Something is wrong . . . I hear only one shower running . . . Why aren't they all running? . . .

No peace in that country of the mind. . .

I don't have to wear a mask . . . Only a number . . . A number in the anonymous ant world . . . *Take the knife* . . .

Where did I get this knife? . . . Absurd, a kitchen knife . . . Who gave it to me? . . . Faust's magic . . . I hear the waterfall running from magic . . . My love, my love, I cry out to you across the endless ocean with its ruined, lost cities--Atlantis, Atlantic . . . Why don't I hear from you? . . . I don't believe Enders' feeble reassurances . . . You are dead . . . You are better off dead . . . The white wall of love . . . Winter is coming with its points of ice . . . The cities lie in ruins . . . Beneath the rubble are buried thousands of victims . . . Revenge, no, justice . . . No pity in the world of ant shadows . . .

When we lose pity we are going into the night . . .

No, Ingolstadt . . . You cannot find salvation in words . . . Their meaning shatters apart . . . The flies have had their wings torn off too long . . . The barbed wire shines in the night . . .

Slowly . . . Open the door . . . He won't hear because of the water's noise . . . *According to the Judgment of the Court of Honor* . . . Wait . . . I can see him . . . Draw back in the shadows . . . That's not Major Weimann . . . That innocent nakedness is not Weimann . . . No place to pin medals on a naked body . . .

My first impression of a Jew revolted me . . . Remember the ceremonial reading from *Mein Kampf?* . . . But you weren't there, were you Weimann? . . .You had to leave early so you weren't responsible . . . *No one is responsible* . . .

What am I doing here at the edge of the ocean?. . .Return to Germany . . . There is no Germany to return to . . . *I want you to teach the children* . . . No, I'll never hear from her again . . . This childish American task of re-education when there is no education . . . *I don't believe you, Enders* . . . We learn by rituals, ceremonies, deep in the earth . . .

A gay death, sparkling . . . The steam from the shower sparkles in the light . . . *Tomorrow will come with the stare of understanding* . . . Accept the truth, Ingolstadt . . . Accept the night . . .

Approach while his back is turned . . . How straight he stands . . . *That with the height of Gods man's dignity may vie* . . . Forget the performance of *Faust* . . . A naked man has no dignity . . . A fly ready for the ants . . . How white his body is . . .

I don't believe in despair . . .

Neither do I, Major . . .

If our cities are smashed to rubble they can be reconstructed . . .

Not by you, Herr Major . . .

The German spirit cannot die . . .

Closer . . . The lights are as cold as the stars . . . While his back is turned . . . No, there is soap all over his body . . .

Turn around, Major . . .

With the smash of water . . .

Don't cut it too deep . . .

The water is as cold as the stars . . .

Ants crawl through blood trickling from the naked

body . . . They come from all directions . . . They cover the white, naked skin . . . Water is flooding them, threatening to swamp their world . . . Turn off the water . . .

Where is the fly, the leader? . . . Tear his wings off . . .

Too heavy, the weight of time on his shoulders . . . Without his uniform the fly has no power . . . What is the meaning of bravery? . . . Medals, nothing but medals . . .

Where the stones move, there is hatred . . . They don't move any more . . . Motionless . . . *Unite all things . . . Let One become One* . . . Why are the stars in this room so cold? . . . The new ant leader prepares to ascend the throne . . . Look back with hate . . . The bodies of thousands of ants lie in the rubble . . . No one will ever bury them . . . She is dead . . .

It cannot be . . . I am alive . . .

Fall on him, ants, tear his arms and legs off, tear the life out of him . . . The chant, rising, rising in intensity . . . *We worship hate, Pure becomes Pure, Cold becomes Cold* . . .

A white wall blazes . . . White skin . . . Love . . .

What do you believe in? . . . Draw God . . .

Whose voice? . . . Strike through the ants . . .

. . . see how much stronger the wise man . . .

A star flares across the sky . . . Shooting stars they call them. . .*Knifing stars. . .*

I'm proud that you teach the children . . .

Whose voice? . . . Can't remember . . . Teach the ants now . . . Teach them that vengeance is justice . . . Eye filled with coldness, with barbed wire . . . End the ceremony . . . Enthrone the last ant body . . . *All brands shall be in the shape of stars instead of swastikas . . . Hail! Hail! Hail!* . . .

She stretches her arms . . . Run . . . Faster, faster . . . *She is there waiting . . .*

The white wall of stars . . .

Enthrone the ants frozen in the night sky . . . The fly is torn from his throne . . . Begin the triumphant chant . . . *Pure becomes Pure, Cold becomes Cold . . .*

She is dead . . .

Who? . . .

Joyous death, sparkling . . . Thousands, millions, an

infinity of ants crawling beneath the stars glittering like the sparklers children play with . . . *Tomorrow, the stare of understanding . . .*

It is tomorrow . . . White walls converge . . . The ants climb them, creep through the sparkling night . . . *999 . . . 999 million of them* . . . Over the body of the fly . . .

Look . . . The ruins are gone . . . Buildings rise again, barracks . . . Savage, cold, surrounded by cutting wire . . .

Cry out! . . . My words ring in the long vault of darkness . . . No words, only sound . . . Someone is screaming or crying perhaps . . . Hard to tell as the ants flow on in their triumphant formations, filling the night with exultation . . . How steady, how rhythmical is their victorious chant . . .

THE AMERICAN BARBED WIRE FEVER AND VICTORY IN EUROPE

What to do? Send Armind to an army hospital where he'll be alone, although he may get better care? Or keep him here as his friends urge me. I call Jameson. We decide to keep Armind in our clinic near his friends for the time being.

When I see Armind for the first time after the knifing Lieutenant Stackton, our medical officer, comes out of the room to talk to me. He looks worried and asks, "What's this about ants?"

"Ants?"

"Armind's babbling about ants."

It's happened then. I try to explain about Armind's background. *What's the use? How can Stackton ever understand? I can't explain what Armind has come to mean to me. Give Stackton the bare details for his official medical report. That's the only way Armind can avoid standing trial for murder . . .*

"What a story," the doctor whistles. "I don't blame this guy for blowing his top. Well, the worst is probably over now. I'll do the best I can for him. I've seen a few prisoners like this in other camps. Barbed wire fever we call it . . . "

Barbed wire fever . . . "Can I see him?"

"It won't do much good now. I've given him a strong sedative."

"Will he recover?"

"Who can tell?" Stackton shrugs. "He's got a chance. It may take a long time. I've never seen an extreme case like this where a man was killed. Violent death can cause an extreme regression. He'll need special psychiatric treatment. He can't get that here."

"Maybe we can arrange it."

"The real problem is confinement," Stackton confesses. "If he were free . . . That's why we call it barbed wire fever."

"Take care of him. He's important. We want to use him back in Germany to help out with military government."

"That'll be difficult. Even when he gets back to Germany he may have to go into a sanitarium for the right kind of treatment. This fixation on the ants seems to have shocked him completely out of reality. Can you tell me anything more?"

"I've told you all I know," I lie. "Let me see him for a

moment."

"All right." Stackton leads me into Armind's room. Armind is lying on a cot, his eyes open staring at the ceiling as if something were crawling there. The Arab sits near him on a chair watching him silently. I go over to the cot and look down at Armind.

"I told you he wasn't likely to recognize you," whispers the doctor.

Slowly I turn to leave the room. The Arab remains seated. His eyes barely acknowledge my presence. As I walk out of the room behind Stackton Armind screams suddenly:"*Come back! Come back or I die!*"

Frozen I halt in the doorway and turn around. Armind is still staring at the ceiling. *Was that really his voice?* The doctor holds me back. "He's not talking to you."

The words are not so easy to detach from my flesh. "What the hell do you mean? Who is he talking to?"

"God knows. He's in his own world. That's what happens in cases of extreme shock. The knifing of the German officer is just the final push. Along the way who knows how many obstacles there've been. Of course the loss of his wife that you mentioned is a major factor."

Of course . . . How many obstacles . . . In the corridor I get dizzy. The walls spin as if the unreality of Armind screaming *Come back or I die!* will fly away.

Stackton grabs me by the arm. "Are you all right? Better sit down. I know it's tough. You'll feel better in a minute. How about some coffee?"

Coffee is the god damn American cure for everything. I start breathing deeply, slowly. Suddenly I feel an obsessive desire to leave this building. "No coffee thanks," I tell Stackton. "I've got to get back to my office."

Hurrying into the night I try not to stare back at the clinic. My head turns automatically. The flat, bare building seems absurdly small beneath its large Red Cross. Two enlisted men walk by whistling softly. They catch sight of me, salute. Mechanically I return the salute, wishing for a surge of authority to flow through my body. I glance at my watch. Almost 5 A.M. The sun will be up soon. Once when I was a boy I stayed up all night with some friends to see the sun rise. My parents were furious. *That's what I want to do now.* I walk down to the beach. Somehow I want to see the water glisten as the sun rises over the Atlantic to the east . . .

Armind does not improve. He will not talk at all. Army psychiatrists who examine him are pessimistic in their prognosis. The Arab plays records to him. With the Arab I resume the operatic programs. Opera no longer affects Armind except in a passive way. His friends come to read to him. At first they try German classics. Then they explore modern masters, Mann, Wassermann, Hesse. He accepts everything indifferently as if words have become merely soothing.

My visits settle into a daily evening routine. He never acknowledges my presence. The Arab takes him for walks along the beach. Standing by the shore staring at the gulls circling over the lapping waves they make a uniquely silent duo.

The first issues of *Der Ruf* are published successfully. Letters flow in from prisoner of war camps throughout the country praising the paper, requesting and submitting specific articles. With the war's end approaching our program begins to have an effect on the camps. Books banned by the Nazis are reprinted and begin to circulate. A film program starts. This proves to be particularly useful in loosening Nazi control. Finally we're helping to stir up a new ferment of ideas among the prisoners. As the Allied armies advance into Germany the Nazi leadership in the camps crumbles. Jameson is able to fend off congressional and military investigators who sound constant alarms about our program.

One day Fischer brings me the beginning of an article that he discovered in Armind's possessions. As I read the title, *Me Into Myself: The Inner Banishment of Emily Dickinson,* I realize with a start that Armind actually began to carry out his instinctive pledge to write about the New England poet for *Der Ruf.* When I visit Armind I take along the few pages and notes and leave them with him. He gives no sign of recognition or interest in his work. For some reason I persist. The next evening I read him some of Emily Dickinson's poetry. No reaction. After several poems I begin the one that

I heard him read to the Arab in the Trinidad Guard House--*I have no Life but this--To lead it here--Nor any Death--but lest/Dispelled from there--Nor tie to Earths to come--Nor action new--Except through this extent--The Realm of you--*

Armind's withdrawn expression does not change. Impulsively I read the poem again into his lowered eyes. This time, without looking at me, Armind puts out his hand slowly and touches me. He doesn't say anything. The touch is eerily abstract. My flesh tingles. Is it only another twitch, an unconscious gesture through the darkness of his isolation? Perhaps the touch is not really intended for me like his earlier scream *Come back or I die.*

Stackton is encouraged by this brief contact. "At least it's a beginning even if it doesn't mean much in the way of concrete recognition. Even an abstract contact is hopeful. The point is to keep him in touch with some kind of intimate environment. Then in Germany he'll have a chance of recovery."

So I keep struggling to arrange time to insure regular contact with Armind. His friends read him articles submitted for *Der Ruf* as if he were present and active in their staff meetings. He sits silently without comment. One evening the Arab hands me a scrap of paper on which Armind has scribbled:

Me from Myself--to banish
into the arena of ants--
How have I peace
except by subjugating
Consciousness?

"Can you make anything out of that?" Stackton asks puzzled when I show it to him.

"Strangely he's run together his experience with the ants in the Trinidad desert and some lines from Emily Dickinson. I don't know why . . . "

"Even this fragment is a breakthrough. Try to get him to write more. Don't lose your patience. Don't forget sometimes it takes years for people like this to recover if they recover at all."

Though we persist in urging Armind to write he shows no recognition of these requests. Only occasionally does he write fragments as if driven by his own impulses that have nothing to do with us. They are always in English as if he cannot bring himself to confront his native language. Often I recognize the presence of Emily Dickinson's curt lines in the fragments. Is he incorporating her isolation in some curious way into the mosaic of his isolation? Are her lines somehow a substitute for the loss of his wife? No, the fragments seem too distant, impersonal, formal. They read as if he's deliberately stepping backward into time to avoid present entanglements. They are almost meditations for oblivion. As Stackton says there's nothing to do but wait . . .

Hitler's dead, a suicide. American troops are converging on Berlin. Maybe we'll get to Germany now! All of our prisoners participate in eager plans to transfer our programs to their homeland. Only Armind seems untouched by the end of the Nazi state.

Suddenly Jameson summons me to Washington. He won't tell me over the phone what's up. When I get there he tells me the Re-Education Program has been dissolved. Just like that. *Dissolved* is the peculiarly correct word that stuns me. We are not canceled. We are highly praised and abruptly dissolved. Is this the new form of exorcism for controversial projects? In the formal letter from the Provost Marshal General ending our program, Colonel Jameson is praised as a great civilian scholar and a valiant, perceptive fighter against Nazism. He is awarded the Legion of Merit. All his staff officers receive Commendation Ribbons. My Commendation Ribbon, praising my "constructive work with German prisoners of war and the newspaper, *Der Ruf,*" arrives in an official military mailing tube six months after my discharge from the army. I pin it to the back of my bathroom door . . .

There is no way to protest, no way to discover exactly why our program is dissolved. Jameson hears that the chief American Military Government official in Bavaria, where we planned to take our anti-Nazi prisoners, is a former Dies Committee congressman, celebrated for his investigation of "un-American Red activities." On that committee in the

1930s he achieved fame by interrogating the distinguished woman who headed the Federal Theatre Project about their production of Marlowe's famous Elizabethan play *Doctor Faustus.* He asked her the penetrating question that reverberated with shocked laughter in the newspapers: *"Was Marlowe a Communist?"* Maybe he came to suspect our program's relationship to Marlowe and fought to prevent us from threatening his new Bavarian domain.

Probably he doesn't deserve sole credit. Jameson's appearance before the House Military Affairs Committee was apparently too successful. The chairman of the committee, a veteran congressman from New Jersey, praised Jameson's testimony publicly. However the congressman expressed his laughing concern that our anti-Nazi prisoners might be a lot of "masquerading Communists." Several months after the war ends this congressman is to be indicted for graft and bribery, convicted, and imprisoned only for a few months due to his "distinguished record of public service" and his ill-health. Maybe the influential congressman was a key participant in the maneuver to praise us out of existence. There's a subject for you-the killing power of American praise. . .

I try to pretend that I don't really care. My first duty is to myself not to some god damn German prisoners of war. Civilian freedom is opening up. Time to get my own career on the road again. Before I leave Washington to return to Rhode Island Jameson asks me to his apartment for a private farewell. Farewell day turns out to be Victory in Europe Day. As I leave my hotel Washington is in a frenzy. I walk through the streets in a dream journey. Through joyous mobs I fight my way toward Jameson's apartment. . .

Deafening. Cars are all sounding their horns. Everyone is shouting, screaming with joy. Cars bulge with strange passengers. They drive a block or two, drop riders, pick up more, exchange kisses, flowers, bottles, circle around aimlessly. A merry-go-round of cars honking, cheering, grabbing, lifting girls, driving away. Hats, coats, dresses, sail out the windows into the warm air. . .Farewell to clothes. . .

The mysterious interior. . .Swept along by happy, screaming wanderers *(Peace! It's all over! We've won! Do you hear that, Armind, wherever you're going, it's victory over the ants),* I'm rushed despite my struggles into the interior of hidden Washington. Streets of black faces appear. The Army has just been desegregated. No more isolated black units. In front of a brightly lit church a huge sign commands SAVE YOURSELVES AND SING BROTHERS AND SISTERS. A crowd is clapping, singing, dancing. I don't believe it. Black and white dancing, singing together:

> It's the Promised Land, Brother,
> It's the Promised Land,
> We're gonna dance
> Into the Promised Land,
> We're gonna sing
> Into the Promised Land . . .

I'm dancing with an enormous black woman. Her grin's as wide, as full of white teeth as the moon above. Holding her strong hand is like holding on to a tree while a heavy wind tries to whirl you away. Be my tree, lady, be my tree.

The tree whirls off. I'm clapping beside a big, black Sergeant. He wears a white Military Police armband. His gun is still strapped around his waist although he's lost his cap. He lifts his police whistle and blows the rhythm of liberation. EEEEEEP. Incredible improvised music occupies the night, garbage can lids banged, drums rattling, glasses clinked, tables pounded. High above the jammed street in a tenement window a boy is playing a flute. The MP Sergeant unbuckles his gun. Watch out . . . He throws the bullets away one by one. Eager hands reach to catch them. A woman dances with a bullet between her teeth. The Sergeant throws the gun as high as he can into the sky. Maybe in his glee he thinks it'll stick up there like a glittering star. The gun falls, disappears. Someone else hurls it into the air again. A new game. The gun gleams as it soars, falls, soars, falls . . .

A police car pushes slowly through the throng. Someone has pasted a sign on it, PEACE CAR. People keep climbing into it, riding on the hood, clinging to exchange greetings, dropping off. As he inches his way along the cop waves a newspaper out the window. A big headline announces

UNCONDITIONAL SURRENDER. Voices sing again:

It's the Promised Land, Brother,
It's the Promised Land,
We're gonna dance
Into the Promised Land,
We're gonna sing
Into the Promised Land . . .

Swept out of the Mysterious Interior I float back to the center of Washington, Frantically I grope my way toward Jameson's apartment. High above all the windows are wide open. Perched on the sills men and women are drinking, cheering, ripping up phonebooks, shredding newspapers, floating them down to the street, the end of bureaucracy. Little pieces of paper nestle in my hair. A sheet of S's from the phonebook falls into my hand--*Simon, Simple, Simplon* . . . No one exists with those names. Tomorrow everyone will have new names.

My god, the enormous, endless offices . . . The secretaries seem to be throwing records, files, out of the windows. Maybe I can catch my service record as it falls down--*Peter Enders, Army of the United States, four years of socalled Limited Service, private to Lieutenant. No one is saluting any more. No one will ever salute again . . .*

When I arrive sweating, exhausted at Jameson's apartment, he pours out huge, sympathetic martinis. He's just fought his way home too through the jubilant mass hysteria. He wears a silk Chinese robe with a dragon embroidered on the back. I hardly recognize him. It's the first time I've ever seen him out of military uniform. Maybe he's struggling to shift quickly back to civilian--distinguished professor, author, political expert on Germany. He doesn't look too German in that Chinese robe. Why should I be so surprised that he's a sensuous man? A highranking uniform permits only the expression of an authoritarian masculinity.

"Here's to civilian life," Jameson says as we clink glasses. Then he falls into a silent gloom as if suddenly aware of his efforts to create a false joviality. I feel his frustration. He's never made any secret of his ambition for power that he feels he deserves. Now he's trying to reconcile the program's failure, the mistakes he may have made, with the achievements we were just beginning to realize. *Ask him about Armind. If anyone can tell me about Armind he can. Don't push it . . .*

Jameson sits with his bare feet in slippers up on a coffee table. Although he forces himself to talk to me it seems as if he's trying to convince himself about his future. "Look, Peter, we did the best we could under impossible conditions. We learned how too much secrecy can destroy a program. We had to spend all our time fending off attacks. They never wanted us to go to Germany. So forget about our program. Go back to college, finish your degree. Get a job that really interests you. It's time to look after your own future."

A little irked by the nagging, conventional advice I complain: "It seems so damn futile. We worked so hard and so little was accomplished. To have to stop now. . ."

"It's too easy for us to get bitter," Jameson reflects drawing on his pipe. "You're too damn serious, Peter. You're going to have to learn to change style. You think progress consists in righteously smashing the villains and riding free into the future on one of your triumphant California prairie schooners."

"Come on, Colonel." I try to laugh.

"Don't call me Colonel any more. Pretty soon people your age will start calling me Professor or Doctor again as if I were some kind of healing physician . . . "

"Herr Doktor Professor . . . "

"Screw your god damn academic Germans. I'm looking forward to being a professor again." His body sags into another gloomy silence and he takes a long drink.

"Are you really?"

"Sure, I want to teach and write again, make something worthwhile out of this damn experience." Suddenly he leans forward and points an accusing finger at me. "Do you think I liked being stuck here in Washington? I tried like hell to get to Germany. It really hurts not to go."

He's almost crying. All I can say to console him is "It's going to be tough going back to college after running a reeducation program."

"Let's have another drink damn it." Jameson gets up and pours us two more martinis. My head wanders in a maze of fantasies from the V.E. Day Celebration to Jameson's Chinese robe to Armind . . .

"Here's to the end of re-education and the beginning of education," Jameson glares at me and we clink glasses again. "Damn it, Peter, if we learned something about our ability or inability to change it's been worthwhile."

"I know you're right, but . . . " *Change, god have I changed in four years.* My parents, my brother, Frau Hedda and her cat, Holzreichl, Limited Service, Trinidad, Weimann, Armind . . . The characters change so rapidly they blur into each other. *Armind, he's the one I can't focus on clearly . . .*

"You're not listening. You're off in fantasy land."

"I'm sorry. I was thinking about Armind after he killed Weimann when he screamed *Come back or I die.*"

"But you said he wasn't screaming at you. You can't blame yourself."

"It doesn't make any difference. Even though he wasn't speaking to me I was there. Maybe if I'd done something. . ."

"Look Peter," Jameson grabs my arm, "In a few months Armind will be back in Germany. You may never see or hear of him again. Yet you'll still be involved with him more intimately than with many of your American friends . . . "

"That's what bothers me. Why?"

"Who knows how the process of change connects people mysteriously? Sometimes I think the world divides into those people with imagination and compassion that forces them into deep relationships even though they may never meet or meet briefly, and those people who are destined merely to develop their own day-by-day materialistic security. The ones with imagination and compassion endure the greatest torments because they are open to the greatest changes. Also they tend to make the greatest discoveries because they're obsessed by their fantasies."

Obsessed by their fantasies . . . Armind and his ant-spectres . . .

Jameson stares at me over his pipe, waves his glass, and grins. "Do you want to hear me sail on?"

"Please, I don't think I understand . . . "

"Some day I want to write a book about this. In this country we spend most of our time trying to rationalize the soul out of its mystery. We know psychology, but we don't know the psyche. What if the particles of the soul, of the imagination, are like the atom's particles, infinitely small and mysterious, capable of endless transformations . . . "

"If you write a book like that they'll run you out of Political Science."

Jameson chuckles. "Political *Science* is a lousy term anyway. Politics has more to do with the fantasies of art than of science. The more rigid and institutional society becomes the greater the hidden fantasies. Think what politics would be like if we knew more about the fantasies of politicians. Is it true that the more power they have the greater are their fantasies? How can these fantasies be controlled unless they're brought out into the open? What are the fantasies of Stalin, Mao, Hitler? What were the fantasies of Jefferson when he spoke publicly against slavery and yet owned slaves and was probably involved with a slave mistress?"

"But how do you discover those fantasies? Isn't the art of politics to conceal what you really think in order to make a workable compromise?"

Jameson grimaces at me and gives me a mock salute with his glass. "I'll be god damned, Peter. You're turning into a political scientist."

"Can I come and study with you?"

"Never," Jameson says firmly. "I don't want any friends for students. You can't be just with friends. There are too many fantasies between you."

Friends . . . Now it's I who can't talk . . .

Jameson continues, "You ask the right question, how do you discover the hidden fantasies? Maybe it's impossible completely, but often it's a matter of putting unusual facts together and reading the right *tone* of things . . . "

"Tone?"

"The real sound of meaning beneath the words. When Hitler used to rant and repeat everything deliberately I want to investigate his fantasies of power. I want to show how even after his suicide he's left a unique burden of Nazi Fantasies to cope with. I want to try and analyze how those fantasies are related to the fantasies of power in our own country."

"Good luck. Tell me how do you think your sense of Nazi fantasies are related to Armind?"

"I'm not sure. Time will tell. Prisoners like Armind have created their own world of anti-Nazi fantasies. They hide in those dream-worlds the way Armind has done."

"I'm not quite sure what you mean about fantasies, why not ideas?"

"Because ideas are too rational. A war brings to a crisis all of man's deepest fantasies. What you feel for Armind has to do with some kind of hidden compassion, hidden loyalty. That's where you're involved with him--in the fantasy world."

In the fantasy world . . . "But I don't feel *loyal* to Armind. After all he's a German. I'm not responsible for him. I've got enough trouble with my own fantasies."

"Of course, but there's a different element of change involved in your relationship with Armind because of your different experiences. What I call the compassion of loyalty may spring up through the greatest barriers, across national boundaries, beyond rational human friendships, beyond mere language even . . . "

Armind and the Arab . . .

"Maybe this hidden fantastic relationship exists even beyond admiration, beyond love," Jameson continues. "Sometimes I think you can hate someone for what he's done and still feel this compassion of loyalty because of the deep qualities of imagination that connect you."

I don't hate Armind, I don't hate him . . .

"Even though you may admire Armind in certain ways and feel sorry for him, you may also hate him for his situation and what he forces you to do . . . "

"I don't understand."

"As an American you can't really sense how freedom of choice deteriorates in a society created by Nazi Fantasies. Yet you feel something heroic if futile in the experiences that Armind has endured. You admire his courage as compared to yours. Maybe you even hate your lack of experience compared to his."

"That's true. I never thought of it quite that way."

"So you feel yourself attached to him by mysterious, guilty ties. Yet you'll be glad to be free of him. You'll be glad to get out of the prison world. In a few months you'll forget him, but certain links will remain. Even though the two of you are separated the chain of possibilities, of connecting fantasies will remain."

The chain of possibilities, of connecting fantasies will remain . . . Even though I never see Jameson again how can I forget this? As we part we speak of future meetings. We promise to keep in touch. I tell him I want to hear about his book. He tells me how he wants to help me with any recommendations that I may need.

We embrace, shake hands warmly, a final touch that I can still feel. Our promise to keep in touch results in only a few brief letters. In two years Jameson will be dead from a sudden heart attack in his university office. He will leave the usual papers and a mass of notes, but no manuscript about his theories of political power, his concern with Nazi Fantasies. His final ideas will never be deciphered by some eager Ph.D. candidate. They disappear unfinished in space and time . . .

Outside of Jameson's apartment the Victory celebration still surges wildly through the streets. Night seems to have increased the frenzy. Who's ever seen so many animals wandering loose around a city? Dogs, cats, monkeys on people's shoulders, a cow (where'd she come from?), policemen's horses decked with flowers. Soon snakes will be crawling along lawns, lions and tigers roaming the parks, buffalo grazing on the wooded hills. The Peaceable Kingdom . . .

Irresistably the tide of rejoicing surges toward Lafayette Park across from the White House. The White House blazes with lights. Inside they must be dancing triumphantly. Everyone is watching the White House dance from the crowded lawns of Lafayette Park. Cars driving by throw us bottles. We're drinking Cutty Sark, Ballantines, Lafroig, you name it, the most expensive brands. Ice cubes are thrown through the air. They melt in your fingers. Paper cups and real glasses. Around the park you can hear glasses smashing against rocks. All of the cupboards in Washington are empty. Tomorrow's a new time. It's good to forget the whole damn prisoner of war program.

As I'm standing on the grass watching the White House blaze in its Victory Dance a girl calls me and grabs my arm. She's young, attractive, ready to travel anonymously like everyone else this night. As we stride along through the park she throws away her shoes, liberated. She urges me to take off my shoes. "Relax, soldier," she laughs, "The War is over."

"It's not over," I want to argue suddenly. She throws away my shoes and they sail through the air. She rips off my lieutenant's bars. The grass feels good on my feet. *Green how I love you green.* No grass in the ant world. We're striding along again over an infinity of tangled couples. Invisible faces in the moonlight. The park is a garden of strange, white shrubs. On closer inspection the shrubs turn out to be branches of arms, legs, occasional bottoms. Jumping over one of the human shrubs she stops, grins at me, and pins one of my lieutenant's bars to the seat of a pair of pants. A cry of rage soars.

We race on. A mad race that seems to repeat the same territory. We're journeying through some magic garden of peace. At last exhausted from our dream journey we sink down into the tall grass. No one has ever cut it. It's grown throughout the war especially for this night of celebration. So green. The grass is so cool. Her eyes glint at me through the green grass. *Das Phantasieren--"This is the act of fantasy-making which begins with the games of children."* Relax . . . We're playing the game of Victory . . . It isn't true . . . There's no such game . . . *The war isn't over . . .*

"Look at you," she laughs, her arms around my neck. "Mr. Civilian Bedroom Eyes. What's your first name? Don't tell me your last name."

"My name is Peter," I say kissing her. Across the park the White House goes dark suddenly. Everyone inside has gone to join the Victory celebration . . .

The Coast Guard station always seems to reject its identity as a prisoner of war camp. For a moment I expect to see another blaze of Victory Lights over the gate. *The war is over! Long live the war!* An overcast sky threatens rain. Gulls huddle bleakly together on the shore. The prisoners have heard about the termination of our program. They're anxious to hear how this will affect their return to Germany. I try to reassure them. Soon they'll be free to return. They'll be free to accept any jobs they wish. *Free* . . . Fortunately they're too excited about the war's end to think of any difficulties they may encounter in Germany as a result of the program's termination.

The news of Victory doesn't seem to pierce Armind's isolation. His routine of silent meditation, walks, occasional scribblings, listening to records and readings continues. There is no news of his wife. No one mentions her any more as she seems to be one of the many nameless victims in the increasing horror of the concentration camps. The Arab indicates that he doesn't want to go back to Africa. He wishes to accompany Armind to Germany. I promise to inquire, but I tell him it seems impossible.

Only a few weeks pass before my discharge comes through. I can't wait now to leave the camp. Nothing is worse than to hang on in a place where a plan has stopped, where a function is lost. Our camp ceases to be a community. Everyone is occupied with his private projects and dreams. Most of these projects consist of attempts to contact lost friends and relatives in Germany to explore job and educational possibilities. I spend my time writing ironic, formidable letters of recommendation into the unknown. My contacts with American authorities have been severed. All I can hope is that the letters will become part of the prisoners' files. I write out the qualities, the anti-Nazi record of each prisoner, without knowing if anyone in Germany will even bother to read these letters. Each letter is addressed TO WHOM IT MAY CONCERN . . .

When the last issue of *Der Ruf* is published we have a farewell party. I buy wine and refreshments though liquor is forbidden in prison camps. Armind is invited. He is given a position as guest of honor. He seems to enjoy it although he says nothing. The Arab sits beside him filling up his wine glass. They both drink solemnly. Fischer and other prisoners tell me they're forming a group to publish *Der Ruf* in Germany after their return. "We want you to come along as a civilian," they urge laughing.

"What could I do to earn a living in Germany?"

"We'll hire you as--what do you call it?--our American expert in Public Relationships," they chorus happily.

I don't ask how they're going to raise money to publish the paper in Germany. I don't question how they're going to get permission to publish it from the American Military Government. By the end of the evening we're singing songs with Fischer at the piano. For the last time I hear the Ballad of the 999th Division. Armind and the Arab get a little plastered. We have to help them to bed. Armind's friends swear an oath to see that he gets proper treatment back in Germany.

Unfortunately when I leave the camp the prisoners remain. Orders have come through to alert them for transportation to a Port of Embarkation. Still I feel like an officer leaving a ship before the crew. My final act is to say goodbye to Armind. He's down on the beach walking silently with the Arab. When I approach to say goodbye I take his hand. The clasp brings a final surge of regret. There is no return contact. The Arab gives me another piece of paper on which Armind has scribbled. Without looking at it I put it in my pocket. When I turn away I almost expect him to scream *Come back or I die!* Nothing except the wild cry of gulls overhead . . .

On the train clicking toward the Discharge Center where I'm to be formally processed I remember the scrap of paper. Trembling I take it out of my pocket:

Myself is only part of you
In silence--By waves and shore
The silence of the wind
Moves with us into silence--

For a moment tears flow. Then I realize this scribbled verse is no more for me than the scream. *Yet we are involved . . . The chain of possibilities, of fantasies will remain . . .*

After my discharge I visit my parents. My father is married again, happy with new projects, turned resolutely against the past. My mother is struggling hard to save herself from depression by working on a book about Navajo myths that she has collected. I make plans to return to college and finish my degree on the G.I. Bill of Rights. What profession to pursue? After my experiences with *Der Ruf* I have a yearning toward journalism if I can find the right position, the right kind of writing. Plenty of time to work this out. Relax even though it's impossible. Learn to enjoy life again with other veterans who haunt the campuses. Yet I feel adrift in the civilian world . . . Ridiculous after my army experiences . . .

Slowly facts filter in about the prisoners' return to Germany. Despite their special abilities and anti-Nazi records none is given a position of importance by American Military Government authorities. Evidently behind the screen of official praise the suspicion of our program remains. Most of our prisoners become avid neutralists. They look warily on any plan for Germany put forward either by Americans or Russians. Several prisoners turn into important writers, educators, lawyers, newspaper editors. What we achieve by our Re-Education Program is small, suspicious islands of independence in post-war Germany. From these isolated islands eyes are constantly alert to any sign of American or Russian invasion. To revive the German economy indiscriminately as long as it benefits American power we manage to swamp these small islands of resistance with tidal waves of American money. Volkswagens, Porsches, Mercedes appear proudly on American as well as German highways . . .

In Germany I learn Armind is sent to a sanitarium highly recommended for its treatment of schizophrenia. I write to him several times and lose track when he doesn't answer. In a brief note of acknowledgment a doctor at the sanitarium writes that Armind remains silent but that he is now writing scraps of poems in German. Evidently, after being permitted to accompany Armind to Germany, the Arab has been forced to return to Africa and has vanished there . . .

A year later I read in a German magazine that Armind is receiving sudden critical attention for a small book of elegies that he has written called *In the Ant World.* In a literary magazine one German critic calls him *"Another Mad Hölderlin."* Basking in the limelight of Armind's sudden creative recognition, the sanitarium doctor is enthusiastic about the possibilities of Armind's recovery. Armind is beginning to speak. Evidently his words are extremely controversial and provoke violent debates on the meaning of sanity. He refuses to leave the sanitarium.

After a long delay when I get a copy of his book of poems they don't seem at all like Hölderlin. Emily Dickinson is a much stronger influence. Lines from her poems are incorporated into his in a strange mosaic like the scraps of paper in English at the coast guard camp. As in Emily Dickinson the poems echo the search for love, the loss of love. The images are wild, surrealistic, violent, full of American desert spaces, satirical funeral marches, knifed victims, gulls dying on nameless New England beaches. How can readers unfamiliar with international prison camps comprehend these poems? Slowly the world's been forced to discover the new secret power of prison camps and the strange courage and lyricism of soul that it takes to endure there. As Camus writes: "A hundred and fifty years ago, people became sentimental about lakes and forests. Today we have the lyricism of the prison cell." So Armind's ant world shines with a secret American tone despite its metaphysical air of satanic disorder that one might expect of Mephistopholes updated to World War II camps.

I write Armind a note of congratulations on the success of his book. No answer of course. One day in the midst of my studies I find in the library a German magazine that contains an interview with Armind in the sanitarium. The interviewer is none other than Fischer who is now a music critic and conductor of choral groups in Munich:

Question: The doctors say you are free to leave the sanitarium. Why do you stay here?

Answer: I am not here for retreat, but to learn how to attack. Quite properly the world has no use for isolation. If I left here I would only go to an isolated room. Here I am still participating in the institutional nature of our time.

Question: How do you mean 'institutional nature of our time'?

Answer: The useless are confined to institutions where they are used, or at best tolerated. Recovery means what? Do animals or insects recover after confinement? The return of the isolationist. the defeated, to participate in social change is only possible through individual attack. In my silence I am studying the means of individual attack.

Question: By 'individual attack,' do you mean through your poems or through political methods?

Answer: Conventional politics are useless. For the moment my attack is the word. You call them poems. I do not know what they are--some expression of the flesh that helps me to endure, to learn the nature of rebellion.

Question: What do you mean by rebellion?

Answer: Unlike the communal insect world, man must study the methods of individual attack. The attack must be strategic, not merely hostile and aggressive. One must absorb a million strategies, develop millions of mysterious techniques. To begin words are perhaps a necessity. Only the word can spread its hidden, physical meanings across the crude barriers that are called national frontiers. The word is useless if it doesn't spread to gesture, action, physical contact between the isolationist and his environment. One must cast off words like Rimbaud and assert his or her place proclaiming, "Here I am, not a statistic for the state to count, but an individual whose destruction must be honored." When the state from its gigantic institutions answers "No" to this request for recognition, the problem of individual attack comes into focus.

Question: Isn't this 'individual attack' rather hopeless against the social and military forces that exist?

Answer: It depends on the imaginative power of the individual attack. One visionary attack of sufficient magnitude can defeat an army. Also it depends on the number of individual attackers that one can educate.

Question: Once you were a teacher. Do you still believe in the power of education?

Answer: The power of education does not exist unless a channel of flesh, a visionary tunnel, exists between teacher and student. Education today is only another blind institutional growth.

Question: In your concept of 'individual attack' don't you face the danger of violence?

Answer: I reject the nature of violence, but I recognize its presence. I have killed a man and seen men killed. If you ask me am I sorry that I killed this man or witnessed the death of other men, at the moment I can only answer 'Yes and No.' Before violence can be cured and redeemed it must be recognized.

Question: If you reject the nature of violence, what possibility is there for rebellion against the great nationalistic powers that exist today?

Answer: American as well as Russian power must be resisted. The real revolutions of the future may come from uniquely fantastic actions by the aged to attain their rights and their dignity in the face of death. All those resilient spirits who learn to survive modern institutional life will join and help to create the rebellion of the aged. Only where individuality is established can there be a real community. Youth is important in this regard and is hopefully learning to oppose the force of institutions. But youth is often too impetuous and strikes blindly out of idealistic frustration. This kind of pseudo-revolt merely masks man's basic desire for power. As we grow older we become more resigned to our isolation. With age we become shadows of ineffectuality. The discovery of possible liberation from these shadows may be the new revolution. When we discover how to make our isolated shadows active there will be freedom. Real communities will flower . . .

When we discover how to make our isolated shadows active there will be freedom . . . As I walk across the western campus under the dry brown hills I think of those shadow words. *The real revolutions of the future may come from uniquely fantastic actions by the aged.* Absurd, but the world is aging. Is there any connection between this fantasy of Armind's and Jameson's belief in a chain of fantasies? I can't believe it even though I'm about to enter the age of fantastic demonstrations. Meanwhile I remember a green New England shore with gulls flying overhead. The Arab, lost in Africa, walks there with Armind. Their silence vibrates magnetically. I run down the beach toward them. They disappear into the water. The echo of a scream sounds through the crisp air: *Come back or I die!* But the scream is not for me. It is for time, for the spirits of shadows, for those who struggle to be redeemed, for the rebels young and old who survive the camps and institutions that our growing technologies create. The scream is for us.

THE END